RETURN TO THE
PLEASUREZONE

RETURN TO THE PLEASUREZONE

Delaney Silver

First published in 1993 by
Nexus
332 Ladbroke Grove
London W10 5AH

Phototypeset by Intype, London
Printed and bound by Cox & Wyman, Reading, Berks

ISBN 0 352 32882 7

This book is a work of fiction.
In real life, make sure you practise safe sex.

Contents

Dedicated to *The Transformer* . . .

. . . the one I've transformed?

THANK YOU AGAIN

Prologue

Sex on the brain? Looking for something unique and special? Your wildest erotic fantasies can now be realised in absolute safety. We can make your most bizarre dreams real, and if you're feeling adventurous, create new ones especially for you.

If you think you can afford us – and you dare take us on – access PLEASUREZONE INCORPORATED on code 0000000####000#01 ... and prepare for the ultimate fulfilment!

Should she change it? Isis wondered. No, perhaps not ... Why change something that had always worked so well?

Okay, on to the next phase ...

Ever wanted to step out of your own sex life and into somebody else's? Ever wanted to make your fantasies real? Try things you never dared? Do things your partner won't? Take risks? Ever wanted to do all these things but not done them because you've got more sense?

In that case, welcome to PLEASUREZONE INCOR-PORATED. We can give you anything and everything in absolute safety. The only risk is to your bank balance.

So why not spoil yourself? Do yourself the biggest favour of your life and run wild in the world of sensual fantasy. There's a full refund after the first session if you can't stand the pace ... but we dare you to take us on and push yourself to the limit. And beyond.

Access code 000000####000#01A/P for details of our

fees and how to pay them. And don't forget . . . We challenge you to challenge us and experience the magic of PLEASUREZONE INCORPORATED!

No changes needed there either.

'Only the brave, the bold, the curious . . . and the astronomically horny would ever answer such a preposterous advert,' was what she'd once said to someone quite special – but it was astounding how many people there were around who were all of those.

Pleasurezone was an even more irresistible temptation now than it had ever been, and Isis herself would have answered the advert like a shot . . . if she hadn't been the woman who'd written it.

1

Sweet Dreams are Made of This . . .

Isis had always been an orally inclined person. She liked eating ice-cream, drinking cocktails through a straw, and most especially, making love to a man with her mouth.

And right now, she was doing the last of these to one Joshua Jordan Mortimer – and revelling in every second of it. It was a pastime she'd dreamed of often and vividly during the long, long months of his absence, but no amount of fantasising could ever match the delicious reality.

His taste was salty and tangy and spermy. Isis adored the bigness of him and the slickness; she loved the way he made her cheeks bulge and her lips dribble. She was mindful, too, of the gentle way he thrust so as not to make her gag.

In the privacy of her mind she smiled; an ancient female smile Josh would have recognised if he'd seen it. She almost *wanted* him to be rough. There was a deeply piquant thrill in simply being used, but with her mouth full of his hot male flesh, there was little chance she could tell him so.

Nor could she tell him that her ignored quim was getting wetter and needier the longer it was denied his attention. The heavy aching frustration was building into a pleasure as perverse as it was exciting and powerful. She couldn't hold her body still any more, or keep her hands from grabbing at his tensing buttocks. Her hips pumped and lifted of their own accord, rising in search of a phantom tongue or finger.

'Oh God, yes! That's good!' she heard him gasp as his prick popped noisily out of her mouth and smeared sideways across her face. Across her bad side, she acknowledged wryly, yet felt her lust coil and surge, fuelled by the simple coals of her genuine affection for him.

With the velvety tip of his sex, slick-wet with his juice and her spittle, Joshua Mortimer was paying her a divine homage; intimately caressing a face that might well have made a lesser man droop.

Isis had a scar. Oh boy, did she have a scar! It wasn't a small blemish or flaw that could be covered by make-up. No, Isis's mark could be neither masked nor ignored – it was the great mother-goddess of all known scars, a convoluted rosy-purple cicatrix that sprawled balefully across the right-hand side of what was an otherwise lovely face. At one time she'd cursed it as hideous and resigned herself to never ever having a man again. Looking in a mirror, all she'd seen ahead was a sterile, sexless existence with only her own fingers or some poor inanimate object to satisfy her. It had been depressing to think she'd never have someone to snuggle up with and whisper sweet nothings to in the night.

Then one day, she'd looked into her mirror more carefully . . . And first laughed, then shouted aloud with elation, astonishment and hope. She'd seen her scar's true nature and been almost grateful for the pain that had given it birth.

Etched into Isis's face was a design something like an intricately crinkled sea-shell. It looked like a flower too: a rare, cultivated orchid. And it also looked like something that was just as exotic and – since the Garden of Eden – far more sought after.

Isis smiled beneath the butterfly touch of Josh's stroking flesh, amused – even after all this time – that the mark on her face should echo almost exactly the moist, pretty, pouting thing that simmered between her long slim legs. Engrained upon her cheek, for every red-blooded man to see and want, was a map of her most intimate womanly

2

topography: her pussy, her loveplace, her tender loving quim.

In recent months, it had become increasingly obvious to Isis that leaving off the veil she'd once believed so essential tended to have an unexpected and peculiar effect. Far from repelling them, her saucy, sexy scar drew men into her orbit in droves.

Of course not everybody noticed its special significance. There were still flinches, averted eyes and cruelty. But Josh Mortimer – bless his heart and his sweet, dirty mind – had spotted it straight away and was still quite patently in awe of it. Isis found it rather scary, but it almost seemed that he wanted her *because* of it.

Here in his bed, though, with his prick sliding across the stigma's roseate pattern, she wasn't about to argue the point with him.

All she could do was lie beneath him, watching his strong body moving above her, looming like some magnificent sex-god as the unstoppable wanting ache kept building and building between her slowly scissoring thighs.

He was kneeling astride her now, supporting her neck with his hand and gyrating his hips to drag the tip of his cock slowly over the lines and whorls of her scar. The backs of his strong thighs brushed tantalisingly across the peaks of her sensitised breasts. His skin felt hot to her nipples and she imagined the heat pumping in his muscles as they held him taut and poised above her.

'Josh . . . Josh . . .' she murmured, stretching her neck to reach him, pointing out her tongue to taste the flesh she craved. She tried to fix on the waving rod, to sight it, then dart like a snake and engulf it. But having temptation this close meant her eyes couldn't focus – and despite her rampaging lust, the idea of her going cross-eyed over his cock made her break into a fit of the giggles.

'What's so funny?' her lover enquired huskily – quite accustomed, she knew, to her not being a conventional bedmate. Humour could be erotic between a pair of true intimates, and she and Josh had shared almost as many laughs as they had orgasms.

3

'You're making me go cross-eyed, you tease,' she complained, swiping sideways in an attempt to snare his cock-tip with her lips.

But the sexy devil evaded her, flicking his pelvis and sending his long, stiff penis swinging clear of her hungering reach.

'Josh, please, put it back in!'

'But where, my sweet?' His voice was smoky, naughty.

'Please, baby, let me suck you,' she heard herself pleading as she craned her neck to bring her mouth to his glistening glans. Meanwhile, another part of herself was agog with astonishment. Tut tut, Ice, this isn't like you. When was the last time you wheedled and begged? Never. It's not your style . . .

Oh but it is, the interior voice taunted as Josh finally allowed his cock into her mouth. His taste was a potent drug; a truth serum that worked on both her lust-dazed mind, and between the moist, puffy lips of her sex.

Yes, my girl, it is your style, she admitted in wonder, licking and suckling the swollen bulb between her lips. Dabbing and darting with her small, delicately furled tongue, she heard the cool analyst in her mind just laugh and laugh and laugh.

I love this, she thought dreamily, probing his tiny love-eye and making him moan and sway.

I do. I love being nothing but a slave. Negative to his positive. A slavering, panting willingness that accedes to his every sexual whim. A naked body. A wet quim that sizzles when he comes and waits and waits in an agony of need until he allows *it* to come too.

I love this, she thought, opening her throat to his short sharp thrust; then whimpering aloud with loss when her fleshy comforter was suddenly withdrawn. Oh no, not when she'd just rationalised the idea of being used.

'Josh? Ooh, Josh!' she pleaded, feeling childlike and out of control.

'I'm hungry, baby,' he whispered, and Isis watched him across the plain of her own nude body as he scooted down the bed and crouched between her splayed thighs. She trembled as he cupped her buttocks in his big warm hands and lifted her to his mouth like a ripe, split fruit.

'I want to taste honey...' The words were muffled as his mobile, questing lips burrowed towards her nether ones, his long tongue cutting a swathe through her soaking, silken pubic bush and probing for the titbit they both prized so much.

Oh God, yes!

Isis wasn't sure if she'd cried out or not. She only knew that her hands were deep in the tangled blackness of his unbound hair, and that between her feverish thighs was a miracle.

Josh Mortimer's tongue had every bit of the skill that hers did. After one searching plunge into the pot of her juices, he flicked it gracefully up the full length of her slit and tantalised her aching bud with a series of firm, glancing stabs.

'Yes! Oh God...'

She did shout this time, mashing her loins into his face, trying to open herself to him in a way that was more than physically possible. She wanted him to kiss her clit, yes, but she also wanted to be so wide and accessible he could almost climb inside her. It was submission again, she realised dimly. She wanted to be every available thing to him. To surrender all her sex, to *be* all sex. To be totally available...

'Caress your breasts,' she heard him mutter through her silky-soft, tabby-coloured hairs, 'Do it, Isis,' he commanded. 'Play with your pretty little tits.'

Obedient, she curved her nimble, scarred fingers around the fruity globes of her breasts. The scars were sugar-pink lace against the white skin of both hand and breast; another legacy of the accident that had tattooed her face, another distinction she had, at last, accepted as charming in its own right.

'Do it!' Josh growled from between her legs – and Isis flew up off the bed, her quim spasming from his hard little suck on her clittie.

Heat was beating between her legs... It was difficult

5

to make her hands work ... They seemed to belong to some other woman, not the one who was bouncing and babbling, wracked by orgasm, and being fed on by the ravening man at her crotch.

'Please,' she sobbed, not knowing what it was she begged for. It certainly wasn't that he stop chewing her clitoris between his pursed lips. It certainly wasn't that his long fingers should withdraw from the jungle-hot crack of her bottom. It certainly wasn't that he stop tickling the tiny puckered hole there.

'Oh God! You bastard! Yes!' she heard herself howl as his finger poked and pushed. 'Yes! Yes! Yes!' she yowled as it pressed on, then grossly waggled in the tightest opening of her body. It was monstrous. Unthinkable that she should respond like a mindless animal when a man pushed his finger inside her bottom. And licked her clitoris like a god at the same time. Her whole body, and her pulsing, dripping sex, seemed to spin slowly between the twin poles of shame and elevation.

And Isis could not tell which one was which. The slow drag of his tongue against her throbbing bud; or the relentless vulgar finger that moved in her anal canal.

'Don't,' she whimpered as it went deeper, and without thinking, she bore down on the intrusion.

'You don't mean that at all, you dirty little girl,' said her tormentor, lifting his face from her loins and smiling up at her. 'You love it.' He was moving upwards now, his finger still in her rear, 'You love it, or you wouldn't be riding it like this, would you?' The finger pushed harder, and seemed to knock on a spot inside that was connected to the root of her cruelly abandoned clit.

Isis groaned hoarsely.

The cry was stifled as Josh kissed her lips, his tongue stabbing against hers in time to the pushes of his crudely inserted finger.

Isis groaned again, the sound a gabble around the tongue that filled her mouth. She could feel her juice flowing fast now, trickling down over her perineum and coating Josh's hand as it curved around her bottom.

'You're drooling, lady' she felt him murmur against her lips, 'This really gets to you, doesn't it?' He pushed more. 'Doesn't it?'

Distracted, Isis tried to shake her head, but ended up nodding as he took away his mouth. There was devilment in his brown eyes as he stared down, impaling her eyes as surely as he did her twitching behind.

'No! None of that,' he said, taking her chin and shaking her face gently as she tried to close her eyes and turn away. He'd knelt up beside her now, and was looking down straight into her eyes. 'I want some straight talk out of you, Isis my darling. Some honest answers about your body . . . Do you understand?'

Again, she nodded, feeling like an exhibit, an exotic flower or bird, spread for an experiment and pinned by the finger lodged deep in her arse. A strangely apt image, thought the detached observer inside her who could still manage to think. Although *she* was the one who was a scientist . . .

'Tell me you like *this*,' Josh said, smiling as his finger curled wickedly inside her.

'Yes, I do.' Isis's face was all red now; it wasn't just her scar that was glowing. She was burning up with embarrassment, yet the hotter she got, the wetter she got. Her slit must be a lake by now, a great, soft chasm full of bubbling juices. She'd never felt more aroused in her life.

'Say it properly.'

'I like having your finger inside me.' Oh yes . . . I do! I do! screamed the voice of her fluttering quim.

'Inside where, Isis?'

'In my bottom.'

'Where? Speak up.'

'I like having your finger up my bottom,' she answered, almost crying with mortification and the rawest need she'd ever felt. 'Oh God, Josh!' she squealed as he took her clitoris between the fingers of his free hand and manipulated gently to the rhythm of his anal prodding.

Isis felt the fiery approach of orgasm, then really did sob as he took away both of his hands and left her high and dry, her pelvis lifting involuntarily to seek out the stimulation she'd so suddenly lost.

'Rude girl,' he teased, and Isis couldn't have cared less if he'd called her 'slut', 'whore', 'bitch', 'she-cat' or a dozen other even fouler insults. All she wanted was to be done, and done well. To be rubbed and probed and humiliated in any demeaning way he fancied... She wanted to be plugged. Anywhere. Fingered and stroked. She felt like gripping her own knees, and canting up her body from the bed to expose her holes as explicitly as she was able. And then, with both her entrances displayed, she'd beg him to fill either one of them.

'Show me what you've got, sweetheart,' he told her softly, and without thought she did just the thing she'd imagined – pulling apart her thighs as she curled upwards, then feeling herself lifted higher by his hand at the small of her back. Her juices slurped obscenely as her vagina stretched and gaped, and she felt his hardness brush against her flank as he leaned over to study the view.

'Beautiful...' she heard him whisper. 'A man could die in either.'

He stared at her sex and bottom for what seemed like hours. Isis panted weakly, wishing he'd touch her – or let her touch herself. But all he seemed to want to do for the moment was look.

'I'd like to take your arse,' he said suddenly, punctuating the statement by touching the tip of his forefinger to her anus. There was no entry this time, just the lightest of pressures; yet Isis's clitoris leapt wildly and she groaned aloud.

'You're very tight,' he observed almost absently, 'Maybe I should put something inside you first? To stretch you...' The finger stayed perfectly still and Isis felt a tear trickle from the corner of her eye. 'I could get a carrot from the kitchen. One of those big fat ones with the top still on. I could push it in you and leave it there for an hour or two to hold you open.'

She was sobbing again now: frustrated almost to the point of a spontaneous climax by the vision of herself like

8

this before him but with a giant carrot protruding horridly from her bottom . . .

Oh God, no! Some things were just too much. But if so, why did the idea of a vegetable inside her make her almost scream aloud to come?

'Or perhaps you've got a love-toy we could use?' The supporting hand seemed to heft her slightly, as if she were a baby he was dandling on his knee. 'A sensuous woman like you must have a dildo tucked away somewhere. Something big and wide and black perhaps? Something donkey-size I could coat with your nectar then push slowly, oh so slowly into you . . . Right into your bottom, Isis . . . Into your pretty, quivering bottie. You'd like that, wouldn't you?' he asked, returning to his pattern of vocal torment.

'Yes,' she croaked, her lips dry, her sex awash.

'But maybe you'd just like me in you?' The finger tickled infinitesimally, and Isis felt the hole beneath it flutter.

'Oh yes,' she sighed, arching back her head, her throat bared for a vampire kiss as she offered her rounded woman's rear for buggery.

'So be it, my angel,' her lover purred, gentle now as he rolled her over, and urged her, bottom upwards, into a cat-like crouch. 'Oh God, you're perfect,' she heard him say, then felt him kissing the globes of her rudely exposed rump. He seemed to be whispering a litany of nonsense against her pale satiny skin, murmuring a catechism to the finely honed musculature of her gluteous maximi. She sighed with approval as – just once – he kissed the tiny hole he'd soon be plundering.

From a million miles away, she recognised that their equation had changed again. She was still, in a sense, the submissive . . . and yet Josh was paying the deepest of reverence to her offered bottom. Mentally, she heard the voice in her head dismiss the debate. Whoever said sex made sense?

And she knew the sight before him was worthy of worship . . .

Her body, despite the odd faint scar, was smooth, well-shaped and sensually inviting. Her backside was full, yet

9

taut, and she'd admired her own anterior cleavage in the mirror often enough to know that Josh would love it.

Sensing him right behind her, she flirted herself towards him and was rewarded when his fingers returned to her warm, waiting crack, sliding beneath first, to her vagina, to load themselves with her juices.

There was plenty there for the taking; she was quite indecently lubricated. It was running down her legs, almost as far as her knees – and as fast as it overflowed her quim a thick, new oozing took its place.

'Juicy lady,' Josh hissed against her back as he curved himself over her, scooping out love-juice from her slit.

Beside herself with need, Isis fell forward, cradling her head in one arm and pressing one side of her face into the pillow. Vaguely conscious that it was her good side she'd hidden, she reached down beneath her arched body and slid her searching hand between her legs. Her rubbing fingers met Josh's and for a few seconds they duelled in the pool of her moisture, working together on her slutty, sex-crazed body: she, scrubbing almost viciously at her clitoris; he, plunging two fingers into the maw of her aching vagina.

'In here first,' he said, pushing them in further, then withdrawing to leave the way clear for his cock.

Isis nuzzled the cotton against her face, cooing with content as he entered in one long, smooth stroke. This easy, familiar shafting wasn't going to last long, but she was damn well going to enjoy it while it did. Pinching her clittie, she gasped into the pillow, her quim grabbing at Josh in a light, sweet orgasm.

He was gasping too, and sweating heavily; she could feel the wetness of his torso slapping rhythmically against her back.

But this was only the entrée... Even though she'd already come – beautifully – this gentle, normal rhythm was just the prelude to a more primitive coupling. He slid in and out of her for a few more minutes, the beat of it steady, almost leisurely, then drew out and back, poising himself in readiness.

Isis could feel the head of his cock almost floating against the insloping of her right buttock. It was almost as if he were asking silent permission to violate her; and without waiting for a spoken question she nodded, then murmured a ragged 'yes'.

Edging the weight of her body onto one shoulder, and burying her face in the pillow, she reached behind her and eased herself open with her fingers; widening the shaded cleft so Josh could anoint her anus with juices he'd drawn up from her quim. Aware of him rising above her, she felt a strong sense of being 'mounted' and gathered herself for an act that was both ravishing and primal. She felt his glans pressing in the groove, finding the spot, beginning to probe. And when it lodged against the rumpled hole, she wrenched mercilessly at her bottom cheeks, widening the orifice to ease his way in. As he pushed, the tension on that small ring of muscle seemed to jerk by proxy on several different parts of her body at once; the most urgent being her sodden quim and the tiny throbbing nut of her clitoris.

She moaned again, not in pain – not yet – but with an excitement more keen and clear than she'd experienced in ages. This was danger. A exquisite love-hate badness that was a potent caress in itself.

And then he started pushing harder.

Isis bit her lip, unable to decide whether it was pain she was feeling, or a crazy, wrong-way-round pleasure. Biting harder and tasting blood, she bore back against him, awed by his unforeseen hugeness as he forced his way into her resisting, untried entrance.

Oh Josh, you're hurting me, she told him silently, her eyes watering from the obscene sensations in her bowel, yet feeling happy, so happy that she'd selected this special man – a man she was truly fond of – to take the first meal at this bizarrely erotic table.

And she still couldn't properly distinguish whether it was discomfort – liar, pain – or a luscious yet grubby delight she was feeling in her partially penetrated rear.

Progress was slow. In spite of all the bossy games he'd

played with her earlier, Josh was both a gentleman and a gentle man. Isis could sense his restraint, sense him curbing his strength and the power of his lust to minimise the shock to her sensitive interior.

Oh Josh, don't be such a sweetie, she almost cried out to him as she butted up and back to meet his frustratingly considerate onslaught. Yet still her body resisted him, wouldn't let him properly and deeply into it . . .

'Relax, baby,' he whispered in her ear as he climbed up over her back, adjusting the angle of his onslaught, 'Relax, sweetheart . . . Go loose. Let me in. It's what you want . . .'

Isis quivered heavily, her whole consciousness focused in the groove of her partly speared bottom.

It *was* what she wanted. She wanted his chunky, veiny prick inside her, distending the passage no other man had breached. She wanted her rectum filled and plugged, the relentless pressure squeezing the juices of her sex until they ran like a thick creamy river down her legs. She slid her fingers into her quim and tapped gently on her clitoris, drawing the fire of her senses back to the seat of her pleasure and away from the burning ache in her anus.

'Yes, my sweet, that's it,' she heard him mutter, his voice not quite steady any more. 'Touch yourself. Stroke yourself. Make it nice . . .' She felt him shift slightly, taking his muscular weight on one arm as his free hand went beneath her to cup a dangling breast, then squeeze its stiffened nipple.

A circuit formed, a tight loop between her breast and her clit. Pleasure surged along the powerline and Isis grunted into the pillow, her empty vagina contracting as she thrust hard and backwards to meet her lover's forward thrust.

Oh God, he was enormous! Flesh that was generous on the outside seemed ten times bigger inside her. Her quim still pulsing, she seemed to hang suspended in space from the great hot club that was buried to its hilt in her bottom. Its massive presence must be displacing her organs inside her. She could almost feel the thickness of it pushing in her throat, her innards bulging impossibly against the back of her eyes. She was packed with him. Stuffed. Wadded. Engorged. Her bowels surged hideously as he moved inside her, her abused nerve-ends sending sly, shitty messages to her reeling, befuddled brain.

Yet even as she fought the automatic urge, her clitoris quickened anew, leaping in a wicked orgasm triggered by her unthinkable visions of soiling the man who pleasured her.

Holding herself perfectly still, feeling Josh freeze sympathetically above her, she rode the wave of pleasure and shame until both her quim and her roiling bowels calmed. In her mind's eye she saw a vivid tableau: a dark man sprawled across the back of a woman who was paler than pale, his face buried in the shimmering, brindled waves of her hair, his penis invisible, lodged right up to his balls in the forbidden hole between her smooth white buttocks.

It was lewder than lewd. Disgusting. Fabulous. She still dare not move, but she felt sensation stir again in the tissues of her cunt. In the beautiful stasis, she let Josh nudge aside her fingers with his own. He'd abandoned the dangling pear of her swollen breast to turn his caressing attentions to her clitoris. She felt his cock throb softly inside her as he massaged and teased. Another circuit had formed, she understood dimly, a loop within the generous man who possessed her, a feedback between the giving of pleasure and its taking.

'Oh yes, Josh, yes,' she purred as he took the tiny, exquisitely sensitive berry between finger and thumb and tugged it in the way she loved best. Shuffling beneath his weight, she pushed her slim hand down beside his, flexed her wrist and thrust two fingers roughly into her own vagina. She could feel – through the thinnest of membranes – the great heated bar of him as he began to move slowly in her bowel. She fluttered her fingers slightly and felt him gasp into her hair as she almost stroked his cock from within her own body.

Josh made an inarticulate noise and went still inside her – as if better to appreciate her off-beat caress.

Isis protested, 'No! Please! Keep moving, Josh . . .

13

Please. Do it. Fuck me, fuck me! Please!' Without knowing why, she wanted him to be almost brutal. To take her. Debase her. Hurt her, even. She wanted his great prick to slam into her, ream her out. She wanted him to move only for his own satisfaction, and when he reached it, to fill her outraged rear with a full, hot load of his semen.

'Use me, Josh, use me,' she begged, her words muffled as she mewled and chewed the pillow beneath her face.

'But I can't use you,' he answered, sounding almost fearful of her, even though he was taking and fucking her in the most demeaning and ungiving of ways; dismissing her womanhood as redundant while he plowed the furrow of her resisting arse.

'Yes you can!' Impatient, she dashed his hand from her crotch and began beating hard on her own clitoris and forcing her bottom upwards to make him go deeper.

Drooling and biting the cotton pillowcase, she writhed in ecstasy as her dear, empathic lover grabbed her by the hips, got full purchase on her bucking body and went at it with a savage frenzied violence.

Triumph flared inside her, and the world reduced to a microcosm that was simply the tight, impaled orifice of her rectum and the steadily pulsing bead of her clitoris. She whined and groaned and keened, coming in one long, continuous internal undulation that licked and rippled out from the twin focuses of arsehole and clit to bathe the whole of her belly in hard golden light.

Out of her mind, she felt her spirit rise up and watch Josh biting her shoulder – an animal in his rapture – while his fingers gouged deep into the thin flesh that covered her pelvic bones. Sinking down again, rejoining the tumult of pain and pleasure, Isis heard his breathing go ragged, and felt the gust of it on her neck as he gasped and panted against her sweat-dewed skin. Her nether moisture poured out in a rich new stream; her vulva bathed his slapping balls as it pulsated against them in climax.

Weeping with joy, she heard his fierce shout and felt his boiling seminal flood pump long and sweet inside her.

'Isis Isis Isis . . .'

14

It sounded so tender and loving. A chant of unalloyed affection and gratitude murmured close, so close to her face, still pressed to the tear-soaked pillow.

Glowing satisfaction made her giddy, and even as her body still radiated its afterpleasure, Isis felt a strange shift of perception as the world seemed to rotate slowly on its axis and leave her reclining, on her back, on a smooth, leather-covered couch rather than the coiled, crumpled sheets of a well-used bed.

'Easy, baby . . . Relax. You're back,' said a familiar, melodic and utterly feminine voice. A soft hand brushed the damp hair out of her eyes, and everything went first dark, then light as Isis let her eyelids flutter open.

The smile that hovered above her was not Joshua Jordan Mortimer's and after a quarter of a second she didn't really expect it to be. Instead of Josh's brown eyes and handsome masculine features, she was looking up into a face of the most stunning and supremely female beauty she'd ever encountered.

And a pair of huge, glittering jewel-green eyes that were quite unmistakably Tricksie Turing's.

2

The Sorceress's Apprentice

Isis let her eyelids close again and seal in the beautiful image. Red lips, milky skin, eyes like huge chips of emerald.

'Are you okay?' the vision enquired, stroking Isis's shoulder, touching the warm bare skin with a gentleness that was breath-taking.

'Yeah ... I'm fine, Trix. Just ... Wow! Oh God, that was sensational!'

'Wasn't it,' Tricksie murmured, and dimly Isis realised the experiment had been a success. She flicked open her eyes again. In a few moments she'd be herself again – her real self – and able to analyse ... But for now she could do nothing but float.

'Do you want anything, sweetheart?' Tricksie asked, taking Isis's pulse as she'd been taught to, then stroking her arm lingeringly.

'Yes, a blanket and a glass of Astrapure. But don't rush, love. See to the debug programme first. I'll be okay for a minute. I just need some space to think ...'

'Sure thing, boss,' said Tricksie softly as she made to turn away.

Struggling out of her limbo, Isis grabbed her friend's wrist. 'You did a slick job, Trix. Beautiful ... I need time to get my head back together, that's all.'

'You got it ...' Tricksie's smile was brilliant, joyous, blinding, and incredibly Isis felt her body respond to it. It was crazy. She was rousing again, getting hot, and she'd only just finished an adventure.

16

Not really wanting to, she let Tricksie go, and as the woman set about her diagnostic tasks, Isis began her own less tangible analysis.

Both physically and mentally she felt fantastic. Her body was warm, relaxed and comfortable, and her psyche was still thrilled by what she'd dreamt.

The inimitable Josh Mortimer, how she'd missed him. It was months since they'd shared their one night together, but she supposed it was her constant thoughts of him that had made this last trip so real and wild. Closing her eyes, she let the images reform on the black velvet screen of her mind . . . She saw Josh's fine brown body. Felt his heat, his hardness, the erotic rudeness of his final slow assault. His presence in her arse, the hot flood of his come, the glorious weakening of submission. The raw sensation of a long, loving buggery. All these still seemed real to her, and 'remembering' them rekindled their pleasure.

Stirring slightly, she sent her hyper-tuned senses winging around the poles of her body; reliving each sensation at the site, checking, assessing, enjoying.

She was unplugged and unfettered now, thanks to the gentle deftness of Tricksie. The lovely woman had a feather-light touch; it was no wonder all the clients adored her.

Her mind flitting from Tricksie back to Josh, Isis wriggled her bottom against the smooth white leather of the treatment couch. It was one solid piece again now, and the intimate probes were gone. Her pussy and her anus were her own, but there were faint, sensual echoes of the dildos that had so efficiently filled her. Mounted on those fat sexy presences were the Pleasurezone transceivers, the minute alchemic chips patented by Isis herself, that both recorded sensation and created it, taking pleasure from without to within.

A lightning of a kind was still there. Joy in the hot pulpy wetness of her quim, the invaded looseness of her rear . . . Delicate flickers of it teased her. Soft pulsations. Crying out quietly, she arched, pressed her hand to her crotch, and came. Moisture bubbled between her fingers

17

as she squeezed her thighs together, then ran, thick and gelid and sultry, down the warm peachy crack of her arse.

'Yes, love. That's it. Give it up . . .' Warm arms were suddenly around her and other fingers floated across her belly and covered her own, pressing down lovingly on the hand that coaxed out her pleasure. Still coming, Isis fell against Tricksie's lush bosom and sobbed.

'You look so beautiful when you come,' whispered Tricksie, smoothing her free hand over Isis's unbound hair.

It was a tender gesture, and the words were spoken in sweet good faith, but to Isis such statements were forever open to question.

'Me? Beautiful?' she said, raising her face from Tricksie's perfumed cleavage and showing the mark that would never go away. What the accident, years ago, had done to her.

'Yes. Beautiful.' The voice was firm, but the fingers that touched Isis's scar were thistledown, tracing its purple-whorled shape with all the delicacy and skill that she used on the thing it resembled: the intricate crumpled-petal structure that lay between Isis's pale thighs.

It was a strange phenomenon, a backwards kind of recompense, Isis supposed, but whenever someone caressed her scar she felt the same sensation in her quim. She shuddered violently when it happened now, and whimpered like a child when Tricksie went one better, petting both face and body at the same time.

'No! No, sweetheart, no!' Isis moaned. She meant 'yes'. Meant 'yes yes, more more, don't stop'. And marvellously Tricksie understood her, coaxing spasm after spasm from that sweet hot coruscating place.

It took a while to recover. For Isis, at least . . . But eventually, with a soft, luscious kiss on the mouth, Tricksie issued an instruction.

'Take five, boss,' she ordered after fetching the blanket and the glass of water.

Isis allowed herself to be coddled, drinking the mineral water obediently and staying still and quiet while Tricksie wrapped her in the blanket before returning to less intimate tasks.

Snuggled in the cozy woollen cloth, with her body relaxed and her sex still fizzing, Isis felt both guilty and amused. She was tickled by Tricksie's bossiness, and guilty because she had let herself *be* bossed. It wouldn't do, all this loafing about. She was the scientist, the inventor, the one who should be reviewing the new data. Tricksie was as smart as a whip, and an amazing natural technician, but the truth was she wasn't a computer expert. She'd never been to any kind of college or secondary school; and her previous, and still sometimes current occupation was whoring.

Isis couldn't actually remember which of them had suggested this novel career move – star-spangled prostitute to lab-coated therapist – but she could vividly remember the circumstances.

They'd been in bed together.

Isis and Tricksie had been occasional lovers since they'd very first met, but it was only in the last six months that their relationship had grown so deep. Hugging the blanket tighter around her, Isis considered the cause.

Primarily, it was the simple female need for mutual sympathy. Shoulders to cry on and bodies to cling to for comfort. Comfort, because they had both lost a man. In Isis's case 'mislaid' was probably a better description, but for Tricksie the condition was more radical.

About a fortnight after Josh Mortimer had made love to Isis, then departed to 'fix a mine', as he so modestly put it, another man known to Isis and Tricksie had also disappeared. But this one had gone like the criminal he most probably was, dissolving smoothly into the night without a word, a message or a kiss.

Goddamn you, Diabolo! thought Isis now, angry again with the absent Moon Devil on her own behalf, but oh-so much more so for Tricksie.

Diabolo had been Tricksie's pimp, Isis's helper at the 'Zone, and an occasional and sensational bedmate to both of them. Pleasurezone and Isis were coping quite adequately without him; but unfortunately Tricksie was in love with the bastard and his midnight flit had devastated her.

She'd not shown it, of course, and Isis had been awed by her friend's indestructable composure. Tricksie had twinkled and dazzled as she always did, turned more tricks than ever, and continued to reduce grown men to quivering wrecks with her adorable face and her superbly fuckable body. But inside she'd been dying.

Only Isis had seen the tears and the agony. Only Isis had been there to wipe away those tears and hold that marvellous body, then caress it passionately, touch it, kiss it, and finally content it. Consolation had never been sweeter . . .

It had been a strange night, that night when everything had changed between them. Beautiful. Intense. Unexpected.

Isis had started out on a mission to make Tricksie happy again. To give her as much pleasure as possible as often as possible, with her hands and her lips and her body. But it had been Tricksie who had ended up doing the giving. Isis's quim pulsed deep and hard just thinking about it; her flesh remembering the night as clearly as her brain did.

Her friend had kissed her there. Down there. Delicate butterfly kisses that turned into voracious sucking; sucking that had turned into a long, untiring licking: Tricksie's hot wet tongue on Isis's clitoris. Orgasm after orgasm, flaming in her loins until she cried out for mercy; the victim in place of a cold-hearted man who was absent.

It had been Tricksie's way of fighting back, this great glutting of pleasure; and in the end, Isis had been too drugged by it and too high on it to reason or argue. Since then they'd been lovers, friends and working partners in Pleasurezone, but Isis still had a nasty suspicion that if Diabolo walked in right now, Tricksie would fall down on her knees and crawl across the floor to reach him.

'Bastard!' she hissed and Tricksie looked round curiously.

20

'Beg pardon?'

'Nothing. Just thinking about something irritating,' answered Isis, throwing off her blanket and dropping neatly to her feet. The action was deliberate. She'd shown Tricksie her naked body as a distraction; to take her mind off the man they both knew was far more than irritating.

What am I thinking about that shit for? Isis asked herself as she shrugged into a white lab coat and joined Tricksie at the console. Still barefoot, she slid onto a stool and reached first for a headband to hold back her thick, tabbycat waves, then for a pair of half-moon granny specs that she popped on the end of her nose.

There were much much nicer men to think about, she decided firmly, peering at the data display, frowning and stabbing at a key. Decent men with feelings, Joshua Jordan Mortimer for one, and it was time to find out what Tricksie had thought of his recent 'performance'.

'Okay. This all looks very satisfactory, Trix, but it's what *you* experienced that matters. To put not too fine a point on it – ' She couldn't resist giggling. 'How was it for you?'

'Utterly sublime. When can I meet him for real?'

Tricksie's voice was nothing less than a purr; it made Isis's heart leap with excitement. They *had* had the same adventure then.

For a while now, Isis had been working on improving the therapist's ability to monitor the adventurer's experience. Visuals, via the computer screen, had always been available, but initially Isis had resisted any kind of 'eavesdropping'. Fantasies were strange and private. Many were frankly bizarre. It had seemed unethical to spy on them.

Increasingly though, clients had started asking her to 'join' them; either as a character in their scenarios, or simply as a watcher. Men seemed to get off very strongly on the idea of her observing their sexy foibles, and the data indicated – in all cases – that her 'presence' enhanced their pleasure.

And this was the clincher. The prices she charged were high because her initial borrowing to set up the 'Zone had been astronomical – but she did believe in value for money. If her clients got more of their rocks off with her in their dreams, she felt honour-bound to be there for them.

Monitoring had been the name of the game today, and what she and Tricksie had just run was the ultimate in overseen adventuring. The fantasy had been born in Isis's mind and the pleasure physically experienced in her body; but Tricksie had 'lived' the whole thing with her. An electronic representation of it had been fed straight to her brain via inducer chips held in place against her temples.

How effective the process was, only Tricksie could reveal. Isis had monitored one of Tricksie's fantasies yesterday – a predictably Diabolo-filled episode that had made her blanch, shake, then orgasm wildly – but she didn't consider it a true test. Her own imagination, dream-capacity, call-it-what-you-will, had been unnaturally enhanced by her own invention. Tricksie was pragmatic, down-to-earth and she hadn't adventured that much; if *she* believed in the perceived experience the process of monitoring was valid.

'He's coming home soon, Trix, and I want this lot up and running when he does. Now please, tell me. Does it work?'

'Oh, it works all right ...' Tricksie's voice was soft, awed. The look she gave Isis was solemn. 'It's like magic, Ice. I was there. I was you.' She reached out and brushed her fingers across Isis's brow. 'You're so lovely ... It makes me forget how clever you are. You scare the shit out of me sometimes, love. Honest. It's like being with the high priestess of some ancient religion. A shaman. A sorceress. And I'm your apprentice ...'

Isis was moved. She didn't know what to say or do, except get on with the task in hand.

'Can you describe what you experienced?'

'Okay. Here goes.' Tricksie settled herself on her stool, then reached up to brush a tendril of hair from her eyes. The silky burgundy-coloured strand tumbled down again immediately, but she didn't seem to notice.

'You were in bed with Josh Mortimer. In his flat, I

22

think. I didn't recognise the room. I . . . The action seemed to start with you having him in your mouth,' Her green eyes darkened, went wide, seemed to double in size. 'He was delicious. And big. And so responsive.' She sighed then, and Isis was pleased she'd made Tricksie dream of warm, wonderful Josh instead of that cold swine Diabolo. 'Then he pulled his prick out of my . . . your . . . Jesus, Ice, it *was* me! It was as real as that!' Her eyes flashed and she grabbed for Isis's hand.

'Go on,' whispered Isis. The feelings were starting again for her too. The pseudo-memories. Her damp sex stirred and fluttered, but a faint guilt pricked her. What would Trix say if she knew the whole thing had been a total fiction?

'He did a beautiful thing . . .' Tricksie's voice was thick now, slightly gasping. Her words disjointed. 'He rubbed himself all over my face. Against the scar. I could feel his wetness. His juice. He was smearing it into the scar with his penis.'

Scientific detachment was forgotten for both of them; Isis couldn't concentrate and Tricksie had lost it completely. Arousal was a thick mist in the air, aphrodisiac . . .

'Then he let me suck him again,' the dreamer went on, her face rapt, her eyes like stars, her nipples hard and dark beneath the thin white stuff of her smock. Isis had never seen her friend look more beautiful. 'And it felt so good. So hot . . . And then he sucked me. He was eating me. Licking me. He opened me right up . . . He was licking my clit and touching my bottom. Oh, God, oh God! He pushed his finger into me. Right into me. He was rubbing and pushing . . . He made me want to be gross. Rude. I had to show myself. Show everything . . . Clit. Cunt. Arsehole. Everything held wide open . . .'

There was an obscene magic to Tricksie's explicit litany, and suspended somewhere between an electric myth and the warm flesh-real seductress at her side, Isis couldn't keep her shaking hands still. She pressed her crotch through the cotton of her smock, aware of Tricksie doing the same, and wriggling on her stool, just inches away.

It was Isis's turn now to be awestruck. She watched the ancient female pattern of fingers and pumping loins. Watched Tricksie lift her short white skirt, spread her thighs wide, then use both hands to open herself.

The exposed scarlet curls were dark with juice. Fluid shone on each silky hair. And as she went on dreamily with her description, Tricksie seemed almost unaware she was masturbating.

'He said wicked things to me. Terrible gorgeous things. He kept turning me on and on. He wanted to stick things inside me. In my bottom ... He wanted his prick in there and he knew I wanted it too. He touched me up. Fingered me. Stroked every part of me. Made me crazy for his cock in my arse.'

Tricksie's fingers were moving so nimbly now, that Isis couldn't follow them. She could hear them though ... The thick squelch of liquid. Tricksie's grunts, her slurred attempts at speech. The rude fabulous glooping sound as a finger pumped hard in a soft, tight channel. Two hands worked in immaculate co-ordination. Stroking and penetration. Clitoris and vagina. Two expert hands whose sweet touch Isis knew well.

She was desperate to masturbate again herself, To join in ... Isis's sex ached for the treatment Tricksie was giving hers, but she didn't dare move for fear of disturbing the woman she'd bewitched. The accolyte she'd ensorcelled with erotic dreamery.

'Then he pushed it in me.' Tricksie's voice rose. Wavered and cracked. 'The first time ever ... It was luscious but God, did it hurt!'

Now this, Isis knew, was *her* fantasy. There was no way a working girl like Tricksie could not have been buggered at least once in her life. She'd mentioned it often enough. Had it in her own adventure. It was just Diabolo's style ...

With difficulty, Isis stayed quiet. She wanted to come now, she needed it, but to make it happen would distract her, and make her miss Tricksie's orgasms.

Isis bit her lip as Tricksie shuddered and moaned. She loved the sights and sounds of another woman's pleasure.

Loved knowing what was happening within. Imagined contractions, flesh grabbing and grasping. Rippling. As Tricksie slipped and started to tumble forward, Isis slid to her feet and caught her, cradling and holding as she herself had been cradled and held. The urge to make free with such perfection was like a physical pain; but she stood fast against it.

She could wait. Tonight, there'd be peace, a bed, soft lights, comfort. They'd do it properly. Love each other beautifully, unhurriedly.

Holding Tricksie so tightly, Isis could barely tell which of them was shaking.

Yes, she'd wait. It would be worth it.

Two hours later, Isis was in her shower, in her flat adjoining Pleasurezone, and still waiting. But not for much longer . . .

They'd eventually finished the debug. The post-climactic Tricksie had been deliciously businesslike. 'Okay, boss, that's *that* done with. Shall we get on with the job?'

They'd analysed the data, using both the computer records and Tricksie's account of what she'd monitored. Her second description was cool, rational and utterly precise in spite of its content. They'd finalised the program and fed it into the system for working use.

Now she'd proved its feasibility, Isis was excited by the implications of piggy-back dreaming. Pleasurezone for couples would be the first innovation, and Isis was as fired up by the therapeutic implications as she was by the potential revenue.

Imagine . . . A couple estranged because they were too inhibited with each other to share their fantasies. A partner who couldn't describe what he or she wanted. In the erotic ambience of the 'Zone, such barriers could be smashed and lovers united in mutual knowledge. Full sense monitoring would be safer too. Even for solo adventures. There was always the odd adverse reaction . . .

Isis smiled in the streaming water, remembering the time a very toothsomely half-naked Josh Mortimer had woken up too fast, gone ape-shit and threatened to kill her. Fortunately, he had still been restrained.

And *that* sent her fingers to her sex. Her supercharged memory painted wondrous pictures . . .

Josh on the couch: wired, dildoed and dreaming.

God, that man had looked so beautiful in his straps. Smooth brown skin against pure white leather. His fine body stretched and vulnerable. The rise and delectable rise of a truly exceptional prick.

Delicately prising open her labia, Isis laid a finger experimentally on her clitoris. She couldn't resist touching herself and she didn't try. Her adventure. Tricksie. Memories. It was all too much and too strong. She'd wanted to wait tonight . . . To make herself simmer first, and then bubble and boil.

But Josh Mortimer had been the last and most incendiary straw. A remarkable lover and a memorable man, he was a rampant sexual sweetheart who would soon be back on the scene, thank God.

Things might get a bit involved then, of course; what with adventures owed and new lovers to consider. But surely they could work something out? Maybe she and Tricksie could share him?

The idea hit the spot even as she thought it, and the flesh beneath her fingertip jumped in approval.

Josh *and* Tricksie? Maybe she could run it through the 'Zone first? Try it without commitment by sneaking it into adventures? See how she – and they – liked it?

She imagined positions. Combinations. Two pale bodies and one darker . . . Sandwichings. Circles. Hands, mouths, sexes. One stiff cock, two needful quims. They'd organise it somehow.

'You're beautiful, Queen of Tricks. He'll love you,' she murmured as the water teemed over her.

And this is no use, she thought, smiling up into the warm stream that caressed her scar and sluiced her thick hair flat against her back. I've been in this shower ten minutes now and I haven't washed anything. Except the bit between my legs.

Lazy self-serving bitch! Here she was in the shower, masturbating to all kinds of glorious fantasies; and Tricksie was left behind, cleaning up after her. Not that the sweet thing minded.

Isis often left Tricksie to shut up shop. In her own flat the beautiful whore was maniacally untidy, Isis could vouch for that, but here at the 'Zone, Tricksie seemed imbued with a truly scientific sense of order. The minutiae and routines delighted her. She enjoyed closing down the systems, sprucing up the two treatment rooms, and generally making good. She actively asked to do more about the place, and it was always pin-neat when she'd done. Isis was no lover of chores herself, and just said a silent 'hurray' and let her friend get on with it.

Pleasurezone had affected Tricksie in other ways too. Iris shimmied in the hot flow, indulgently reviewing them . . .

In her determination to appear more like a technician and less like a lady of the night, Tricksie had subtly altered her appearance.

She'd revamped her hair; muting its natural flaming fire-engine red to a refined but still eye-catching burgundy. She'd also started wearing it in a succession of plaits, pleats and chignons. All very fetching, very classy, and though she didn't seem to realise it, even sexier-looking than when she wore her hair loose. She'd also toned down her flamboyant make-up style and acquired a wardrobe of cool, sharp, business-girl suits and chic understated little dresses.

All this amused Isis no end. Mainly because as Tricksie was sex incarnate, a walking talking love goddess, there was always some exquisite little give-away. A neckline that dipped an inch too low. Black needle-seamed stockings instead of taupe or beige. That one maverick tendril of hair that would not stay in place and insisted on coiling down her milky neck and pointing to the lushness of her frontage.

The truth was, Tricksie Turing was physically incapable

of not looking edible . . . and right now Isis felt crazy to taste her.

Fingers working furiously, she slumped in the corner of the shower stall, the ghost of Tricksie in her mind and in her mouth. She drew her own taste to her lips and imagined it her lover's.

'You're a naughty girl, Ice,' said an arch, creamy voice, slightly filtered by the water and lust, 'You said you'd wait for me.'

Tricksie was standing half in, half out of the cubicle, her thin smock painted to her body by the moisture. Her rounded breasts stood out like glory, the nipples huge beneath the sodden cloth, their dark tips distended and corky.

With a small lost cry, Isis abandoned her crotch and reached out, grabbing.

'Hey, let me get this off first.' Tricksie tugged at her soaking smock and peeled it off in one smooth heavenly action.

She was nude beneath it, as always, and her exhibited body was as fine and angelic as the sleek silky way that she moved.

Isis sighed. She'd learned to love her own body. Its shape, its lightness, its suppleness, its unfailing good health; all these pleased her greatly. But beside Tricksie's unparalled gorgeousness, she merely felt adequate . . .

The woman before her had breasts that were large and sculpture-perfect. Classic white orbs, heavy but high, with nipples that cried out to the hand: puckered, innocent and fresh-looking. Isis wanted to cry and laugh and smile at the paradox. This lush, eve-like shape, this whore's working body that had been mauled and possessed and abused and worse . . . How could it still look so untouched? So pristine, so faultless and dewy?

Tricksie was a miracle. And as she stepped fully into the stall the water was already hanging in drops on her bush, clinging like diamonds to a forest of pure coiling scarlet.

Wet, she was more delectable even than dry. The shower

had already demolished most of her sophisticated make-up, and the rest of it went as she slathered gel over her face, her arms and her breasts. Isis watched, entranced, as she slipped a double handful of foam between her long white thighs and submerged her thick crimson pubes in a sea of exuberant bubbles. With mock-innocent gusto, and a sly glance in Isis's direction, Tricksie began to 'wash' her nether parts: stirring the froth wildly and working her hips in an easy, syncopated rhythm.

Isis watched, still as ice, the element she was nicknamed for, yet inside on fire . . . Transfixed, she sobbed as Tricksie brought herself off in a quick, jerking orgasm.

'That's better,' the sated woman said casually. She seemed to need no recovery time at all; she was already reaching for Isis. 'Now let me wash you.'

Isis nodded, weakened and thrilled, yet content as she conceded command. With her hands dangling loosely by her sides, she adjusted her stance. Her thighs parted, her loins tilted. Her crotch seemed to bulge and wave obscenely. Wash here first, it pleaded, the hips that carried it flaunting helplessly forward, begging mutely for the grace of release.

Tricksie chose, instead, to wash Isis's hair. Taking another good dollop of the cleansing gel, she rubbed it into the whole thick multi-hued mop, working quickly and thoroughly to shampoo and rinse, then smoothing her hands caressingly over the planes of her lover's wet face. Her fingers lingered reverently on the lurid scar, then she leaned, warm and close, to press a kiss to its graphic pink shape. Isis felt a tracing tongue, and the sweet hot waft of breath against the evocative mark on her cheek.

It was a shadowplay. The same would soon happen below and her quim pulsed softly in hunger. 'Oh please,' she moaned, her lips close to Tricksie's, longing for that clever red mouth. Breathing deeply, she drew in the fragrance of woman and the faint, sharp fruit-scent of the gel. She imagined sucking the stuff off Tricksie's labia, licking it from her clitoris, grooming it away with all the measured precision of a cat. She wanted it laved from her place too, consumed like an unction from the contours of her lovelorn quim.

Isis quivered and raised her hands, desperate to touch this sumptuous woman who excited her. Tricksie dashed them away, chuckling wickedly. Slithering like an eel, she kept her distance while her own hands slid toyingly over Isis's arms and shoulders.

I can't take much more of this! cried Isis inside as Tricksie took her open mouth and devoured it. Strong, flexible soap-covered fingers went expertly over her body, massaging thighs and buttocks, tracing spine and ribs, washing everywhere evenly. Canny fingers delved into every last crevice and dent. Except the one that needed it most. The swollen-hot folds of her sex . . .

In her enhanced mind's eye Isis could see how it must be down there. She saw engorged flesh. She saw rose-pink and livid blood-fired redness, her heavy, puffy love-lips, her clitoris standing proud and grossly swollen, pulsing silent and slowly in a code of unbearable, spirit-breaking lust.

Isis found a use, then, for her redundant hands, gripping the stainless steel shower-stall handles like fury. Her knuckles went white as Tricksie's fingers shot between her thighs from the back and started lathering the sensitive cleft of her arse. She whimpered as Tricksie rubbed her vigorously yet studiously avoided moving forwards to the hot wet zone that – had it had a voice of its own – would have been screaming aloud for her touch.

'My clit. My clit, please,' she begged, vaguely remembering a similar plea, one that had echoed in the confines of her electronically stimulated brain.

'No no no,' said Tricksie gaily, still hard at work. 'I know what you want, you dirty little girl. You dreamed it for me.' She pushed lewdly to illustrate her point, 'You want something in here.' She pushed again and Isis groaned. 'You want something in your wicked little bottom, don't you? Don't you?' She poked crudely and Isis nodded, almost climaxing in delicious humiliation.

'Turn around,' Tricksie ordered.

Isis obeyed and grabbed tight onto the handles again, bracing her feet on the shower's ridged floor as Tricksie positioned her. The whore's practised hands were smooth, soft-skinned and gentle.

What? Oh what? Tricksie was edging her legs further apart . . .

What? Oh Lord, Isis, tell the truth . . . You *know*!

Two strong thumbs pressed into the inner cheeks of her bottom, and she put her feverish forehead to the cool of the streaming wet tiles. She was opened, completely, and her anus rudely exposed to the relentless rush of the shower. The pounding water itself was a caress, as was the sensation of a small vulgar orifice being perused by laser-green eyes.

'Oh God,' she gulped as a hot, pointed tongue touched that same unholy place.

'Relax, baby.' Tricksie's voice was a zephyr across her twitching bottom, the tiny lip-movements a blessing. Isis felt her lover's tongue dart up and down the crease, then return to the hole itself, furling to delve deep inside. She opened her mouth against the smooth whiteness of the tiles, smearing her anguished face against them and slobbering mindlessly as her sweet, bad love-monster probed her.

Tricksie's thumbs bit wickedly as she pressed in sideways and outwards. Isis felt mercilessly opened, speared by the stiffened tongue that moved in her spit-wet channel. She sobbed and pressed back against the intrusion, wanting, needing to touch herself, but not daring to let go of her handholds lest she tumble in a spasming heap to the floor of the shower. Her abandoned quim was bursting but she loved it, loved it, loved it. Clever Tricksie had perfectly recreated the divine, aching, craving, shaming sensations of the adventure, and Isis knew that at this moment she would have given the sweet whore anything. Truly. Anything.

Isis heard uncouth bubbling grunts coming from her own wet mouth as Tricksie's tongue waggled indecently inside her. The rhythm was rock solid, and Isis felt saliva

31

trickling down the incurve of her bottom, its bubbly texture a contrast to the sleek aseptic water. She heard the sounds of voracious gobbling, and felt her own thick juices oozing out to join the spittle. Her backside was waving crazily now but Tricksie clung on like a leech. First sucking, then stabbing, but always driving onwards and upwards in her pursuit of erotic supremacy. The moment when Isis lost her pride and her mind completely in a maelstrom of deviant pleasure. It, and she, the sucked and stuffed one, would come any second now. Become just a filthy, howling sex-thing, climaxing involuntarily with her quim empty, and her behind full of stiff plunging tongue.

Even as she thought it, it happened. Tricksie thrust jaw-crackingly deeper and it melted some discreet inner barrier. Her tongue-tip barged against a place that Isis had never known about. Some profound sexual trigger . . . And with a long broken wail, she started coming.

Her unfilled cunt heaved and pulsed. Sensation washed out from it and engulfed her, then dwindled at light-speed to a hard bright blast at the jumping root of her clitoris. She slumped against the tiles, snorting in air, and felt Tricksie slump with her, that devil-woman's tongue still lodged in its outlaw haven.

Consciousness wavered and drifted, but the small sweet prod stayed in place, dabbing imperiously.

'I . . . I can't,' begged Isis, but obediently, subserviently, she climbed onto her knees, raised her rear, and offered up her body for more . . .

3

Welcome Home Mister Mortimer

PRIORITY. PRIORITY. PRIORITY.

Isis stabbed a button, cut the red flashing light, and
eyed the message screen in her bedroom narrowly. Who
the devil had been trying to contact her in the middle of
the night?

Some crank, probably – which was why she had the
machine in the first place. Working in the sex business
laid you open to all kinds of weirdos and freaks. Most of
these odd-balls went on to be the 'Zone's best customers,
but it was always best to be on the safe side. This way she
could filter out the nasties from the ones who were just
plain delightfully strange.

She took a swig of coffee from her mug and sighed,
appreciating another of Tricksie's consummate skills. The
angel! She'd left a full pot of Blue Mountain for Isis to
wake up to.

Still savouring its peerless aroma, Isis pressed a button
on the machine that would show her the message's point
of origin – often a useful indicator as to who or what to
expect.

Holy Moly! Who the hell did she know *that* far away?

For a moment, the location completely flummoxed her.
The distance was unimaginable. Then her whole body
loosened, shuddering heavily. The tremor was so sudden,
intense and downright pleasurable that she put down her
unfinished coffee and clapped a hand to her fluttering
loins.

Of course she knew someone . . .

Memories of last night's adventure hit her like a runaway truck. Beautiful pictures of sucking and being sucked. Of rampant, moaning copulation. Submission. Of dirty, delectable, perverted sex all overlaid with a tenderness that was strangely aposite.

Then, in a moment of disorientation, true recollections blended with the *faux* ones. Josh in the Pleasurezone at *her* mercy. Josh on the night he'd left. Gentle, naked, gorgeous Josh in her bed and in her body. Gentle, naked, gorgeous and *big* Josh.

'Oh, Josh,' she whispered, pressing her tingling mound and reaching out with her free hand to cue the lovely man's message.

The screen filled with a slightly phased image of a face that was intimately familiar. A dark, wickedly handsome face, but one that was also – at the time of recording – quite endearingly and boyishly nervous.

'I hate these bloody machines!' complained Josh's dancing electrons. 'Look, Isis . . . I don't know when you'll get this, but I'm on my way home. I'm not sure when I'll get in, but I'll try to be in La Selene tomorrow night – ' He appeared to consult his chronometer, and the momentary sight of his strong brown wrist gave Isis goose-bumps. He had such superb hands. Engineer's hands with long clever fingers that could get into the tiniest and most sensitive of crannies. 'That's about eight o'clock, your time. I – ' He looked to the left, out of Isis's line of sight, and frowned. 'Sorry, Isis, this slot is about to close. We'll talk tomorrow . . . I . . . Oh God, this is hopeless!' The image leapt, then started rolling with stomach-churning speed, but just as the recording dissolved into static, his voice leapt desperately from the speaker, 'Dammit, Isis, I've missed you!'

'And I've missed you, Mister Mortimer,' whispered Isis, re-cueing the call, running it without sound then freezing it at a particularly awesome frame. Beneath her pressing fingers and her kimono, beneath its sleep-crushed mat of curls, her quim rippled in a long, deep wave. It was a special kind of man who could reach out across the aether and caress her as if he'd been there in the flesh.

Special, yet as soon as he arrived, things were going to get complicated . . .

As a paying Pleasurezone customer, with four adventures still owing, Isis didn't think she ought to take him to her bed. Well, not immediately anyway.

The lines between business and pleasure were decidedly blurred where the 'Zone was concerned, but Isis had made it a house rule never to get involved; that is, to have straight sex with her clients. To be lover as well as therapist could distort their confidence in her. She had, at certain delicate moments, to project an aura of total clinical detachment. That couldn't really happen if they'd seen her have an orgasm . . . seen her lose all her control. Heard her scream and groan.

Okay, so she had made love with Josh just before he'd left. Several times in one night. But that was only because she'd taken the goddamned machine to bits and it had stubbornly refused to go back together again. He'd been leaving for a long tour of duty at an unbelieveably remote mining facility. There were no women there, and precious few comforts of any kind. He'd been entitled to pleasure of some sort before becoming celibate for months on end.

But he was coming back as a client again now. It was a whole new ball game, and the man himself a sore temptation. Last night had proved to her how vulnerable she was.

But there was nothing unethical, awkward or complicated about pursuing her private scenarios, was there? Her solo sex . . . Simple straightforward secret garden daydreams with no electronic assistance whatsover.

Well, no bolt-on extras apart from her own augmented imagination.

A born dreamer, Isis had created stories and fantasies for as long as she'd been able to think coherently. Since puberty, those inner worlds had been almost exclusively sexual, and this rich fund of dreams had formed the basis of the Pleasurezone databank. She'd devised most of the set pieces from her own erotic stories – and now the process was becoming reciprocal. She fed the 'Zone and the 'Zone fed her. Wickedly.

And she could use that wickedness now, couldn't she? In the service of her attraction to Josh.

Okay Mister Mortimer, let's roll, she told his image within her, locking the door then gathering all the pillows from her bed and mounding them in the squashy armchair beside it.

If the white leather treatment couch was the cradle of fantasy, this poor old chair was the very throne of masturbation. She'd had some fine times in this chair, preferring it even to her bed, and as she threw herself backwards amongst the pillows, she saw a dozen lightning freeze-frames. Shuffling, she stretched one leg straight out, and draped the other languidly over the chair-arm.

The pose itself was another habit. With her thighs flung wide, her quim was open and exposed, accessible to questing fingers and the cooling caress of the air. Sighing and closing her eyes, she parted the wings of her delicate Japanese kimono.

And travelled.

In the world behind her eyelids, she was dressed to kill and sitting in the centre of La Selene, the nightclub through which clients gained entrance to Pleasurezone. It was a place she loved, and somewhere she seemed to meet all the important people in her life. Surrounding her now were the members of what she liked to call her 'court'.

Tricksie was there, lush and exquisite, locked in the arms of her beloved Diabolo – that icon of sinister Latinate beauty whom Isis's imagination had conveniently retrieved from wherever. The couple were caressing uninhibitedly, fondling each other's genitals through their clothes, but not once did their combined gaze move from Isis.

Also present was Guido – the handsome young La Selene barman for whom Isis had a soft spot – arm in arm with another watcher.

In the dreamworld Isis nodded, acknowledging her cousin, St Etienne.

You are one peculiar person, Ett! Isis thought for perhaps the thousandth time in her life. She laid her fingers teasingly on her belly, then slid them lower. It was a good thing she and St Etienne were only marginally related; some of her feelings weren't cousinly at all. St Etienne was mad, bad and sublimely beautiful, even if she did spend most of her time dressed as a man. She was also one of the most innately erotic individuals Isis had ever met. More insatiable even than Tricksie, Ett was a hedonist and writer who indulged in every kind of sex known to man or woman. With either gender, and preferably in numbers exceeding two. She'd made passes at Isis for as long as they'd known each other, and there was a tacit but unspoken agreement between them that one day, Isis would succumb . . .

Having assembled her audience, Isis wriggled her bottom more comfortably into the chair and brought on the star of the show.

Out of the shadows stepped Joshua Jordan Mortimer, clad in black as he had so often been during the course of their all too brief acquaintance. In this interior pseudo-reality, it seemed the most natural thing in the world that he should walk through the throng towards her, then fall on his knees, take one of her slender feet in both hands and raise it up to his lips to kiss the perfect arch of her instep.

He eased off her shoe and fondled her nylon-clad foot, and in both worlds her quim grew hot and sticky. She slid two fingers into the feverish groove, struck up a rhythm, and hurled herself deep into her fantasy.

As Josh had the benefit of nuzzling and sucking her toes, it seemed only fair that the onlookers get a share of the thrills. Unbuttoning her tailored jacket, she pushed roughly at the camisole beneath and freed her hard-nippled breasts for the pleasure of the assembled company. With the bunched fabric wedged beneath it, her bosom was lifted and lewdly displayed, and she added to the show by pinching her own teats and squirming. Stimulation leapt in an arc from her breasts to her still-concealed sex.

Feeling her in motion, Josh looked up from his kissing. His gaze was a fire that seared her most intimate membranes – but still she gave him only her foot.

In the real world, Isis put her free hand up to one breast; mauling the berry-like nipple and stretching out the whole soft mound into a long, cruel, extenuated cone of pain. In the fantasy there were two cones and she moaned softly, enjoying both the suffering and the pleasure. As Josh's lips nibbled at her ankle, it was time to make dream and reality match. Her clitoris was mad for attention.

When she lifted her skirt, a cheer went up. She was wearing no panties and her pretty, brindled pubes were visibly wet. Squeezing harder on her nipples and opening her legs wider, she spoke in a husky, yet authoritative voice.

'Pleasure me, Josh. Use your hands. Use those beautiful brown fingers, Josh. Make me wetter... Make me ache ... Make me come. Do it now!'

He needed little encouragement. Isis watched him make a small show of rolling up his black denim sleeves, adjusting the way he knelt, then placing a hand flat on each of her thighs with his thumbs pointing inwards. There were no nerve-ends in her pubic hair, but she could swear she felt his thumb nails touch it.

'Go on,' she whispered, and with an industrious little digging movement, he parted the soft, lush fleece, then snagged an outer lip with each thumb and opened her up like fruit.

More murmurs of approval ...

Isis wafted her held-open quim in a salacious gesture of triumph. Let them see the juicy, crinkled lips, the tight oozing hole, the purply-pinky-peachiness of her aroused and wantful body. Let them see how big her clitoris got when she needed an orgasm. Let them see Josh obeying her every lustful whim and making her come in precisely the manner she'd specified.

She felt the heat of their stares on her tugged-apart sex and imagined her juices sizzling and popping like grease. The exposure made her engorge more than ever, but she was proud of her own sexual succulence. She was also getting tired of waiting for her orgasm.

'Do it, Josh!' she commanded. 'Put your fingers inside me. Two! Use two!'

When the two slid in, her hot silky channel made a grab for them. Greedy little thing, she chastised her own body. You want more, don't you?

'Josh . . . Put three in. Touch my clitoris too.'

Phantom-lover complied, opening her entrance in a rude, uncomfortable stretch. Her clitoris jumped violently, and a finger settled on it in seconds, pressing with the lightest of emphases. 'Josh! Oh god! You bastard!' she screamed, coming like a comet as the voices gasped in adulation.

Beat. Beat. Beat. Her vagina sucked hard on her fingers as the waves swept out from her clit.

Pulse . . . Pulse . . . Pulse . . . Slower now, and calmer, as the spasms ebbed and she opened her eyes to an empty room and an absence of both lover and watchers.

'Where do you get it all from, Ice?' she asked wryly, sliding out her fingers and flipping her robe across the gooey sexed-out mess of her quim.

Probably some pathological exhibitionist streak, the analyst in her forebrain told her. A backlash against her flawed face that found expression in fantasies of exposure.

'Or maybe you're just a horny bitch?'

Chuckling softly, she leapt to her feet. The sweet sap of lust was a truly glorious thing . . . but lordy, did she need a shower.

But some hours later, at approximately eight o'clock that evening, her sap was rising again. Isis felt its heavy cling between her legs when she walked into the foyer of La Selene. Pausing before the long rank of mirrors, she checked her looks and made a moue – half of irritation, half of pleasure.

It seemed helpless, somehow, to get all wet between the legs at the thought of seeing Josh again. She felt slutty and ridiculously hormonal; precisely when the ability to behave like a cool emotionless scientist – a sort of female Mr Spock – would have been so appropriate and useful.

She was irritated with her face too. Over the years she'd nearly come to love her scar, but ever so often, at times like these, she resented it.

Get real, Ice, she told herself viciously. You can't take a graft, and thick make-up looks stupid. You're stuck with it. Angling her face this way and that, she consoled herself with the one major improvement in her appearance since Josh's last visit. At least her eyes matched these days. A full schleral lens, made from a new hypo-allergenic polymer, gave her two hazel gold orbs instead of one and a muddy bloodshot damaged one.

She was pleased with the rest of herself which looked, she decided, pretty stunning: groomed to perfection, in black, hair pinned back beneath a hat. What's more, her unpredictable Gemini nature forced her to admit something else ... She *enjoyed* feeling randy. Especially for a stone fox like Josh.

Earlier that day, she'd run her purely ethical dilemma by Tricksie.

'You could always let me supervise him,' the whore had pointed out in deceptively casual tones.

Isis, sensing scrutiny, had looked up from her client list and found Tricksie's bright green eyes drilling into her.

'Hmm ...' It was a good suggestion, but the jealous pang it brought was as sharp as it was surprising. What had happened to the idea of 'sharing' all of a sudden? Isis wondered. What to do about Josh was a thorny question, but her primal reaction was not to let her voluptuous and provenly irresistible friend anywhere near him.

'Don't say a word,' Tricksie laughed softly. 'I wouldn't dream of making a move unless you wanted me to. And anyway, why would he want me when he can have you?'

'He doesn't "have" me.' Isis feigned primness to cover her inner heat. 'I feel a responsibility towards him, that's all.'

'I know exactly what you feel towards him,' Tricksie countered, moving closer and running her fingertips evocatively over Isis's face. 'I've been in your head, remember? And quite a lot of what you feel for that guy is down there between those long silky legs of yours.'

'It's unwise to get sexually involved with a client. We both know that.'

The words were emphatic, but Isis's voice wasn't. Tricksie's delicate stroking of the scar was having the effect it usually did. Isis wriggled on her stool, her quim congested and running, as if Tricksie really had been fingering her there, rather than simply tracing the replica.

'Stop that, Trix,' she croaked. 'I know you're only trying to get round me.'

'Okay,' Tricksie ceased the torment, but leaned over to seal it in place with a single soul-stopping kiss. 'But he's the one that should be getting round you . . . If you get my drift?'

Maybe he will, Trix my sweet, reflected Isis now, picking out her favourite spot at the La Selene bar and installing herself there. Tucked away in a shadowy corner, she could lie in wait for Josh. She wanted to see him before he saw her, and this little nook was ideal. She ordered a glass of iced water.

Today had been weird. She'd spent a lot of time devising Josh's welcome home adventure, but she'd really had to work hard at concentration. Especially later, during an afternoon session in the 'Zone. Even then the punter had been a swarthy, rather dishy individual who looked – to her – disturbingly like Josh Mortimer. It had been criminally easy to coax him into a scenario she'd chosen . . . Then translate the monitored images she received into the figures of Josh and herself.

Happily, the client had been over the moon with his trip. Afterwards, he'd walked from the facility on air, barely noticing how quickly his therapist had hustled him out. A therapist who wanted to lie down on her own couch, spread open her legs and finish what the fantasy had started.

Isis smiled at the thought. Then set down her drink with a suddenness that nearly spilled it. As discreetly as she could, she flicked down the veil of her stylish black felt toque; because Josh Mortimer had just walked into the bar and was standing not ten yards away from her, looking searchingly around the room.

God, he looks fabulous! thought Isis in despair. She could not feel detachment. She could not be rational. All she could feel was a bouncing heart, and a great surge of wetness below.

As pulse and quim pounded in synch, she imagined her sheer satin knickers getting moister and moister . . . And no wonder. In the few seconds before her inevitable discovery, she visually devoured him. That familiar fine-boned face. Those dark chocolate eyes. That awe-inspiringly hard-packed groin encased in sinfully clinging black denim . . .

Jesus God, how she'd missed him.

Suddenly her black leather suit felt too tight. It was custom-tailored to her measurements but now she seemed to bulge from it, swollen with juice and sex as if lust had turned her whole body into one aching, weeping vulva.

And he hadn't even seen her yet.

But when he did, Isis was glad of her veil; it gave her just the breathing space she needed. In contrast, Josh gave his feelings away immediately. His mouth dropped open, his eyes blazed and he strode the few yards towards her as if no one else in the room existed.

In the blink of an eye, he was standing before her: sleek and menacing in the all-black outfit she'd uncannily dreamed of him wearing. She wanted him now more than ever . . .

'Hello.'

'Hello.'

In spite of her disfigurement, Isis was rarely embarrassed or tongue-tied. But she was right now. All possible

42

openers seemed banal, and she suspected that whatever she said, it would probably run counter to her recent decisions.

'What's with the veil again?' Josh's voice was slightly sharp – as if he were as nervous as she was.

'I thought it might be better,' Isis offered cautiously, pursing her lips to keep in all the outrageous things she wanted to say.

'And *I* thought we might ... Well, I thought we'd be taking up where we left off.'

Isis lifted her veil, ashamed of her own evasiveness.

Josh Mortimer was a very tired man. Without the lace screen, Isis could see the evidence. The burden of his long, long journey showed up plainly in his eyes and in the tightness of his smooth brown skin across his elegant cheek-bones. It suddenly occurred to Isis that even if she did agree to go straight to bed with him, he'd probably be better off sleeping.

'Look, Josh,' she reached out and placed a gloved hand over his bare one – and felt a tremor pass clean through both of them, 'We can't take up *exactly* where we left off ... but we can get quite close to it.'

'How do you mean?'

'You've got four adventures to have first and then maybe –'

'Stuff the bloody adventures!' His hand twisted quickly and clamped around hers, 'I want *you*!'

Her body quivering, Isis let her hand remain inert, 'Does that mean you're rejecting what I've got to offer ... my finest creations?'

There was some sort of snap inside him, and he smiled tiredly, his gentling like a great spear of heat to her loins.

'I'm sorry, Isis. Really ... Travelling turns me into a total bastard.' He shrugged and his containing hand assumed a softer, more accepting quality. 'Come on, tell me about those creations.'

'Boy, have I got some treats in store for you, Josh Mortimer,' Isis purred, her confidence back. She'd hooked him now, she could tell. He'd only been weary. He still liked her. 'You surely don't think the technology's been standing still while you've been away, do you? We've got a whole new set-up in there.' She nodded in the direction of the discreet red baize door at the back of the room – the portal to her palace of electric dreams.

An interesting gamut of emotion crossed his handsome face – frustration, lust, curiosity, excitement – then the dawning of his familiar and uniquely sexy smile.

'Okay.' He sighed and shook his head, the soft light glinting on its jet-black squeaky-clean gloss, 'All these months and you *still* win. But can the condemned man have a drink first?'

'Of course,' murmured Isis, hiding exultation, success burning hot between her legs. It was all she could do not to whistle for Guido's attention.

Her burning was a flash-fire by the time she had Josh on the couch.

Preparing him was just as difficult as it had always been. Not because he was uncooperative; just the opposite. Once he'd decided to put himself in her hands, Josh was as docile as a lamb, and merely sighed, grunted or moaned depending on which part of his firm brown body she was handling.

The problem was within her. What the sight of him did . . .

Everything about the man pleased her, and having him there – stripped, secured, plugged and wired – made the state of her sex almost explosive. It felt bloated, shivery; its juices running like a river. She was wearing one of Tricksie's lab coats and that only made matters worse. It was short – very – and Isis hardly dare move in case it rode up and revealed her sopping condition.

And she knew Josh was watching for just such a moment. For the tops of her thighs, shiny with nectar. For her knickers, soaked and dark and incriminating. 'Love the new smock,' he drawled, his voice blurred and dreamy as the first batch of relaxant took hold. 'C'mere . . . Let me see if you've got any drawers on.'

'Don't be so silly,' she answered pertly, dragging a groan from his lips as she adjusted the stretchy sensor-cuff around the tip of his cock. Compounding her crimes, she took a firm grip on his hips and bedded him more snugly on the anal probe. He was probably half into the adventure by now, and half out of his mind with the sensations, but it didn't stop him straining his strapped-down hand towards her thigh.

Flicking away from his groping fingers, she turned towards the console and picked up the monitor headset, fitting it in place and arranging her wayward hair so it didn't interfere with the inducer chips at her temples.

'What the buggery is that?'

Josh giggled and Isis smiled. His drug-addled brain had probably heard that as a screamingly funny pun.

'One of the new developments, sweetheart,' she murmured, 'This time I –' she tapped the lightweight headpiece, 'I go with you.'

'Oh yeah . . .' Josh sighed, and Isis felt her last qualms dissolved. This man had always wanted to share his dreams with her. 'You gonna be in it too?'

'Oh yes, Josh, if you want me to.' He nodded, smiling beatifically, and she decided to spring her other surprise. 'And there'll be somebody else you know too . . . Sort of . . . You've never met her, but you do know her.'

'Twice as nice . . .' His voice was barely audible, and his face relaxed and angelic as she fixed his eyemask in place. She was almost certain he knew who she meant.

'Sleep now, Josh baby,' she whispered, not sure he could even hear her. She settled herself more comfortably on her stool, grimacing at the sweet wet squelch between her legs. If she was like this now, what on earth would she be like when 'Egyptian Magic' was over?

'Let go, Josh. You're going on a magical mystery tour . . . to somewhere ancient and beautiful. Listen. Can you hear it? Hear the water . . . Hear the breeze rippling over a famous river . . . A river of life, Josh. The river of a great, great queen.'

She reached out, pressed a switch ... and she could
hear the river lapping too.

4

Egyptian Magic

Gods help me, I must have fallen asleep on my feet!

Mikhmet swayed precariously in her hiding place and cursed the softly lapping Nile for its dangerously soporific effort. If she toppled over now, her mistress would probably walk in, catch her and have her executed. And then Mikhmet would *never* see the sights she craved so dearly!

Though maybe it would be better to die. To surrender her life at the Queen's order and be shot of this endless torment, this intimate aching itch she was forbidden – by her low station at court – to scratch. Sighing under her breath, she touched herself through her thin pleated skirt, knowing the crevice between her legs was already damp, just from the simple process of *thinking* about . . .

About *her*. The one. She. She who was more beautiful than the night outside, and more bright and glorious the day just past.

She. The divine Neferhapset, ruler of the Upper and Lower Kingdoms of Egypt, Queen-Goddess of the sacred Nile, beloved of Amun, daughter of Isis.

By rights, the Queen should hardly even have noticed Mikhmet, a lowly serving girl. But she was Neferhapset the Insatiable, and she noticed many things. Noticed them, but because she had everything, *was* everything, had no need under the hot Egyptian sun to do anything at all about it.

Only this morning Mikhmet had blushed and died under the royal scrutiny as she'd brought in the Queen's goblet of wine. Her wilful young body had roused before

47

those long, glittering, black-outlined eyes. Had she imagined that slow, near-legendary smile? The ghostly curving of the most exquisite lips in the dual kingdom? Or the flick of that gaze towards Mikhmet's slender loins and small but rounded breasts with their hardened nipples that betrayed her state of arousal.

Had she seen? Taken note of her wine-bearer's silent lust? Mikhmet had prayed herself discovered; then prayed herself not. A servant could be put to death for such sacrilege against a living goddess.

In the confines of her fertile imagination, however, there were no such restrictions. Mikhmet indulged in long protracted viewing sessions that took in every detail of the Queen's unapproachable body. Both the portions she'd already seen and the lush, more tantalising regions that were not normally exposed to a cup carrier on the lowest level of the palace's pecking order.

In her mind Mikhmet would see the Queen's smiles of pleasure as – in fantasy – they caressed.

Languor would soften that cool imperious beauty: the peerless structure of her facial bones, the black-brown glitter of her khol-painted eyes, the bizarre allure of the divine lotus-flower tattoo that adorned the smoothness of her velvety cheek. Mikhmet would tremble at the image of her mistress's soft red mouth, then taunt herself with the vision of her Majesty's unclothed form. Ripe breasts, the pure symmetry of her belly and thighs, the fecund delta below, that moist oasis of bliss that Mikhmet would never ever get to see.

Unless she put her life in jeopardy and hid behind the wall hangings in the Queen's most private chamber!

This night's escapade was gross insanity, and Mikhmet knew it, but this obsession possessed her by throat and heart and crotch, and in all honesty she didn't even want to be sane again!

Neferhapset. The queen of her madness . . . She pressed a hand to her aching pubic mound and felt her own heat sear her right through the thin cloth of her knee-length linen kilt.

My lady! she pleaded, willing the Queen to appear in reality, then gasped soundlessly as, like the deity her subjects believed her to be, the monarch of all Egypt answered Mikhmet's mental prayer.

The chamber doors were thrown open by the tall Nubian guards, and in a swish of diaphanous pleated white, a sparkle of gold, blue faience and precious stones, and a great gust of a delicious and blood-stirring perfume, Neferhapset the Queen strode impatiently into the room – still crowned with her regal diadem and carrying the sceptre and flail that symbolised her sovereignty. Close on her sandalled heels came her Babylonian body-servant Tumet, and Tosis, the slim black mute whose only function was to wave his giant fan and keep the good Queen cool.

Mikhmet barely noticed these others. Her eyes, as always, and the running cleft between her thighs, were attuned solely and entirely to the lady herself.

Neferhapset the Insatiable. Renowned for her prodigious sexual appetite, and the numbers and stamina of her lovers – both male and female – the Queen was apparently without a paramour tonight. Which might account for her slightly fractious demeanor.

Although, of course, she *could* be planning to cavort with the mute and Tumet?

Quite possibly, thought Mikhmet, shivering with lust, and silently furious at the idea her Majesty might share sex with some of her servants and not with the poor frustrated wretch lurking behind her wall-hanging! The Queen's carnal capacity was fabled to exceed a dockside whore's and it was unlikely she'd let a night pass without some kind of stimulation. Even as Mikhmet watched, there was evidence of her hunger.

With a gesture of exasperation, the Queen threw herself into her great, carved, throne-like chair and groaned softly, like a soul in torment. The pleats of her sheer linen tunic rustled like the Nile breeze as her slim legs moved sinuously against each other, and her body shifted uneasily in the luxurious seat – almost as if she were afflicted by an itch as lewd as Mikhmet's own. Locking her eyes on

49

the regal loins, Mikhmet shook with an almost irresistible urge to offer herself as the scratcher; even though exposure was likely to bring with it an almost unthinkable punishment.

Mikhmet had been most careful in the choosing of her hideway. The hanging she was tucked behind was well away from the light-pools created by a proliferation of linseed-oil lamps; and yet a cunning peep-hole cut in the cloth's elaborate design meant she had a perfect unobstructed view of the Queen without her having the slightest inkling she was being observed.

Or had she?

Suddenly Mikhmet had a sensation like a viper sliding down her back. Gods! What if the Queen *was* aware of her? More than that ... What if she sensed both her watcher's presence *and* that watcher's consequent arousal? And approved of both.

Even as the thought occurred, the Queen's sultry, slumberous gaze seemed to fix on Mikhmet with killing accuracy. And then, as if deliberately, the symbolic flail fell to the floor and the Queen drew the chunky head of her golden sekhem – the sceptre of her regnant power – along the inner slope of her sleek, thinly clad thigh.

Mikhmet shook and dug her nails into her own thigh, praying that the small pain would help contain her vaulting desire. She saw the heavy sceptre snag on the fine pleating of the Queen's filmy robe, then begin to ruck it up and expose more flesh. There was a sibilant hiss as long thighs moved slowly against each other, caressing the sekhem between them as if it were the rod of some secret lover.

The pale skirt moved higher, showing pale skin beneath. The Queen was lighter-hued than most of her people; her complexion more delicate, finer, far more precious and rare. Mikhmet longed to touch her – a privilege she'd never enjoyed and no doubt never would.

But for the moment she could look.

Look on as her beloved goddess nodded magisterially to the obedient Tumet. The servant moved forward; not exactly confident, it seemed, but sure at least of what was required of her. The Queen lounged deeper in her throne, her braided hair fanning out over its richly padded head-rest, one slender arm dangling languidly at her side as the other pressed the sekhem firmly into the vee of her crotch. It seemed now that Tumet's task was to assist in her mistress's masturbation.

The henna-haired servant took the hem of the Queen's white robe and started folding it delicately and reverently upwards. The sovereign sighed slightly and impatiently, then lifted the rudely placed sceptre so an even ruder tableau was created. Milky linen folded against a tiny waist, lily-pale skin, a neatly trimmed cluster of shiny russet curls; the golden bulb-headed sceptre sliding smoothly back to its position.

Mikhmet was biting now instead of gouging. Gnawing at her lip to keep the groans behind it. She felt a sudden violent urge to be turned into a thing of beaten gold – to be the sekhem and be lodged between the Queen's match-less thighs. Her own quim trembled and dripped, and her mouth felt strangely sensitive as if it longed to take the place of the inanimate metal rod. To kiss, to suck, and to probe with a tightly furled tongue.

Locked in intolerable immobility, Mikhmet had a great and almost painful desire to shake her head – toss her skull and the brain inside it to dislodge the base and impudent thoughts.

This was the Queen! the living goddess of the land of Egypt . . . And in her mind Mikhmet was taking unbeliev-able liberties that she wouldn't even take with a woman of her own class. Simply to *see* what she was seeing now would probably incur the penalty of blinding.

But still seeing, her eyes were riveted to that obscene knob-headed sceptre. The thing was huge! And in spite of the Queen's vigorous and legendary sex life, Mikhmet couldn't imagine the royal quim being big enough to take its bulk. In her mind's eye she'd imagined the Queen being quite dainty between the legs – everything tight and snug beneath that soft fluffy bush of pubic hair.

Mikhmet held her breath as her royal mistress humped like fury at the sekhem, mashing her tender flesh against its hard gold head. Great Gods, she *was* trying to get it inside her! Some women, Mikhmet knew from whispered conversations with her peers, could get a grown man's fist into their vaginas, but the Queen of Egypt it seemed was aiming to accommodate something far more unforgiving. And the idea of such a hideous stretching drove Mikhmet to utter distraction. She gritted her teeth, her young face contorting with effort as if someone were shoving the huge golden club inside *her*!

'Tumet! Tosis! Assist me!'

The Queen's voice was ragged with lust, yet still entirely regal. Her servants leapt to obey.

Tosis, the slender Nubian, laid down his fan, came around to kneel before the Queen and replaced his lady's grip on the sceptre with his own. Tumet meanwhile leaned across her mistress's body, put both her hands between the royal thighs, and eased apart the Divine One's labia. With nothing left to do now but open up, Neferhapset reached immediately for her own clitoris, which she rubbed wildly as she grunted and groaned, exhibiting far less than a holy sovereign's finesse.

Gods, she's an animal! thought Mikhmet in torment. Her naked breasts were swollen and rubbed uncomfortably against the heavy hanging . . .

And between her legs? Everything there was swollen, slippery and distended, it was only fear of detection that kept her from rubbing herself furiously. Oh Gods, great Gods, she prayed, give me one chance to love her then I'll go happily straight to the afterlife!

'Tumet! Oil!' the Queen shouted hoarsely and the servant, as ever, rushed to comply. Abandoning her mistress's abused flesh for just a moment she went across to a nearby table and brought back a carved alabaster jar. From this she poured a thick stream of scented unguent directly onto the Queen's beseiged vulva. When the vessel was completely emptied, she returned her fingers to their original task; attempting to split the Queen of Egypt right down her exquisite erotic middle!

Mikhmet felt her own median pulse obscenely as the seemingly impossible happened. Driven by a steady measured pressure from the mute, the gross bulb-headed power sceptre slid slowly into its living sheath. The Queen gave an uncouth, almost bestial grunt of satisfaction, settled firmly onto the rod and increased the speed of her frenziedly moving fingers.

'Tosis! Fuck your Queen!' she commanded, clearly dissatisfied with the sceptre being immobile. Waggling her curvaceous hips she encouraged her slave in his endeavours, and within seconds a rhythm was set up, the sovereign wafting her impaled pelvis to meet her servant's shallow pushes. Her primary task completed, the enterprising Tumet had now lowered the top of her mistress's robe, pushed up her elaborate and priceless jewelled pectoral necklace, and was kneading the Queen's immaculate breasts in time to the action below.

I could do that! wailed Mikhmet in silent torment, knocked sideways anew by the sight of two palely perfect ruby-tipped globes. I could do that! she thought, the feel of that warm skin almost real beneath her trembling fingers.

The Queen's breasts weren't large, but they were marvellous. They fit perfectly into the lucky Tumet's caressing hands, and Mikhmet wished to the gods they were in hers instead. Or one perhaps, in her hungry salivating mouth. Amun, how she'd kiss! How she'd suck! Taste the perfumed sweetness there, before moving onto other zones. Especially the one now enspeared by the fat golden sceptre.

It still seemed astounding how the sekhem had fit in there, how it could plunge so deep into that tight, sacred channel. And yet more astounding that Queen Neferhapset seemed to want even more of it! She was throwing herself onto the thing: her beautiful tattooed face a snarling mask, and her frigging fingers a blur of self-abusing lust.

And the noise she was making would easily have covered any sobs of yearning that Mikhmet herself might make. A steam of vulgar sex-words poured from the royal lips; she cursed herself, her servants and even the divine gods in a nonsensical erotic litany that was almost as arousing as the crude golden rogering between her oil-coated thighs.

It's too much! thought Mikhmet desperately, leaning back against the wall and closing her seared eyes. It's too much. She's too much. I wanted to peep, but I never bargained for this.

But the sounds still beat into her brain. The Queen's gasps and grunts, the horrid slurping of the rod as it pumped in and out, the soft, reverent words of encouragement whispered by the fondling Tumet. Even poor word-less Tosis was drawn into the cacophony, uttering a thin muffled cry which Mikhmet, on opening her eyes again saw was due to the Queen pulling his hair in the wild delirium of her ecstasy.

One huge shriek, quite unequivocally the Queen's, was the final straw for Mikhmet. Her gaze locked onto that pierced and spasming hole, and she felt the pit of her own belly begin to cramp. She clapped her hand between her shaking thighs and bore down on the heavy ache of her need. She bit her lip again, tasting blood in a life or death battle to keep in her orgasmic scream. Fire seemed to fall through her loins, she saw stars as well as the climaxing Queen, and her long-suppressed frustration was released in a long soul-wrenching climax.

Almost fainting, she fought her own liquefying legs in a supreme effort to stay upright. The transports of the Queen – and possibly her servants too – were momentarily forgotten as Mikhmet struggled with both consciousness and the task of staying concealed while her body was turning itself inside out with pleasure. It was only after a full two minutes that she was able to open her eyes and apply one of them to the peephole again.

The sekhem was just sliding out. Mikhmet watched in fascination as the giant intruder plopped wetly and audibly from Neferhapset's stretched vagina, and the intimate orifice, which had been so very very wide, contracted suddenly and completely to a neat, almost maidenly small-ness. Women's bodies were a fleshy miracle, Mikhmet decided, observing the flowerlike petals of her mistress's sex, the tiny almost invisible hole which had so recently received such a gross thing as the sekhem. She watched as Tosis studied the sceptre gravely. The mute pursed his lips, and a look of anguish passed across his darkly handsome face.

Poor devil, thought Mikhmet, feeling a sudden sym-pathy for the Nubian. He wants to lick it but he hasn't got a tongue.

Mikhmet felt her own mouth start to water. The golden rod was slick and gleaming; there was the hard shine of oil down virtually all its length, but the thick clubby head, the portion that had entered the Queen's fair body, also had a more silvery glint. The distinctive cloudy shimmer of thick, luxuriant vaginal juices ... Mikhmet watched on in kindred hunger as Tosis contented himself with a kiss to the most fragrant part of the sceptre, then knelt back with the anointed object resting squarely across his kilted knees.

Neferhapset herself now seemed to be rousing from her blissful stupor, although neither she, nor the still-hovering Tumet, made any effort to cover up her body. Her mag-nificent broad-nippled breasts rested free and naked above the folded down bodice of her gown, and her pretty oil-shiny quim was open and exposed between her pale, widely spread thighs. Those blood-pink lips and the silky, carefully trimmed thatch that surrounded them, seemed to Mikhmet to be the very centre of the universe.

'Come out! Immediately!'

Mikhmet jumped like a startled ibis, and even if she hadn't been detected before, she most certainly would have been now. The hanging rippled heavily in front of her, and the Queen's sparkling eyes were looking directly towards the peephole.

Even so, Mikhmet remained where she was, paralysed

by a mixture of fear and acute sexual excitement – the latter increased a hundredfold by the former.

'Come out, I said!' the Queen rapped imperiously, still entirely unheeding of her partial nudity.

This time Mikhmet obeyed, thrashing about in her attempt to push aside the heavy hanging, then took two trembling steps forward in the direction of her sovereign. Unable to look the Queen in the eye, and aware, even in spite of her mind-numbing panic, that it was a treasonable offence to do so unless given leave, Mikhmet fixed her gaze on one of the regally elegant sandalled feet and flung herself down on her knees. She heard but didn't see the fact that Tosis moved discreetly out of the way.

'Approach, Mikhmet.'

Gods, she even knows my name!

Mikhmet made to rise, but was cut short, 'Remain on your knees!' Conscious of a severe lack of grace, she shuffled forward to take the spot Tosis had so recently occupied. She was aware of the eyes of the Queen, the Babylonian and the mute all focused tightly upon her, but more than that, she could almost feel the heat of the divine exposed membranes that seemed to simmer just inches from her nose.

'Speak!' The command was soft, but carried all the power of a full-throated battle scream.

'Forgive me, Majesty,' she stuttered, conscious of the saliva that the Queen's fragrant genitals induced in her apologising mouth, 'Forgive me, Divine One. I've committed a heinous crime, I know, but my senses have been addled by your sacred beauty. Forgive me, my Queen . . . I wanted only to worship before your loveliness.'

'You're a smooth talker, young Mikhmet,' the Queen of Egypt answered with a comforting amiableness. Mikhmet's fear lightened a little as she remembered the royal predilection for younger lovers. 'You please me. I've noticed your body as you've served me. You won't suffer for your insolence this time.'

'Thank you, Madam.' Mikhmet risked a kiss to the sandalled foot before her and sighed inaudibly when she wasn't kicked away, 'May the divine Amun bless you anew for your clemency.'

'I smell something, young Mikhmet... A muskiness not of my own making.' The Queen's smile was as subtle as a cat goddess's. 'What were you doing behind that curtain? Besides watching me, that is?'

Her tone was arch, and as feline as her smile. Mikhmet looked up, and felt as if Bastet herself were using her supernatural vision to look straight through a layer of linen and see the sodden state of her trembling subject's sex.

But she hadn't masturbated, had she? With the image of the Queen at her pleasure before her, Mikhmet could honestly say she hadn't needed her own hand. The orgasm had been spontaneous, and as a Queen-Goddess had the right to demand absolute truth, she decided to reveal it.

'I... My Lady...' Mikhmet faltered, aware now of interest in the handsome Tumet's eyes too. The Babylonian servant was eyeing her speculatively, her gaze zooming in on Mikhmet's crotch and uncovered breasts just as avidly as her mistress's.

'Daughter of Isis,' she began again, a deep shudder running through her at the honorific. Was this truly the offspring of a goddess? The daughter of fertility... Forged from the spirit of... of Isis. Mikhmet shook her head to clear it, unable to account for her moment of dizzying disorientation. 'Daughter of Isis, forgive me. I didn't touch myself... The sight of your pleasure... and your great beauty... overcame me. I... I...'

'You came without benefit of your fingers?' The Queen's husky voice might almost have expressed admiration. 'That is indeed remarkable. I wonder how many orgasms you could have if you were properly stimulated? Perhaps we should investigate?'

Mikhmet threw herself down again, and was just pressing her lips slavishly to the Queen's perfumed instep, when the import of what she'd just said struck home.

57

Great Amun! Did she mean ... Could she possibly ...
Would she ... Oh Gods, pray it was so!

'Tosis! The sceptre. Let our young friend taste the product of *my* pleasure.'

As Mikhmet looked up again, utterly befuddled, she saw Tosis holding forward the sekhem, with its bulbous head leading the way. Dazed, but with a bounding heart and a throbbing quim, Mikhmet touched first her lips, then her tongue to its still warm surface.

The Queen's taste was pungently musky, delicately salt. Like the kiss of the holy Nile and yet like nothing else in the insubstantial world. This was the true essence of a goddess, the flavour of eternity, the taste of a mighty sexual deity for whom Mikhmet would gladly have laid down her life ... She could die right now, perfectly, with the taste of her Queen on her tongue. But it seemed that Neferhapset didn't want her death.

'You find me savoury ... Sweet? Or both?'

Mikhmet nodded, unable to resist drawing her tongue across the sceptre again.

'And the sekhem? Humongous, isn't it?'

She nodded again. It was true; with the thing this close to her face, Mikhmet boggled again that it had really gone inside a woman.

'It stretched me, Mikhmet,' her Majesty continued slowly, 'It abused my tenderest place. I feel inflamed. I need to be soothed ... Something soft and moist against me. Just here – ' She touched a long elegant finger to the tiny opening of her vagina. 'Perhaps you could help me, Mikhmet?'

'My ... My lady?'

'Why so coy, Mikhmet? You know what I want of you.'

'But – '

'No buts, girl! Soothe me!' With sinuous grace, she eased her body further forward. Wet and pink, her vulva seemed to speak to Mikhmet as clearly as her commanding voice did. More clearly ... In flesh they were equals; not Queen and servant, simply a naked roseate cunt and warm willing lips to pleasure it. If Mikhmet had salivated before, right now her mouth was awash. She leaned forward, paused, and watched the intimate flesh ripple as if impatient; flutter as if ruffled by the proximity of red-hot worshipping breath. Its aroused odour was ravishing; delicately fresh and marine, yet headily musken.

'Mikhmet!' cried Neferhapset, her tone more urgent than angry.

Furling her tongue, just as she'd imagined, Mikhmet dove in and obeyed, licking as slowly and smoothly as she could, desperately trying to forget whose sovereign flesh it was she was tasting. She's just a woman like me! she told herself as she flicked cautiously up the pungent valley, returning again and again to explore each crumpled petal, and teasing by denying a direct contact where it most mattered. She's just a hungry delicious woman, Mikhmet repeated silently, darting and diving in response to that woman's small agitated cries. She's just a sexy she-cat who loves being licked! she decided, drawing the swollen labia fully into her mouth and sucking them clean of the most superb and abundant of juices.

'Yes! Yes! Oh, Gods! Yes . . .' the Queen growled from what seemed like a long way away. 'Oh yes, Mikhmet! Ungh! Oh yes! Yes! Please!'

The words, fragmentary as they were, descended once more into animal grunts. The Queen was noted as a states-woman and orator but when pushed to sexual extremes it seemed her vocabulary was limited. Mikhmet felt her head being first caressed, then clasped by long fingers, their rhythmic kneading far more eloquent than the savage sounds coming from the Queen's red lips.

Up until now, Mikhmet had only dared follow orders and put her mouth to the sweet royal flesh; but now she grew bold, took an initiative and slid her hands beneath her mistress's body. Sliding a palm beneath each firm buttock, squeezing hard on each taut mound, she lifted the Queen's slim hips clear of the seat and applied herself to her task with even more diligence. Mikhmet felt her regal victim wriggle around slightly – legs flailing, heels drumming – and realised that her ears were being clamped

59

by a pair of gracefully slender yet extremely strong thighs. Smiling against the warm wet groove against her lips, she applauded the fact that not once in her gyrations had the Queen broken their mouth-to-cunt contact.

Mindful of the original command, Mikhmet began a series of tender probings. Rolling her tongue to a point she pressed it into her mistress's vagina itself, pushing in slowly and steadily, withdrawing then advancing, repeating the act in time to the Queen's long ragged breaths. Lubrication ran thick and sweet, and Mikhmet sucked it up gladly, marvelling at how quickly her Majesty was sopping wet again.

This hole wants a cock! she thought in a flush of lust-crazed dementia, seeing in her fevered brain a vision of the dark mute mounting the Queen while both Tumet and herself, Mikhmet, looked on.

And even as the wild thought occurred, she yelped hard against Neferhapset's squirming body. Then she squirmed herself. One of the almost forgotten watchers had reached beneath her, sneaked a hand inside her kilt and was sliding fingers boldly into her dripping slit.

Until now, Mikhmet's sexual world had been confined to taste, smell and the sensitive perceptions of the tip of her exploring tongue; when she opened her eyes again she was very aware of the other two servants in attendance.

Tumet, smiling slyly, was crouched alongside her, applying deft and delicate stimulation. The servant's hand moved into play even as she caught Mikhmet's eye. Mikhmet felt an almost criminally featherlight massage begin. Her anus and perineum were being gently palpated in time to the smooth rubbing further forward.

Mikhmet froze, temporarily dazed by the pleasure building in her loins, but Tumet nodded furiously in the direction of the Queen's spread legs and the sexual duties required between them. Mikhmet closed her eyes tightly and plunged in again; but not before catching a glimpse of the ever devoted Tosis pulling strongly on the Queen's erect nipples and deforming her breasts into two painful-looking conical masses . . .

'Yes! Yes!' Neferhapset shouted. The mute must be inflicting a quite brutal sensation, but clearly the Queen *liked* her pleasure rough!

The thought made Mikhmet quiver under Tumet's caress. She had a intense urge to come, then felt the surge tamed as the Babylonian backed off skilfully. Perhaps she's a part-time whore? Mikhmet thought wildly, her hips bounding in the orbit of Tumet's grip. Not even the most talented amateur, perhaps not even the Queen herself could stoke and damp, stoke and damp, rouse a lover like this and work them into a state of believing that their whole crotch would imminently explode! Diverting her attention, Mikhmet sucked viciously on the Queen's clitoris and was rewarded by an ear-splitting wail of satisfaction and sandalled heels thumping hard against her naked back.

'Yes, you she-jackal! Yes! That's it! Suck! Suck hard! Go on, you bitch! Pull it! Oh! Oh! Oh, sacred Gods, I'm coming! Agh . . . Agh . . .'

The words dissolved into nonsense again, but even if it had been the most lucid speech of Neferhapset's reign, Mikhmet couldn't have understood it. All signals were scrambled, her entire life-force was first errupting in her pulsing clit, then roiling and boiling deep in her vagina – only to overspill her loins entirely, shoot up the column of her spine, and explode like a firestorm in her brain. Some reflex, or some physic order direct from the climaxing vulva against her face, kept her sucking like a baby on the Queen's clitoris, never once losing her grip, even while Neferhapset wrenched herself about above, and Mikhmet's own hips pumped spasmodically below.

In a few minutes, Mikhmet found herself slumped on the tiled floor with no real idea how she'd got there. Shaking her head, she looked up blearily, only to see the Queen – now stripped magnificently naked of her gown and jewels – being swathed into a soft linen robe by the ever solicitious Tumet. Without thinking, Mikhmet sighed her disappointment aloud.

'Don't fret, young Mikhmet,' Neferhapset murmured

soothingly as first one portion of perfection, then another, disappeared from Mikhmet's view. 'The night is yet young.' Tumet handed the Queen a sash and in an instant the robe was discreetly secure. 'But first we must make ourselves comfortable.'

As she spoke these last words, and nodding to Tumet to step close, Neferhapset lifted her narrow hands and slid them beneath the heavy braided fall of her jet-black hair. She seemed to massage her scalp, then suddenly and shockingly she lifted the dark mass up and away from her head.

She wears a wig! thought Mikhmet in the split second that the false hair was being removed. It shouldn't have been a surprise; wig-wearing was the height of fashion. But she cringed at the thought of a shaven scalp beneath.

She sighed again – but not with disappointment this time – when the true picture was revealed.

As some point in her lineage, the Queen's ancestors must have been as promiscuous as she was, and equally unfussy about the nationality of their conquests; for underneath the monarch's traditional black wig was a boyish cap of curls in a colour Mikhmet was hard pressed to describe in a single word. In contrast to the dark hair of most Egyptians, Neferhapset the Insatiable's charming coif seemed to be a number of different and rather beautiful colours at once. Blonde, red, rich brown; all those tints were there, as well as several more that glinted and shone as the Queen tilted her head in the flickering lamplight.

'Are you going to lie there all night, girl, or are we going to bathe?' she enquired, every bit as imperious with her multicoloured crop as she was in her august ceremonial braids.

Mikhmet struggled to sitting position, stunned by the words 'we' and 'bathe' as the Queen swept impatiently into the bath-house beyond. She wants me to bathe with her! she thought deliriously. We'll be naked together in perfumed water ... Perhaps she'll let me wash her; touch *all* of her body, caress and explore it before ... before ...

Mikhmet was on her feet now, but still dithering, embarrassed – in the presence of Tumet and Tosis – by the orgasmic flush that stained her naked chest and neck. And yet she was aroused again, her sex beginning to engorge, and she could hardly credit her own powers of recuperation. The Queen of Egypt seemed to imbue her with a bottomless pit of sexual energy, that unassailable erotic majesty stirring her humble subject to a state of need far beyond that any lesser being could induce.

'Mikhmet! Get in here now or leave!' the regal voice rang out.

Mikhmet obeyed her queen, almost running into the bath-house, followed at a more composed pace by the Babylonian servant and the Nubian mute.

And it was those servants – male and female – that prepared both cup-carrier and Queen for the pleasure of a mutual bath. Mikhmet had been embarrassed before, but now the sense of mortification plunged to new depths. Tumet and the Nubian performed the most intimate services. For both Neferhapset and her guest ... And, used always to fending for herself in these matters, Mikhmet was bright scarlet in the face by the time it came to step into the huge fragrant pool that was laughingly called a 'bath'. Her arousal had been stoked even higher by the ministrations of Tumet and Tosis, and her nipples were prominent enough to be a source of further embarrassment when Neferhapset's bright gaze homed in on their perky-tipped hardness.

'Very nice, young Mikhmet,' she murmured, lifting one graceful hand out of the milky water to touch the pretty points that amused her. Her slender fingers slipped lightly from one bud to another as Mikhmet's hot blood raced to obey the royal command. Her body felt drawn as if by some mystic charm and in moments she was sinking into the cloudy, scented water beside her mistress.

The Queen however decided it was not yet time to add their love-juices to the mix of water and aromatic skin-softening oils. She abandoned Mikhmet's nipples and drifted slightly away from her.

'Relaxation first, impetuous one. Let the water soothe

away your tension. Let the balm seep into your skin . . . and your flesh and bones . . . And then we'll begin again!' With this she closed her glittering, slanted eyes and slid slowly under the surface, only to rise again after a few moments with water streaming from her lovely tattooed face, and her short hair plastered enchantingly to her elegant, finely shaped skull.

Mikhmet sighed. Even naked, unpainted and soaking wet, the Queen was still every inch the Queen! Every bit the woman she worshipped and wanted.

And the one she obeyed. She hadn't thought it would be so easy to relax in the presence of her sovereign but suddenly it was. She looked on, feeling loose and mellow, as Neferhapset quietly dismissed her two other servants. There was a nice sensation of justice as Tumet's hand slid easily into Tosis's as the pair left the room. It seemed that she and the Queen weren't the only ones there was 'more' for . . . and Mikhmet wished the strange couple well as their footsteps faded slowly away.

The silky, oiled water swirled gently around her, and suddenly the Queen was not so much the threatening sexual commander as the comfortable long-time friend. They floated together in companionable silence for a while, backs resting against the side of the pool, backsides resting on its floor, the water being just the right depth for their heads to be above it and their bodies completely submerged. It was a situation Mikhmet would never have believed she could sleep in, but it wasn't long before drowsiness overtook her.

She awoke with a jolt and a wild thrash of water as the wet heat bathing her quim was suddenly and deliciously compressed. Conditions down there were still as fluid, but now there was a mind-bending suction against her most delicate tissues. The Queen had dived down beneath the water and was busily mouthing her! Mikhmet felt strong hands steady her thighs, and as she stilled obediently and surrendered to the superb sensations, she marvelled at a monarch who would deign to suck her own servant's clitoris . . . and risk being drowned into the bargain for the experience!

Mikhmet didn't know how Neferhapset was managing to do what she was doing, or how long she could do it for; she only knew she didn't want it to stop. She felt as if there were some wicked, exotic leech clamped over her quim, a hard-sucking little beast that seemed intent on siphoning her pleasure out of her by main force. And in the heart of that almost unbearable vacuum, the royal tongue poked and probed, and languorously licked, acquainting Mikhmet with some of the most astounding sensations she'd ever experienced. The Queen was attacking her most sensitive areas with such a prolonged and voracious fervor that Mikhmet seriously wondered if her mistress were prepared to asphyxiate in the process. Only after an almost inhumanly impossible amount of time did the beautiful torment cease and the spluttering Queen come shooting up out of water, shaking her head and gasping and choking for air.

Her flesh trembling on the very brink of release, Mikhmet pushed through the water to offer assistance, 'Breathe, My Lady, please breathe!' she urged anxiously, then forgot Neferhapset's status entirely and slapped her firmly on the back to clear her waterlogged throat. The Queen spluttered some more and Mikhmet pounded her again, observing with an almost dreamlike detachment that her blows made the regal breasts jiggle divinely.

'Enough!' Neferhapset said at last, wiping the moisture from her flushed face and grinning impishly at Mikhmet.

'Majesty . . . Are . . . are you all right?' Mikhmet asked, feeling far more shaken than the Queen obviously was. Entirely unfazed now, the monarch of all Egypt pushed her sodden hair back off her forehead, then sank back into the bath until her chin just cleared the surface. Mikhmet groaned as the searching royal hand found her still unrelieved arousal.

'Yes, Mikhmet, I'm fine.' Neferhapset shrugged and her white shoulders momentarily broke the surface. 'At least my body is fine. Of my mental state, I'm less sure . . .

Sadly, we Pharaohs are sometimes not too bright. It comes from having fathers and mothers who are brothers and sisters as well. Some of my ancestors have been feeble-minded, but for my part I've only been afflicted with a madness of the body.' Her nimble fingers rubbed playfully in Mikhmet's tormented groove, 'I'm insane for love, Mikhmet . . . Do you think you can assist in my therapy?'

'Of course, my Queen!' Mikhmet murmured breathlessly, 'Your wish is my command.' Her eyes closed and her hips bounced slowly in the water in time to the neat, deft movements between her thighs.

'That's good, my slippery young friend. I knew I could rely on your desire to serve . . .' With a delicate torturing flick she removed her fingers from their niche and moved towards the pool's shallow stairs. 'Perhaps we can continue this pleasantness on a more stable footing. Come along, Mikhmet, I want you to lie down here.' Out of the water and superbly, breath-catchingly naked, the Queen indicated a thick heap of linen cloths that were presumably meant for them to dry themselves on but would clearly serve equally well to protect them from the bathhouse's hard stone floor.

Trembling with anticipation, and with her sex almost aflame, Mikhmet followed her mistress out of the water and lay down as directed on the soft linen pile. She stared almost numbly at the blue-painted ceiling, hardly daring to watch the approach of the most beautiful body in the civilised world.

What greater thrill could there be than this? To know that any second now she would be pleasuring a living goddess, the beloved of Amun, the spirit of the Nile, the holy daughter of Isis. As Neferhapset reached her, Mikhmet tried to sit up and embrace her, but the Queen would not allow it. She crouched beside her servant, pressed down on her shaking shoulders and made her lie again.

Once a queen, always a queen, Mikhmet thought blissfully as Neferhapset's long thighs parted ready to straddle one of hers. She wondered now why she hadn't realised the Queen's hair wasn't black; the neat little bush – the mat of curls that didn't conceal the royal vulva one bit! – was the selfsame brindled colour as the hair on Neferhapset's head. Mikhmet watched the glossy cluster descend, then observed the divine one part her own nether lips and heard her sigh long and brokenly as her warm sacred flesh split wetly against her servant's waiting thigh.

Mikhmet could feel every detail of that intimate geography as the Queen rocked slowly against her skin . . . and the look of unalloyed pleasure on that beautiful face was so bright and fine it was almost dazzling. Closing her eyes and sighing, she reached for her sovereign's peerless breasts and was allowed at last to fondle them. She felt hot flesh rippling against her thigh as she slowly pleasured the Queen's hard nipples, each quiver and pulse seeming to induce a melting undulation throughout the length of her own wet vagina. She felt as if she were experiencing the Queen's own pleasure by proxy and that her juices were running as abundantly as the royal unguent that poured out over her snugly held thigh.

Unashamed and uninhibited now, Mikhmet shouted and moaned as the Queen quite selfishly rode her; and with a hand still cupping one perfect breast, she scooted the other hand down to the apex of her mistress's wide-open sex and fingered the engorged and jumping clitoris.

Neferhapset howled her appreciation and bounced joyfully. A heavy ball of pressure seemed to build in the cradle of Mikhmet's own loins, and as she arched helplessly, a beneficent hand was suddenly right where she needed it to be. Mikhmet wasn't quite sure now where her body ended and that of the mighty Queen began. Slender fingers worked roughly on her clit, and as Mikhmet praised the name of every god she knew of in turn, she felt her Neferhapset's streaming quim crush violently against her, and rock its whole climaxing surface rhythmically against the twitching muscle of the thigh it so passionately gripped.

But even in the throes of orgasm, it seemed the Queen of Egypt was ever mindful of her subject's welfare. The royal hand bestowed its final blessing and as Mikhmet's own crisis came, hard on the heels of and merging so sweetly into her mistress's, there was only one salute on her lips and one all-consuming deity who had dominion over her heart, mind and body.

'My Queen! My Queen! I love you! I love you! I love you ...'

5

Intermezzo I

'So . . . What did you hit him with first, then?'

The question was casually phrased but it didn't fool Isis one bit. Tricksie was bursting to know everything about Josh's first night home. She'd been fidgeting, fussing with drinks, giving Isis nervous little grins, doing anything and everything but ask the questions that were obviously driving her crazy.

It was late now and, shaken in a host of different ways, Isis had sought refuge at Tricksie's place. It was an untidy, homey and very feminine little hide-out in a block not far from the 'Zone – small but infinitely roomier than Isis' minute 'over the shop' flat – but whether it had been a good idea to come here, she was seriously beginning to wonder. Close as she was to Trix, there were things – now – she hardly dare tell her.

'Well?' Tricksie was impatient now she'd finally got started. Her eyes were wide, expectant, glittering and Isis fell back on the technical details she could reveal without seeming an idiot. Or a hypocrite.

'I gave him a tuned-up "Egyptian Magic",' she said, keeping her voice light and her eyes away from Tricksie's.

'Sonofabitch! If you're trying to play it cool with him, that's not exactly the one I'd have chosen.' Tricksie sipped her wine, then ran her moist pink tongue around her lips in an unconsciously sensual gesture.

Help me, Lord! thought Isis. I'm having enough trouble sorting myself after Josh without her getting to me as well.

'It's a classic, really,' she began cautiously.

'Classic red hot rumpo ...'

'Okay, it's a very sexy little scenario. But which of them aren't?'

'True,' observed Tricksie, doing the thing with her lips again.

Isis found herself squirming slightly on Tricksie's rose-pink *chaise longue*. Things had been so straightforward twenty-four hours ago. She'd been Tricksie's lesbian lover, and a woman looking forward to a rather nice man's imminent return.

Now she felt strange with Tricksie because of Josh, and unsure how to be with Josh because of Tricksie.

'Okay, so you gave him Good Queen Nef,' Tricksie went on, pressing, pressing, pressing. 'But answer me two things. Which role was he in and who did *she* look like?'

'I ran it with him as Mikhmet. His profile indicates he enjoys his adventures better with a gender swap.'

'And?'

'All right already! I was Neferhapset and you were Tumet. Satisfied?'

What's the matter with me? cried Isis inside, appalled by the fact she'd made Tricksie flinch. I adore this woman ... I think I might even love her. Why the hell am I getting so ratty? After all, she's told me all her secrets. Things most people would never reveal.

Tricksie put her glass down. Very softly, as if deliberately avoiding all sound. 'Come on, sweetheart ... What's up? You're like a cat on hot bricks. He didn't upset you, did he?'

'Yes. No! Oh, shit, I don't know ...' There were tears in her eyes. It was so silly. 'Oh, Trix, I'm so confused. It's dodgy if I sleep with him ... and I feel guilty if I don't. He wants me but he won't force himself on me because he's too much of a gentleman. Half of me wants him to force me and the other half will call him a chauvinist bastard if he does.' She scrubbed her face with her fingers, conscious of mascara and liner going walkabout. 'On top of all that I feel guilty leching after him because I should

70

be happy with you. Oh bugger! It was all so simple yesterday.'

'C'mere,' whispered Tricksie, her fine face bright with wisdom and quiet understanding. It was so easy to slide into her arms. Isis felt fingers moving gently on her unbound hair, then caressing her shoulders above the thin silk top of her camisole. She shivered with pleasure, and suddenly at least one of her complications was unravelled.

Josh was out there somewhere in this city, confusing her, confounding her; but Tricksie was here. Here, beautiful, half naked and asking for nothing more than now.

'I'm sorry,' she sniffed, snuggling closer.

'What on earth for, you goose?' whispered Tricksie in her ear.

'I don't know really . . .'

Isis pulled away, reluctant to part from Tricksie's perfumed heat, but knowing she desperately needed a handkerchief.

She scrabbled around furiously, looking for her bag, but before she could find it, Tricksie had already produced her own hankie; and with infinite and artistic precision she blotted away Isis's tears and tidied up her waterlogged make-up.

'Do you know something, Ice?' she said with a grin. 'For a certified genius, you really are a dumb bunny sometimes. I'm not jealous of Josh. How could I be? He can't do the things with you that I do, can he? He's the wrong gender, silly.'

Isis watched, almost hypnotised, as Tricksie reached out to touch her, resting one long crimson-nailed fingertip on the upper slope of her breast. Intense heat seemed to radiate from the point of contact, like a branding that didn't hurt, a marking of the flesh that left no visible sign.

'What happened, Ice?' she said softly. 'You might feel better if you talk about it.' The fingertip cruised down to Isis's nipple, swirling around its target, delicately teasing and tickling. 'Did you make love?'

Isis appreciated the words 'make love'. Put that way it sounded more acceptable, more valuable somehow than the earthier terms. She hadn't 'fucked' or 'screwed' or 'bonked' with Josh all those months ago, and she wouldn't do now. When they eventually got together in bed.

And 'making love' was what Tricksie was doing too. So subtly and so discreetly beginning the process, pleasuring Isis's breast with an almost ghostly lightness, bringing her doucely to a condition of need.

'No, we didn't,' she said breathlessly. 'I wanted to ... But it didn't quite happen.'

'How so?'

'Well ... um ... Oh, oh yes!'

The contact wasn't so light any more; Tricksie was cupping both breasts now and kneading them, the movements slow, determined, rhythmic.

'What happened, Ice?' she persisted.

'He got aroused again, after he'd woken up. He said it was because the adventure was so gorgeous. Just thinking about it made him get stiff again ...' Isis paused then, torn between the pleasure of now, of Tricksie's long squeezing fingers, and the excitement of then, of Josh's superb erection rising anew from the semen-smeared nest of his silky soot-black pubes.

'Did you touch him?'

'I had to ... to get the cuff off. To clean him.'

Evasion.

'No, I mean ... Did you touch him to pleasure him? Did you stroke him?' Tricksie mirrored her inquisition with action: pleasuring, stroking, going one step further to bare the soft orbs in her fingers.

Flimsy silk bunched at Isis's waist, thin straps slithered down her arms, and she found answering difficult, the memories as distracting as the intensity of the sensation in her breasts. The growing heaviness in the slippery folds of her sex.

'A bit ...' she faltered, remembering his stickiness as clearly as she felt her own, 'But I got distracted.'

'How?' Tricksie prompted without breaking the motion of her fingers and palms.

'He touched me.' Memory and real-time were merging

now, coming together in her breasts and the slow sweet hands that caressed them.

'Where, sweetheart, where?' asked Tricksie in a whisper, as she inclined her lush form forwards and put her mouth to Isis's ear.

'Where you're touching me. My breasts. I was stroking him and he reached out, suddenly, and started stroking *me.*'

It had been so much like this yet so different – the hands that held her now were white as milk, slender, with painted red nails and a fine silver wire ring on each little finger.

Josh's hands were big, square, strong, dark. A man's solid hands, yet still as delicately skilled as a sculptor's. The thin white cotton of her smock had been no barrier at all to his touch. She'd just melted, her knees like jelly and her will as pliant as mist.

He could have done anything, could have taken her there and then, but all he did was fondle her breasts.

'Oh, baby,' Tricksie murmured, her voice husky as if she could see what Isis saw. Feel her pleasure in the tips of her fingers. 'Oh baby, I don't blame him.'

Isis moaned softly, caught between two realities. Josh, spinning her in his arms, then cupping her breasts anew as his erection pressed into her buttocks. Tricksie, face on, but her hands just as tantalising as they squeezed and pummelled and rubbed. Josh, butting her, masturbating against her thinly covered bottom. Tricksie exploring, thumbing, abrading her sensitive pebbly aureoles, working her breast-tips in a relentless pattern of nips and twirls and pinches. Josh, gasping harshly as he came against her, his semen spattering her lab-coat. Tricksie praising, purring and coaxing as Isis surrendered to orgasm, her cunt softly spasming from the pleasure in her nipples alone.

'Just the beginning, my darling,' Tricksie said, her voice muffled as she leaned over Isis's body to kiss the breasts she'd tormented, then moved forward quickly as her victim slumped backwards on the chaise.

Isis gasped, rubbing herself crazily, sweetening the pulsing heat in her quim with her own fingers, not caring now for past or future, or anything but prolonging this moment. Her camisole was around her waist, her leather skirt rucked up to meet it; her pants were dark with juice and her legs splayed. Scrubbing crudely at her body, she was vaguely aware of Tricksie kneeling before her, vaguely aware of how she must look to her. But the only imperative was coming.

'You're so wet, my love,' whispered Tricksie, her breath hot on Isis's crotch and her frenzied fingers. 'So wet.'

Slicking herself still, Isis felt other fingers too, helpful digits joining her own, stroking the soggy cloth of her panties, feathering the inner curves of her bottom, dipping beneath the thin strip of cloth between her legs and dabbling their tips in her fluid. She felt one, a forefinger, slide into her vagina and spear her like a bird on a spit. She whimpered as it waggled ruthlessly, then looked down at an incredible tableau.

A handsome tangle-haired woman crouched between her lover's legs, panting with effort, her hand inside another woman's knickers.

Isis screamed, came harder and flailed on the chaise, then collapsed in an heavy unravelling stupor. Tricksie's finger was still in her body . . .

She came awake again wanting just to kiss. Kiss beautiful unselfish Tricksie who had given without taking for herself.

There was a small intimate moment of disentanglement, then she urged the other woman up onto the *chaise longue* beside her.

She looked at the both of them and grinned wryly. Tricksie was dressed for *her*, for the elegant seduction of a lover, and it made for a warm feeling inside that she'd gone to so much exquisite trouble.

Isis looked down at herself and saw sleaze. Clothes bunched at her waist, breast and pubis exposed by underwear pushed down or aside, nipples reddened, the soft hair of her pussy glistening with her juices. Her belly cramped slightly, her sex excited by her own shoddy tram-pishness, the look of being thoroughly used.

Tricksie couldn't have looked more different; her vinous hair was loose and gleaming, and her clothing, though slight, was tastefully chosen. A wisp of a black silk wrap, and beneath it a teddy in forest-green lace, the thin pat-terned stuff a mere froth on the shores of her lovely swelling bosom. Even her footwear was seductive – fragile black mules with a fat fluffy pom-pom on each toe.

'You look gorgeous, Trix.'

Tricksie's smile was strangely shy, and Isis sensed a strong current of uncertainty in her usually brazen lover . . .

She feels threatened.

It came to her like a flash. Tricksie was frightened; she'd lost Diabolo, and now, with the return of Josh, she was scared of losing Isis too.

You couldn't be more wrong, love, Isis wanted to say. But maybe to speak the words would be to give the doubt more substance?

She didn't want to do that, and examining her feelings – her gut feelings – she knew it wasn't true anyway. The thought of being separated from Trix was appalling.

Equally, the thought of not getting closer to Josh was painful too. Tonight had proved the attraction was as great as ever. More so. She'd been this close to giving in to him; turning in his embrace and offering herself fully, regardless of those notorious 'complications'.

And yet, ironically, it was travel lag that saved them from themselves Gazing at her intently, his wet prick still naked between them, Josh had suddenly blinked. Then blinked again and lifted a hand to his eyes and rubbed at them like an exhausted child would.

And then he'd yawned and they'd both laughed, and the pivotal moment had passed. Either one of them could have revived it, but neither of them had. Leaving Isis confused and wondering, and running like the wind back to Tricksie. The one who never asked 'why' or 'where have you been' or 'who is it', and who – despite her tricky-tricksie name – never played silly mind-games.

'Let me have a look at you, love,' whispered Isis, plucking away the sheer robe from Tricksie's shoulders, then sending the teddy's spaghetti straps slithering. The lace of the camisole caught, though, hanging on her nipples like a vapour, the rough texture of the fabric caressing the nubbly berry-brown coronae beneath. Isis kissed her, and felt the thin barrier slid out from between them.

Their breasts seemed to kiss too: aroused teats rubbing and delicately rotating against each other as their tongues touched and fought.

Isis felt dizzy, but wonderfully happy. The taste, the smell and just the feel of Tricksie were intoxicating, she was the quintessence of woman, a brew so rich and refreshing that not even the strictest ascetic would be able to resist her. Isis was no anchorite and she wouldn't have dreamed of even trying to say 'no.' Smiling against her lover's mouth, she savoured the wine-scented breath, the robust stab of a tongue that knew no fear of her, the moistness that reminded her of other, more pungent moistures.

Struggling now, and gasping, she put her hand roughly between Tricksie's legs, pushing aside the crotch of her teddy and forging through the soft red hair within to seek a greater and more magical softness.

Tricksie shuffled on the chaise, opening her legs wider, offering herself naturally and generously, and whimpering encouragement as she did so.

Her vulva was drenched and silken, the petal-like convolutions all puffed and blood-hot to the touch. Her clitoris stood out like a fat spongy stud at the apex of her labia, and she cried out when Isis gently thumbed it.

'Oh God, yes!' she hissed, the words urgent against Isis's lips and face, 'Please . . . Oh yes, my love, yes . . . Oh God, yes, baby . . . Rub me! Rub me!'

Still kissing, Isis obeyed her, petting the sensitive little organ, making love to it just the way she liked hers to be pleasured. A series of firm, square-on pressures, then feathery flicks, the same number, repeated and repeated and repeated.

As she caressed Tricksie's body, she pondered fleetingly, what, or more pertinently who, the woman was actually thinking about. If she was capable of thinking . . .

In Tricksie's fevered brain, was it Diabolo's hand on her cunt? His fingers that graced her with that first jerking orgasm? His touch that made her scream and howl? His methodical, dispassionate manipulation that made her yell out in bliss and almost deafen her partner? She'd once told Isis that only he could 'do it' for her. That to have a climax, she had to think of him. Was that, still, how she felt?

Isis wondered but didn't ask.

This wasn't the moment for more complications. For questions. Why spoil the simple sweetness of soft flesh fluttering against her fingers? The magic of sending another human soul to a place it could barely understand. Giving someone she cared about the greatest gift she could give.

She hadn't asked but she did get an answer. As Tricksie fell forward, her body loose and boneless, it was Isis's name that she sobbed.

Much later, the two of them lay entwined and drowsing in Tricksie's big pink bed. They were naked now, rosy-skinned and warm, in the afterglow of love; clothing and lingerie lay in several small island mounds, dotted across the room, charting their progress to the sheets.

As she toyed with Tricksie's tangled winy hair, coiling a strand of it slowly round her finger, Isis was suddenly reminded of the first woman she'd ever made love to.

Sandy, predictably, was another redhead; a thin, carrot-topped girl she'd roomed with in Uni. They'd been so young and so intense about it all. Solemnly asking if this was good and that was good, charting each other's erogenous zones with all the scientific precision they had brought to their doctorate theses. It had been tender, too, Isis recalled with a smile; and really good once they'd worked

77

out their shyness. They'd sworn to keep in touch, but letters and calls had thinned out later, when Isis's postgrad work had taken her to remote and exotic facilities.

When she'd returned to the city to take a second degree, the accident had happened.

After that it had seemed kinder to leave Sandy to her memories of two pretty young women experimenting. Let her remember an Isis without wounds and damage.

'Ouch!' complained Tricksie suddenly, and Isis realised she was pulling her hair. She unwound the long burgundy-coloured strand quickly, and kissed the crown of Tricksie's head – the approximate site of the injury.

'Sorry sweetheart,' she whispered, struck anew by the beauty of her lover's hair.

Isis had always found long hair sexy, and Tricksie's extravagant locks were especially so – whatever their colour.

Lush dark red waves lay across both their bodies like a subtle caress, blending in places with Isis's lighter and more unusual mop. She lifted a long tress from each, then merged them into a single wine and tortoiseshell lock.

'Mmmm ... Crazy streaks,' said Tricksie, studying the thick, striated mass, 'Do you think, I should get it done like that?'

Isis stared at her.

'No ... Only joking.' Tricksie laughed softly, and Isis found herself feeling faintly silly. She'd almost believed her.

'I like it as it is, Trix,' she said, fanning the two strands clear of each other, then taking the part that was Tricksie's, she raised it above them, then let it drift down like a Beaujolais film across their naked breasts. 'It suits you. It's sort of hot but subtle.' She caught Tricksie's eye, making a point, 'Like you, I suppose ...' She reached out to stroke the other woman's face and did it with real affection, remembering the orgasms Tricksie had given her. Like precious gifts, without thought of getting anything in return.

'Do you really think so?' Tricksie sat up, her full breasts

swaying and her lovely hair swishing across her shoulders. With no tight curl or elaborate style to constrain it, it reached almost half-way down her back. Isis shivered, thinking of it draped across her thighs as Tricksie licked her.

'I know so,' she said firmly. Reassuringly.

It was an odd fact, but sometimes Tricksie needed reminding of her own superiority. It shouldn't have been necessary. But lately, due to Diabolo's desertion, Isis supposed, her beautiful friend was a victim of low self-esteem. And it was at these times that Isis felt particularly close to her. Who better, she thought with some irony, who better than me to know about rejection and differentness. I could write a treatise on the subject. The art of being less than acceptable.

This was all grim stuff. Post-climactic tristesse, she supposed, giving herself a mental ticking off to clear it.

'But then I loved the other colour too,' she observed, not untruthfully, returning to positivity, and her sensuous thoughts about hair.

'Me too.' Tricksie fluffed a few plummy strands thoughtfully through her fingers.

Watching her, Isis shuddered. Not so long ago those fingers had been moving elsewhere. Working their miracles. Using the skill of years of practice to make a grown woman writhe and weep.

'But this is more classy. More Pleasurezone,' the whore went on, her face deliciously serious as her pale brow rumpled in a small frown. 'And anyway the other colour was far too much like *hers*.'

Under the guise of stretching luxuriantly, Isis hid a little smile.

Chief amongst Tricksie's most lovable qualities were her even temper and her generous knack of giving even the most unlikeable and obnoxious characters the benefit of the doubt. It was a genuine kindness of spirit, and an indispensable asset to both the whore and the legitimate sex therapist.

But even so there was one person, one solitary glitterata

who moved in their circles, who Tricksie Turing couldn't even abide for one second.

'Her?' Isis felt minxy, provocative. She knew perfectly well who Tricksie meant.

'Ett's new friend. Madam Sleazoid. That long red streak of piss . . .'

'Oh, Trix. Your claws are showing.' It was wicked to tease, but she couldn't resist it.

'She's the bitch with claws! She's the cat!' snapped Tricksie, so vexed she'd got her animals mixed up.

'Oh . . . You mean Red Cat?'

'Bloody tramp!'

You're so beautiful when you're angry . . . It was such a cliche, but Isis had to bite her lip to keep it in. Tricksie was so full of rage she was quivering. Her lush hair seemed to crackle around her and her eyes were flashing and glinting like green glass sheared along a fault.

Isis had never quite worked out why Tricksie hated Red Cat – the alternative, nay, downright degenerate female rock star that St Etienne had taken to knocking around with these days. She herself found Red Cat fascinating, and decidedly fanciable in a horrid, almost stomach-churning sort of way. She'd even gone so far as to write an adventure about the woman. Although guilt had made her keep this particular one encoded – so Tricksie couldn't key it up and read it.

Unknown by any other name than her *nom de musique*, Red Cat – with her band The Slaves – was the latest rock and roll sensation, a gloriously fetishistic diva as famed for her fearsome gothic beauty and her outrageous lifestyle as she was for the undoubted quality of her music. She was so bizarre to look at that Isis often wondered if she was just a mass hallucination. It was no wonder St Etienne was hot for her . . . They were a perfect two of a kind!

Allegedly almost six foot without her ever-present four-inch spike heels, the mind-boggling Red Cat was an icon of deviant eroticism. Her figure was lean and her breasts amazonic, and her sublimely toned legs seemed to go al the way up to her multi-pierced ears. A major portion of this spectacular figure was visible to the naked eye for most of the time, and topped off with a great thick mane of almost fluorescent crimson dreadlocks which reached to her perfect muscular buttocks. Which were also often on show. It was the loud hair colour, Isis supposed, that had inspired the singer's name. Or maybe it was just her face ...

Red Cat's features were as surreal as her coiffeur, and hypnotically and unmistakably feline. Wide black-diamond eyes, that slanted up sharply at the corners, were set in a true white complexion. Not the 'milk-white' of romantic novel heroines, but a dense fine-pored dead white; the colour of a birthsheet or a shroud, but silk-smooth, immaculate and flawless.

As someone named after a deity herself, Isis felt a certain kinship with Red Cat. The woman was a demon-goddess, Kali incarnate, an irresistible sexual annihilator. Isis could well believe that the Cat's backing band were really her slaves.

But all this begged another intriguing question. How the devil did the relationship between Red Cat and St Etienne pan out?

Isis's cousin was atrociously frank about her sexual relationships, both by word of mouth and in print, and made no secret of being a dominant. Isis couldn't imagine Ett ever submitting to anybody, but the idea of Red Cat bending the knee was equally inconceivable.

What on earth did they do? Who was the top? Who gave the orders? Who took the pain? Because there was bound to be some ... Isis felt her own sex rouse at the possibilities.

With a sudden grace, two fingers slid between Isis's labia and settled on either side of her clitoris, pressing lightly. She shook and gave a startled bleat of pleasure, realising to her astonishment that she'd been day-dreaming. Suspended somewhere in a bondage of steel and leather while two strong women played with her.

The fingers rocked infinitesimally, then squeezed, and

she cried out again, her hips lifting her moist flesh to meet them.

'You're all wet, love,' Tricksie whispered. 'Do you want to come again?'

'Oh yes,' Isis answered, squashing her guilt as her mind filled with visions of restraint and pain, vague forms of punisher and punished where she didn't quite identify with either.

But we all do this, her last shred of consciousness reasoned as her clitoris was teased from its hood and gently palpated. We all fantasise. We all deceive our lovers and leave them stranded while they serve us.

As she opened her legs wider, the faceless body in her dreams had its, no hers, widened for her. Two acolytes in the classic dresses of parlour-maids had hold of the victim's thighs and were holding her suspended and stretched as a formidable figure moved between them, clad scantily in shiny black. Or was it red?

Tricksie was stroking the unsheathed bud steadily now, wetting it from time to time to tease the sensations slowly and easily from its tender pink tip. In the dream the cruel mistress raised the tiny whip and brought it down hard on the same quivering organ . . .

In both worlds Isis screamed with pleasure and came.

'Don't worry. The man's obviously obsessed with you. I can't imagine him not turning up.'

Isis said nothing. She and Tricksie were in La Selene, waiting for Josh's arrival, and uncharacteristically, the man in question was late.

'Are you going to tell him about *us*?' Tricksie continued, the foxy twinkle in her eyes making Isis happy that there even was an 'us'.

Last night she'd sampled a variety of fantasy partners as Tricksie had patiently fingered her to orgasm after orgasm, but in the world of physical reality she knew she'd have to go a long way to find a lover as skilled and sweet in bed as the woman herself. Even just thinking about some of the things that had *really* happened was enough to stir her again, right here in the bar. It had been lucky that she'd had a free afternoon to rest; there had been precious little sleep last night.

'I dunno . . . Perhaps we should let him pick it up as he goes along?' Isis grinned, infected by Tricksie's perennial sexual devilment. 'Your adventurer isn't due for ages. You could stick around and meet Josh. In the flesh.'

The word 'flesh' produced an instant reaction. 'Don't tempt me,' Tricksie purred, crossing and recrossing her legs.

The movement was sleek, elegant, as everything about Tricksie always was, but to Isis it spoke of the heat between those long, stockinged thighs. Petals wet and pouting. Congestion. A discomfort that was far from unpleasant. The feeling between her own legs now . . . Memories of their own love-making and a hundred other times. With others . . .

Why was this sensation so matchless? Isis wondered, feeling her sex pout and flutter beneath her tailored trousers. She was almost always like this these days. Always wet, always ready to be touched. To take a finger or a penis. There hadn't been many of *those* for quite a while, but in the near future . . . Maybe?

There had been fingers aplenty. And toys too. Either wielded as if part of an art-form by Tricksie; or less refinedly, her own hand, in moments of solitude. All these things were beautiful in their own way, and satisfying, but she had a sudden sharp longing to have a man inside her again.

Where the hell are you? she demanded silently of the man she most wanted it to be.

'Men,' Tricksie observed, taking a sip of her tonic water and grimacing. Isis wondered whether it was the gender or the beverage that had caused the face. Being a connoisseuse of wine and cocktails the alcohol embargo prior to sessions was the one thing Trix didn't like about working for Pleasurezone, 'They go on about us always keeping them waiting, but nine times out of ten, they're the ones that are late.'

The new look suits her, thought Isis, taking a sip of her own innocuous drink.

Tricksie was wearing a chic fawn wool dress that skimmed her luscious figure rather than grabbing it, but it still clung beautifully to the curves of her perfectly toned bosom. The Queen of Tricks had never looked less like a prostitute than she did tonight; but even disguised as a respectable businesswoman she still screamed to the high heavens of sex. Josh was going to adore her.

Observing Tricksie at her second favourite hobby – people watching – Isis wondered what Mister Mortimer would think about their relationship. The whore and the mad doctor. Flesh and science, the melding of the body and the mind.

She remembered the idea of it exciting him all those months ago, but in that he'd not been unusual.

Lesbian scenarios were the most frequently requested adventures amongst men. The entire sex seemed to be obsessed with what girls did to girls in bed, almost to the exclusion of all other sexualities. Josh Mortimer was no exception to this. His fantasy profile showed a marked peak on all registers when he adventured both *as* a woman and *with* a woman.

The ultimate expression of this, of course, was what Isis had planned for him tonight.

Dare I do it? she thought, starting to tremble at the very idea. It would be a stunning thing to do to him. She could imagine how his mind and his body would respond. Readings off the scale and orgasms multiple. It could well be his best adventure yet, but it would be awfully revealing of *her*. And of Tricksie . . .

Yet Josh meant more to Isis than any man had in a long time. She wanted to draw him close, she realised. Make him stay. Enslave him, if you like. Since he'd first got back, the ghost of a crazy scheme had been hatching somewhere in the back of her brain . . . and showing him how it was with her and Tricksie, opening their sexual world to him, was possibly the best way of locking him into her plans . . .

'Yes! That's it! I'll do it.'

'What? What are you grinning about?' Tricksie was staring at her, lusciously puzzled.

'Josh's next adventure.'

'Does *he* know what it is yet?' Tricksie's eyes were huge.

'No. But he won't be able to resist it.' Isis reached for Tricksie's hand, squeezed, and felt her friend's sweet heat through the thin leather barrier of her glove.

'What is it?'

'Me and you.'

It was like lightning passing through them, shared memories passing from heaven to earth along an living conduit. Isis watched Tricksie's pupils dilate, black inside electric green, and her soft mouth part instinctively for a kiss. Were her nipples hard too? Her vagina running? Does she feel like me? thought Isis, quivering.

'Now *that* really is an adventure.' Isis could barely contain herself as Tricksie took the hand holding hers, turned it, and raised it to her mauve-painted lips. If they'd been naked in bed together, Isis would have thrown wide her own legs and masturbated immediately, but as it was she felt her sex ripple in a long deep wave as Tricksie peeled back the thin leather glove and pressed a full openmouthed kiss on the palm of her hand.

She felt confused, conspicuous, turned on. Vulnerable. It was the first time they'd shared such an intimate moment, here in the bar, and Isis wasn't quite sure she was ready for it. Even though there was fire between her legs ...

'Go for it, boss,' purred Tricksie. her tongue flicking against exposed skin as she spoke. The caress was so delicate, so like another kind of licking that Isis felt faint. Heat surged from the tips of her toes to the crown of her head; then rebounded, like a backdraft, to the nexus of all feeling. Her sex. In that instant she wanted, needed, would have died to have an orgasm. Lost, completely, she heard a small sound somewhere at her side. A gasp. At her *other* side ...

Josh Mortimer was standing, his mouth open in aston-

85

ishment, just inches from where she and Tricksie were locked in their erotic stasis.

'I – ' His mouth snapped shut. He was as beyond coherent speech as Isis was herself, yet somewhere in the computer of her brain she managed to log a surge of intense amusement.

Never had she seen a man so flabbergasted. Or so nakedly aroused while still fully clothed.

It was Tricksie, ever the social animal, who stepped graciously into the breach.

'Hello, Josh,' she said, while still smoothing the leather over Isis's moistened palm. Then, without missing a beat, she turned and held her hand out to the newcomer. 'I feel I know you.' Her long, precisely mascara-ed lashes flashed down, just once. 'And I'm sure you feel the same about me.'

Isis almost wished she could retreat into scientific detachment and watch the progress of this remarkable encounter. Josh had 'been' Tricksie once, in an adventure, and now he was meeting her. She tried to imagine how he might be feeling.

It wasn't too hard. His handsome face was flushed, his dark eyes burning, and she didn't need x-ray specs to guess he had an erection. He was currently within kissing distance of what all the data projected as his most potent fantasy. Herself and Tricksie, obviously lovers and obviously hot for each other. She saw him glance from Tricksie to her and then back again, and felt a blast of triumph. The die was cast. If she'd had a remote in her bag, she could have programmed the computer right now.

Josh still hadn't spoken, but suddenly Isis didn't want to waste any time.

'Come on, Josh. I've got something really special for you tonight. And as you're late, we'd better get started.' Hopping down from her stool, she slid her arm into his. He was shaking.

'Nice to have met you, Josh,' Tricksie chimed in beside them, and it was obvious she was dying to laugh. 'I'd tell you to have fun, but I don't really need to, do I?' Lik the courtesan she truly was, she held out her hand again, and Isis couldn't help but admire Josh's swift return to poise. He took it, bent over it slightly and kissed it like a continental chevalier.

'A pleasure, Tricksie,' he murmured, his first words of the evening. 'I hope we meet again soon.'

What have I started? thought Isis as she escorted him to the 'Zone's Suite One. Tricksie had winked at her behind his back as they'd been leaving, and mimed an enthusiastic 'hubba hubba'. The vibes between Josh and the whore had been unmistakable and thrilling. 'Sharing' had just soared to the top of the hidden agenda and Isis wondered how long they'd all be able to hold out against each other.

'Is she still on the game?' enquired Josh as Isis was preparing him. He'd found his tongue soon after they'd left the bar, although strangely he'd said nothing about his forthcoming dream and its content.

It was as if he already knew.

'Occasionally,' she answered obliquely, aware that her teasing would stiffen him. Not that he really needed it. As she'd strapped him to the white couch, his cock was already reaching for the ceiling, a pearl of juice oozing slowly from his glans.

'What's that supposed to mean?' he enquired as they both studied his erection.

'She works for me most of the time now.' Isis's lips were as dry as parts of her were wet. The body before her was so available, so bare. She remembered a night months ago when temptation had got the better of her.

Without thinking, she let out a sigh of longing and placed a hand on his naked chest. The lure was too great, the red, heavily veined tower of his cock irresistible. She drew her fingers down over his belly and his pubic fluff, then took him in a firm, caressing fist.

Don't do it, Isis, she told herself, sliding the skin up and down over the solid core. She'd let him touch her last time and now she was masturbating him. She felt an unspoken barrier grow more friable by the second.

'Whadaya mean?' slurred Josh, his voice drug-altered, as his hips bumped in time to her caress.

'The 'Zone's very busy now, Josh. I have another therapy room. Tricksie's probably doing *this* – ' She squeezed. Lightly. ' – to another client right now.'

Josh went 'mmmm' as the eye of his penis wept on her moving fingers.

'Is she as good as you?' he whispered, almost coming in her grip.

'Oh yes. Definitely. But different . . .'

But is she? Isis reflected dreamily, wondering if Tricksie's frisky couch-side manner was all that different to *this*. In the thrall of her own senses, she went one step further than she'd intended . . .

It was as if she was watching herself from a great height. She looked down and saw a white coated woman lean across the crotch of a man's straining body and take a droplet of love-juice from the swollen tip of his prick. With the furled point of her tongue.

'Oh God! Oh God, yes!'

She heard the cry from the same exalted distance, and saw white spunk shoot from the penis beneath her, then felt it splatter her lips and chin, and drop in thick, pearly blobs onto the stomach of the man in bondage beneath her. Ravished, she rounded up the creamy stuff with her tongue, from everywhere it had landed and let it slide slowly down her throat.

It was a few seconds before she actually realised what she'd done. She hadn't broken the biggest rule, but she'd come awfully near.

Josh had simply come.

She looked up from his groin, and saw that his eyes were closed as if sleeping. He was relaxed in every muscle and his flat brown belly was shiny with semen. His cock lolled on his sticky thigh, still big but soft and slack.

Oh well done, Isis. Really well done. You're up for even more trouble now. She was going to have to arouse him all over again to get the sensor cuff on.

Shutting down the woman in her, and putting the scientist in charge, she took Josh in a firm businesslike grip and worked him quickly back to a full encrimsoned hardness.

She felt almost cruel, but she managed to stay detached. She only felt the faintest stirring – in her own body – when she lubricated his tight, resisting hole, then held his muscular arse-cheeks open with her fingers to let in the plastic bulk of the probe.

Her hands did shake as she cuffed his newly rigid cock, but were rock-steady as she slid the hypo professionally into a vein in his arm. Some functions were second nature; even lust couldn't affect them.

Gently, she covered his eyes, then settled on a stool beside the couch. With her own headset 'live', she pressed the familiar sequence of keystrokes that would initiate the adventure.

'Right then, sweetheart,' she whispered, knowing she sounded like a lover. 'I think we both know what you want tonight, don't we?'

Josh answered her with the very slightest nod of his head.

It was enough.

'Okay. I've set some scenes for you, but *you* decide where it starts . . . Do you understand me?'

'Yeah . . . Yes, I do,' the naked man on the couch muttered, shocking Isis to the core with a voice that suddenly wasn't quite his. The basic timbre was Josh Mortimer, but there was definitely a lilt of Tricksie in there too.

'Right back . . . Yeah . . . The beginning . . .' The tricky he/she voice was strange and scary, but arousing too. 'Right back . . . The first time . . .'

Isis smiled, still trying to assimilate the voice, and wondering vaguely if he'd get the event right or glamorise it. 'A first encounter of the close kind, eh?' she said, more to herself than him, 'That's beautiful, Josh. Really beautiful.'

With that, she pressed the last key and cut into the monitoring system.

In the inner world it created, she saw familiar surroundings and smiled again.

'That's it, lover ... Now go for it! Dream on and on and on and on ...'

6

First Encounters of the Close Kind

Oh God, it's *her* again!

Tricksie blinked twice, glanced accusingly at her glass of champagne, then looked back towards the bar and the mysterious veil-shrouded woman.

It was definitely her. Veils were all the vogue this season, but no one wore them like the stranger. So dense and closely patterned they were nearly opaque. So concealing that they all but covered the face. So mysterious that there could only be the very greatest beauty beneath, and all that was visible of it was a strong but delicate chin, and a luscious rose-stained mouth. Tricksie wondered how well the woman could see.

Who the devil was she?

This was the third time Tricksie had seen the veiled woman here in La Selene, and though under normal circumstances she'd have taken a professional note of someone so elegant, it was the company the woman kept that had grabbed her interest. Grabbed her by the throat with steel-cored fingers of jealous fascination. On both previous occasions the woman had been talking to Diabolo.

Tonight, thank God, the strange woman was alone – sitting at the bar, as chic as ever, writing in a tiny black-backed notebook with a silver pen. Her absorption in her jottings was total, and it gave Tricksie a good chance to study her.

An acknowledged beauty herself, Tricksie paid a silent homage to an allure quite different to her own. The woman had an intellectual air, scholarly, and yet was sexier by far than any academic that Tricksie had ever met.

A bluestocking, she mused, smiling to herself. But professors usually encased their pins in knitted wool, not seven denier silk, and wore heather tweeds instead of slim-cut designer suits that hinted at glorious figures beneath. Tricksie, who made a point of knowing about clothes, recognised the suit's rich fabric. Gros de Londres rib, midnight blue. A sophisticated choice made more so by blue-all-through accessories. The pert hat and its tantalising veil; kid leather gloves; those indecently sheer hose; and classic court shoes that were lower than Tricksie's stilettos but still sufficiently elevated to be saucy.

But it was the prettiest 'something blue' that was giving Tricksie the shivers. A vee-shape of ultramarine-figured satin, a camisole shimmering in the plunge of a deeply serious neckline.

Lord, she's gorgeous! Tricksie told herslef solemnly, quite mad for the woman's identity.

She'd been talking to Diabolo, but did it mean anything? Was she a hooker? An experiment in top-drawer whoring? Some men got off on being belittled.

But never mind men, what is it she's doing to me? wondered Tricksie, sipping quickly at her champagne. A regular client had missed his appointment tonight, but had sent his 'favourite lady' a bottle of Krug out of courtesy. She didn't usually drink this much this early, but the sight of the veiled woman made her feel nervous. She wasn't drunk by a long shot but, looking across the room, she could almost believe she was.

What's happening to me? I shouldn't be feeling like this, she thought, deeply fazed by her body's reactions. By feelings she only usually got for Diabolo.

Unlike some prostitutes. Tricksie enjoyed sex and often had orgasms. It wasn't her customers who made her come, though . . . despite her genuine enjoyment of their company.

Tricksie Turing's pleasure had two unfailing sources: her pride in her own healthy body and its superb erotic skills;

and the presence, in her mind, of her beloved Diabolo at the moment another man entered her.

With these thoughts, she could bring herself to climax in the arms of a total stranger. And if she concentrated hard enough, she could even be wet and ready when her clients slid their fingers into her panties.

What troubled her tonight was that these things were happening to her right now – and had nothing to do with Diabolo. She was wet, engorged and aching because a woman she'd never met was sitting thirty feet away. She gasped, then gulped more wine. As if she'd thought that thought too, the veiled stranger had snapped shut her book and was rising elegantly to her feet. Tricksie felt the ache in her sex gain strength.

Bisexuality and lesbianism were quite ordinary in Tricksie's line of business, but until this moment she could honestly say she'd only ever wanted men. Well, wanted one man . . .

Yet now her breasts felt swollen, too big for her sequinned top, and her poor soft quim felt as if Diabolo himself had just reached into her knickers and fingered her.

And the cause of all this was now walking briskly across the room in her direction.

Tricksie felt numb, locked in a web of heat, and all she could do was tremble and watch and wait.

'Hello, you're Tricksie, aren't you? May I sit with you?'

The voice was as beguiling as the appearance: smooth and cultured, yet insidiously warm. Tricksie nodded, then pushed her glass away, feeling drunk already on the two short sentences.

'Diabolo told me about you. Pointed you out . . . I thought it'd be nice to get to know you,' the woman went on hesitantly, and deep in the middle of her own confusion, Tricksie realised the stranger was excited as she was.

'Yeah, sure,' she blurted out, 'But don't you think you should tell me your name.' She felt disadvantaged with no eyes to look into for clues.

'I'm sorry. Of course – ' The stranger peeled off her

glove and held out a slim hand in greeting. The hand was slightly disfigured by a network of fine pink scars; and as they both seemed to study it, the beautiful rosy mouth twisted in sudden anguish. Even white teeth snagged the soft lower lip, and Tricksie wondered why the woman was so worried. It was only a few pink lines ... Caught in a curious twist of sympathy she reached out and clasped the offered fingers and the veiled one smiled with relief.

'My name's Isis,' she said softly. Her smile broadened, became open and seductive ... and Tricksie's composure slid helplessly away.

What was happening to her? She never lost her cool like this, even with Diabolo. She was falling to pieces. Losing control. Everything she was seemed to be right there in that delicate pink-lined hand.

Isis' fingers were soft, slightly warm and quite dry. There was no tactile indication she was scarred, and Tricksie let her own fingers stay held for seconds longer than normal. She was giving herself away right, left and centre, and Isis could well find such feelings repellent.

I want you. It was on the tip of Tricksie's tongue, even though she only partially understood what it was she wanted.

After a moment, Isis delicately reclaimed her own hand, then turned away to signal for another bottle of wine. The movement made her thick hair fall forward across one shoulder, and Tricksie gasped aloud at its beauty.

On both her two previous visits to La Selene, Isis had been wearing her hair in a sophisticated knot, tucked sleekly beneath her hat and veil. But tonight, though the front tresses were coiled cleverly beneath her chic navy blue pillbox, the remaining great mass of hair was hanging in a loosely crimped cascade that trailed quite a long way down her back. Not exactly curly and not exactly straight, its colour was astounding. Correction: colours. Dark blonde, rich brown, tints of auburn and sienna, the lush, multicoloured fall had a dense erotic gleam that made Tricksie long to feel it ripple on her skin. She imagined them naked in bed together, and Isis smoothing that sub-limely beautiful hair across her belly.

'Is something wrong?' There was alarm in Isis's voice, even though her obscured face revealed nothing.

'No . . . No, it's all right. I was just struck by your hair. It's very unusual. Beautiful.'

Oh God, she must think I'm a complete twit! Tricksie thought glumly as the other woman smiled.

'Thanks,' Isis said shyly, then seemed to regain her confidence as fresh champagne arrived and she busied herself filling their glasses. Tricksie knew she shouldn't have any more, but she still accepted it.

Isis proposed a toast. 'To . . . to us.'

The simple salutation was as intoxicating as the wine. 'Yes. To us.' Tricksie felt giddy, tapped her glass to Isis's and gulped thirstily at its contents. She couldn't wait any more. 'But please. Isis. Who are you? Are you involved with Diabolo? Are you . . . are you like me?'

Isis laughed then, and Tricksie nearly had a climax on the spot. The laugh was so merry and sultry. So young, uninhibited, and sexy that Tricksie would have challenged anyone not to adore Isis simply on the strength of it.

'I'm sorry, that was a really dumb thing to say, wasn't it?' Tricksie stammered, then felt her blood run chill as Isis's merriment disappeared and her lovely pink mouth went tight and sad.

What's happened? What have I said? What have I done to her? thought Tricksie, aching to take the other woman in her arms and comfort her.

'No, it's okay, Tricksie.' The pretty mouth quirked. 'I wouldn't mind being a whore actually. I really love to fuck . . .'

Tricksie's loins throbbed. That 'perfect lady' style was explosive in combination with such a raunchy mouth. In bed, the mix would be incredible.

'I adore sex,' Isis went on, 'but I can't see anybody in their right mind paying *me* for it.'

'Why not? You're beautiful . . . Ask any man in this room and he'd give you a thousand just for the basics!'

Tricksie reached out and grabbed Isis's hand again, although that was the least of the things she wanted to do to her.

In her mind they were kissing, touching each other everywhere, pulling at unnecessary clothes and then stroking and fondling every nook and crevice they could reach.

Amazingly, Isis raised the clasping hand to her lips, then kissed it before placing it neatly into Tricksie's lap.

Something wild was happening between them, yet it was more than simple lust. Tricksie knew now that she wanted Isis as much as she'd ever wanted Diabolo; but she also wanted to know what made her suddenly look so unhappy.

'Bless you, Tricksie,' the veiled one murmured. 'Bless you, but you're so, so wrong.'

With that, she removed her second glove, raised both her hands, and took hold of the lower edge of her veil. Slowly she raised it.

Tricksie's flinch was pure reflex, but in the microsecond after it, she despised herself.

It wasn't only Isis's hands that were scarred.

A large, red-purple cicatrix sprawled luridly across the left side of her face. Starting a little above the level of her glorious mouth, it coloured the whole of her cheek, cheek-bone and eye-socket, then faded away at the smooth arch of her brow. At first sight it *was* shocking. But within seconds Tricksie saw a structure in the huge disfigurement. It was like a flower, but no common one. Its form was rare and exotic. Like an Egyptian lotus. Or an orchid.

Open-mouthed, Tricksie stared harder. And started to smile as she saw more to the scar. More in it. It wasn't *just* a flower . . .

Oh God . . . Yes! How beautiful! Without thinking, she reached out and caressed the face before her as if caressing the holy female thing it resembled. Entranced now, she was no longer scared or shy. She gasped softly as Isis's rosy lips widened in a smile and her eyes glistened, tears shimmering in both the beautiful hazel-gold of her good eye and in the muddy, injured orb that lay at the heart of her scar.

'I still think you're beautiful.' Tricksie drifted her fingers across the very faintly textured skin. 'It . . . it looks like . . .' Jesus, how could she of all people be embarrassed about saying 'cunt'?

'Yes. It does. And just like mine, I've been told.' Isis's grin was impish now, and she raised her own fingers to hold Tricksie's in place. She inclined her strange face a little to the side, and Tricksie almost stopped breathing in anticipation of receiving a kiss.

Rose-red lips touched her palm, lips that were warm and soft and slightly moist. The resonances, the suggestiveness, were both maddening. Tricksie panted as her sex fluttered in response and the slow shift in her perceptions clicked joyfully into place. She did want this woman, her loins were aflame for her, and she was too well-versed in the ways of lust not to recognise the kiss for what it was.

'Crazy, this, isn't it?' Isis murmured, taking Tricksie's hand from her face and returning it – with obvious reluctance – to the table before them. 'It knocked me for six when I first saw you . . . I wasn't expecting it. I had a couple of flings with girls at University, but I thought it was just a phase. I went back to men. I never thought I'd feel hot for a woman again.'

Tricksie felt as if the wish fairy had landed on her shoulder, but there was still one dark shadow.

'What were you doing with Diabolo?' she asked before she had time to stop herself.

Isis eyed her astutely, and Tricksie wondered what the pimp had been saying to her. Or even doing to her.

'Asking for help with a project I'm setting up,' she replied calmly. 'I'm a doctor, a sexologist and I needed the assistance of a male sexual professional. A practical perspective rather than a medical one like my own. An acquaintance recommended Diabolo.' She paused and smiled kindly. 'Yes, I know, I'm being a bit cloak and dagger . . . But it's early days yet and I don't know if it'll work out.'

Tricksie made a decision: based on her new infatuation with the unusual woman before her, and her old knowledge of an equally unusual man. 'Look, it's okay. I won't ask questions. Your business is nothing to do with me. I was only worried about . . .' She let it hover as Isis smiled. Her feelings must be so obvious.

For Isis herself as well as Diabolo.

Isis with her scarred face and her air of mystery. Isis with her grace and elegance and her passion beneath the surface. Isis with her slender throat, her flawed but nimble hands, her lithe body and her legs as sleek as a mannequin's.

Was she wearing tights or stockings? Tricksie conjectured, reaching gratefully for the glass that had just been topped up. She was getting a bit fizzed now, but liked the feeling. It was easier to see the delicious inner pictures with some wine inside her, and much easier to sit calmly at the table with Isis: not talking, but just sipping their drinks and watching the room, its occupants, and each other.

Stockings, she decided, returning to her debate as one of those pictures formed. Micro-sheer silk; broad, navy blue lacy welts; fine, pale skin all sheened up with sweat. And with juice.

Would her panties be as pretty? As moist? Tricksie shuddered, then blushed furiously when Isis looked across and quirked one fine-lined brow.

She's a fucking mind-reader! she thought, awed into silent profanity by the possibility of Isis seeing what *she* saw. Well, get a load of this, lady! She smiled, dropped her gaze to the other woman's navy-clad lap and mentally ripped away her skirt.

Midnight blue lace. Minute. Sopping wet. Hanging heavy with juices when Isis rose to her feet, the soaked cloth thick with desire.

Tricksie licked her lips, trying to imagine the taste. Would she be delicately salty? Her emissions bland and dainty . . . Or would she be musky? Bitchy? Strong and pungent?

Tricksie's mouth filled with saliva but she swallowed, took up her glass and drank again.

Oh God, if only it were Isis she were drinking. If only she wasn't in a public place, and she could reach through the loose, overlapping legs of her trousers and bring ease to her own aching clitoris. If only Isis would slide her slender, pink-etched hand beneath the table and do it for her.

She imagined those beautiful fingers exploring her. Pressing lightly on her mons, aggravating the steady, growing pressure in her bladder. There was a heavy weight of fluid there now, knocking against the root of her clitty. She wriggled, returning happily to reality and the real and wicked thing massing in her crotch. If she'd any sense, she'd excuse herself and slip to the powder room. But she couldn't tear herself away; and the stress from her filling bladder was making the wanting more imperative than ever.

Devil thoughts filled her mind . . . Isis smiling and abusing her, kneading her tortured crotch, trying to force her to pee. She bit her lips, suppressing a whimper as she crossed her legs and her clitoris fluttered in a tiny pre-orgasmic spasm.

'You're beautiful. I want you so much.' Isis's husky whisper piled on the pressure. Tricksie bit her lip, wanting to cry out in her ravaging need and press down hard on her swollen clit.

She knows! She knows! She knows! Tricksie thought passionately. She knows I'm sopping for her . . . Dying for her.

'Shall we get out of here?' Isis went on, her voice urgent as if she too felt torment between her thighs. 'I've got a hotel room. At the St Vincent, across town. I know a short cut . . . If you're up for it, that is?' she was already on her feet, as if knowing full well that Tricksie would follow.

Tricksie nodded and rose in her wake. As she crossed the room behind her goddess, it was difficult to keep herself silent. The sensations between her legs were both appalling and fabulous. Pleasure-pain pressing down like crystal shards, the bloated fullness in her sex, the lewd squelch of her juices as she walked. She imagined she could hear herself slurping, hear her pouched lips jostling in her panties. She half expected people to turn and stare curiously as she passed.

Isis had a walk like a goddess's too; a slight delicious sway, and neat, trim buttocks that rolled with syncopated grace beneath the slim blue tube of her skirt. Tricksie wanted to lift up that skirt – and pull down whatever lay beneath – and kiss her adored one's bottom. She wanted to kiss her everywhere, but at this moment her rear more than anywhere else; the sight of that tight, curvaceous shape jostling rhythmically beneath that classy ribbed silk was making her feel light-headed.

When they reached the relative seclusion of the foyer, Isis grabbed the nape of Tricksie's neck, kissed her once, stunningly, full on the lips, then withdrew and flicked down her veil.

'It's easier,' she muttered, then took Tricksie's hand and led her out into the Mall.

Oh, love, you don't have to do that! cried Tricksie silently from the extravagant heart of her passion. If anybody says anything, does anything, I'll scratch their eyes out. You're beautiful! Can't they see that? All other faces are plain beside yours.

They should fall down and worship you, Isis, she thought in a daze of tormented rapture. Women and men both . . .

For a moment, with shocking clarity, she imagined being a man. Being erect and entering this new divinity before her. The dream of it was so vivid that she felt as if her heart had stopped, then in a flash it was pulsing again, full of life, as fast and frenzied as the hard, heavy beat in her loins.

The discomfort was voluptuous now, every minute movement brought a fresh stab of sensation. Her belly was throbbing, distended, her clitoris on fire to be touched. Every step was a fight not to moan out aloud.

Once in a while, Isis would pause in her hurry, turn

around, and Tricksie would feel an uncanny scrutiny raying out from that dense blue veil. She was convinced now that Isis knew of her critical condition, and understood the bliss of it. Why else would she be forcing her to run in these spindly high heels? Each stride was a streak of pain to her bladder.

'Hurry!' cried Isis breathlessly, 'I need to touch you. I can't wait much longer.'

Me neither, thought Tricksie, bursting. There was a wetness in her crotch that she didn't think was lubrication alone. And you know it, don't you, you beautiful witch? she accused, almost delirious with a thousand sensations.

Panting, she allowed herself to be half-led, half-dragged across the Mall, through corridors and finally out into the cool night air of the city. They passed some rather dubious citizens going about their questionable outside business, but soon they were alone in a narrow, dimly lit alley.

'Thank God,' gasped Isis, flipping up her veil and launching herself forward.

Oh yes, thought Tricksie, sobbing around the wine-scented tongue that instantly filled her mouth, pushing hard against the hand that grabbed for her crotch. Isis palmed her mound, and the balloon of her bladder behind it, and she squealed out aloud.

'Yes, that's it, baby,' the other woman cooed, pressing harder, throwing her weight behind the torturing hand and making Tricksie whimper and wriggle.

'I need to pee,' she gasped, blushing scarlet, tears welling in her tightly closed eyes.

'I know that, pretty Trix,' Isis purred, working hard through Tricksie's thin trousers. 'But don't you like it? Come on ... Admit it. You know you like it.' The fingers squeezed, a white-hot pincer, 'Feel it all. All that fluid, that piss, pressing on your clitty. Making it ache and ache. Is it popping out, sweetheart? Your little bud, peeping from its hood? I bet it's lovely and hard. Would you like me to rub it for you?'

'Oh yes yes yes,' sobbed Tricksie, lost in a hot dark euphoria as Isis bore down. The blatant language had inflamed her. She *was* her clitoris now, it was a star, a red giant between her legs, her body and limbs its satellites. Beside herself, she writhed and pumped and groaned.

'Yes, my beauty, yes,' whispered Isis, soft and wicked in her ear, 'You're bursting now, aren't you? Full up. All that naughty piss inside you ... Pushing on your pretty little quim.'

Tricksie nodded, her voice gone. The pit of her belly was volcanic now and the star, her clit, was huge and violently active. It felt as if it were standing out inches from her labia, projected into space by the sheer force of fluid above it.

'Speak, Tricksie!' her tormentress commanded, 'Tell me what you want!'

'I ... Agh!' A tiny spurt of pee shot out, milked by Isis's crushing grip. Tricksie felt its wetness on her panties. 'Oh, please ... I ... Oh, God!'

'What, little bitch? What do you want!'

'I want you to frig me!' she shouted, exulting in her own coarseness. 'I want you to wank me. Wank my clit. I want you to take it in your fingers and rub it up and down. And I want to piss my pants while you do it.'

Almost fainting, Tricksie felt Isis unfastening her trousers and easing them down her thighs. As the cool air hit her, she jammed her hands between her legs, then skipped from one foot to the other as Isis knelt, pulled the trousers off her ankles and tossed them away into the alley.

She opened her eyes then and the view was dreamlike. A blue-suited woman, kneeling between her spread thighs, face intent, hands slightly raised, scars luminous on both. Her own body looked lewd, an archetypal porn shot, part naked, part covered, her suspender belt white, her stockings grey and filmy, her panties barely existing. She still had on her black high heels. Isis leaned forward to kiss her mound, and Tricksie mewled like a kitten, terrified she'd let her rain flood out across that beautiful purple-marked face.

It didn't happen, and Isis rose gracefully to her feet,

peeling off her gloves as she did so and sending them winging to the concrete to join Tricksie's trousers.

'Beautiful,' she whispered again, drawing the back of her hand up the inside of Tricksie's quivering thigh. Her fingertips danced across the back of Tricksie's clutching hands, then prodded lightly at her lace-covered mons.

'Oh God,' groaned Tricksie, holding harder, holding out against the messages of her frantic nerve-ends. A tiny trickle seeped through her panties and Isis poked her again.

Sweet burning agony jolted her, and little jets of urine sprayed the silk between her legs.

'I can't hold it much longer.' Rocking now, her fingers pressed hard on the sodden cloth and the hot pulpy folds within.

'Yes, you can, my sweet,' Isis's marked face was against hers now; her breath smelt of champagne, 'Just a little while longer.' He fingers slid beneath the elastic of Tricksie's knickers, dragging downwards. 'Let's get these out of the way so I can touch you.'

Strong scarred hands prised away Tricksie's fingers and then the thin pants beneath them. Trickie's pelvis waved wildly of its own accord, and she saw the white bridge of her flimsy lingerie suspended between her parted white thighs, just above the knee. The weight of fluid seemed to bounce like a stone against her clitoris.

'Hold on, pet,' Isis whispered, stilling her, then combing her fingers through the flame-red hair at Tricksie's crotch. Tricksie looked down expecting to see a yellow jet leap out into her fingers . . .

What she did see was one finger and a thumb dive neatly in. Burrow into the hair. Searching . . .

Red lights exploded behind Tricksie's eyes. She was grasped, squeezed, ruthlessly tugged. Liquid bliss boiled in her clit, her quim, her aching bladder. Her whole sex pumped, shooting out her golden fluid and drenching both the long pale hand that abused her and the stretched white crotch of her panties.

And the hand wouldn't quit. It worked her unflinchingly

103

and wrenched out the full power of her orgasm from a vagina that fluttered and sucked.

It was only as the pleasure ebbed that Tricksie heard her own cursing, blaspheming voice.

'Oh God, I'm sorry,' she muttered, grabbing at the tattered shreds of her thinking mind as she stared down at the shining wetness of her loins and thighs and Isis's hand, still touching its tiny prize and coated in a shimmering glove of moisture.

'What for?'

'Swearing and pissing all over you.'

'It's what I wanted,' Isis said quietly, drawing her hand from between Tricksie's legs and shaking it briskly. 'And there's no harm done. It only went on my hand.'

'I . . . I . . . Agh!'

It was still happening; delicious aftershocks rippled through Tricksie's sex and she felt Isis press her again, gently this time, the gesture soft and soothing to her overheated sex. She wriggled contentedly as the sensations peaked, then faded.

'God, Isis, that was wild,' she exclaimed at last as a semblance of order returned to her senses.

'It certainly was.' Isis dipped gracefully, fumbled for her discarded handbag, then dragged out a handful of tissues. 'And if there are any apologies due, they should be from me. I shouldn't drink champagne . . . Well, not that much. It makes me go completely wacko. I start wanting to do the rudest things I can think of.' She grinned, kneeling to blot lightly at Tricksie's crotch and thighs. 'And believe me, in my line of business, I can think of some pretty rude things!'

'Me too,' Tricksie returned the smile as her body sent her head crazy messages.

Oh God, she thought, flexing her thighs to give Isis better access. Oh God, I could start all over again . . .

Strange beauty knelt before her. A face more erotic than any other woman's naked body. Hair that flashed a hundred miraculous colours. Grace worthy of the goddess whose name it bore. Tricksie wanted to join with Isis, absorb her. She wanted to give her back all the pleasure she'd received from her.

Delicate tremors tantalised her quim as Isis completed her ministrations and regarded the sorry wet mess of Tricksie's panties. She grinned up at her and shrugged, the movement enchanting and throwaway.

'Don't worry. I've got tons of things at my hotel. You can get changed there. Can you manage like this for a while?' In a smooth sleight-of-hand action, she pulled up the urine-soaked panties and pressed them snugly to Tricksie's quivering mound. The wet cloth was mercifully chill against her heat.

Tricksie shuddered, knowing she wanted more, but wanting to turn that 'more' about. She wanted to make the sorceress lose her cool; disturb her, disrupt her, dishevel that prim blue suit. Make her lose control, soon. Right here in this alley . . .

As Isis rose, drying her fingers on the tissues and looking around for somewhere to discard them, Tricksie stepped forward, slid her hands into the silken mass of her lover's hair, and pulled her strange face intimately close.

Their lips met with force and this time it was Tricksie who imposed her mouth on Isis, delving with her tongue, sucking and nibbling, keeping lips tight together and pelvises apart. She didn't want that silk skirt ruined altogether.

'But – ' Tricksie stopped Isis' protests with a hand across her mouth. Her left hand . . . Her right one was working on a long row of dark blue buttons.

'But nothing. It's my turn now, sex-lady. *I* want to see *you* come.'

Tricksie felt Isis's mouth go slack beneath hers, and accept her tongue like a pillaging sex. There was no need for words. Not even when Tricksie freed her lips and stood back to put two hands to the task of exposing . . .

'Oh yes,' she murmured as the dark lapels swung open. 'Oh yes indeedy . . .'

Isis was lovely beneath her bright satin camisole: voluptuous without blowsiness, high-breasted, perky, softly conical. Perfectly proportioned, her twinned curves were nymphish and inviting, the nipples small, hard and pointing rudely at Tricksie through the gossamer lightness of silk.

I'll tame you, Egyptian goddess, thought Tricksie, slightly crazed, grasping Isis's nipples each in a finger and thumb, and smiling as the other woman gasped harshly.

She gasped again, almost groaned, when Tricksie pinched each teat, teasing them into a longer and harder erection and stretching the resilient flesh of each breast out and away from the underlying plane of her rib-cage. She did groan, heavily, when Tricksie jiggled and bounced her. But even so, she gave herself away with the slow, frustrated waft of her slender silk covered hips.

'Am I getting to you, sweetheart?' Tricksie felt as if she were flying now, in control, the Queen of Tricks again in her abbreviated sequinned bodice, her white suspender belt and her pants and stockings and shoes soaked with her own cooling urine.

Isis nodded, her pale hands smoothing nervously at her skirt. It was so obvious that she wanted to touch herself.

This should all have been so sordid, observed Tricksie in an odd quiet fugue of detachment, her fingers still gripping Isis's breasts. Two dykes mauling each other in a grungy alleyway. Two lezzies frigging and peeing. It should have been crude and hideous but it wasn't.

Isis had conducted the first act of their drama with gentle playful kindness ... and now she, Tricksie, would conclude it the same way.

We like the same things, she thought wonderingly. Isis was jerking and moaning, obviously in love with the same kind of breastwork that Tricksie loved. The same roughness. The same pinching, tweaking and casual handling. Diabolo did this, she remembered all too clearly, seeing a brief flash of him groping Isis. He was crueller though. Colder. More pain-giving ...

It hurts but it makes me wet, she acknowledged, then longed to know the state of Isis's sex. She imagined her

106

pulsing in the dark beneath her skirt, lubricating thickly into some delicate item of lingerie.

She had to see.

'Easy, baby,' Tricksie murmured, loving her lover's torment. Isis was pressing her knuckles to her crotch now, massaging vigorously, her legs parted and slightly bent. Her sex-lips would be puffy, uncomfortable.

'You want it, don't you, my love?'

Tricksie found the word 'love' came quite naturally. It went well for her with 'sex', which sometimes surprised her given what she did for a living.

But did she love the beautiful Isis? She knew she wanted to 'fuck' her – whatever that meant in lesbian terms – and touch her, taste her, know every part of her that was sensitive, irritated or needy. Was that love?

'Let's see you, then, petal,' she whispered, pulling Isis' slender hands out of her lap and getting a frustrated gasp for her trouble.

Oh God, she's fantastic! thought Tricksie as she dipped down to catch the blue skirt's hem. One minute so together and businesslike, and the next an animal. She's like me ... Thinking with her clit. All she wants is to feed that mouth between her legs ... Oh yes! Oh Jesus, I think I *do* love her!

'Please, Tricksie, help me,' Isis wailed.

'Yes, my darling,' purred Tricksie, hiking up that elegant skirt, bunching it at Isis's waist ...

Then moaning herself at the sensational sight beneath.

The sheer blue hose were hold-up stockings with three inch deep, silver-embroidered welts. Where the devil did she get those? demanded the discriminating observer in Tricksie's brain; while the besotted lesbian lover in her just drooled – everywhere.

And above the glorious stockings, above two tender inches of milk-white thigh, was a sex that took Tricksie's breath away; pouting, glossy-bushed and virtually uncovered.

Where does she get all this stuff? Tricksie wondered again, her fingers drifting compulsively towards a G-string the like of which even she'd never seen. A mere shred of ultra-sheer black silk lace, it concealed nothing – mainly because sometime during the course of the evening, it had ridden up and lodged itself tightly between Isis's swollen labia. Tricksie felt her own body twitch in empathy.

'You're a sly one, my lovely,' she whispered. 'So cool. So educated. And underneath you're a slut like me.'

'Please . . .' The lewd, bisected crotch flaunted towards her hand. Pleading.

'Do you want me to rub you?' Tricksie asked softly, aping the powerful Isis of earlier. Reaching down, she hooked one finger in the G-string and yanked gently upwards.

'Ungh . . . Ungh . . .' was the only answer, and Tricksie laughed with joy, her heart somersaulting in her chest, her own quim hot with a pleasure completely shared.

Isis came hard and fast and loud, her hips jerking furiously, her hand jammed against her mouth but unable to contain her noise. Her scarred face contorted spectacularly and she sucked her own fingers, moaning around them as spittle glistened sleekly on her chin.

Tricksie tweaked the shred of silk a second time. 'Come, baby, come,' she coaxed, sawing upwards with a strong, jerking rhythm. She'd been going to strip Isis, bare her, but now it was far too late.

The climaxing woman was suspended on a cord that created her pleasure, her whole weight rocking on her clitoris. Tricksie was merely the two strong hands that held the cradle taut . . .

Jungle sounds echoed in the gloomy alley: a lioness roaring in triumph, a she-cat howling out her orgasm. Isis threw her free arm around Tricksie's bare shoulder and slumped against her, still wriggling her body on the G-string.

Tricksie felt her own pussy throb as Isis writhed against her. Her own clitoris ached, jealous of the torturing sensations between another woman's spasming thighs. She considered reaching down and caressing herself . . . Then refrained.

Save it for later, Turing. Don't be so greedy. Concentrating on Isis, she hauled hard on the thin lace scrap and cupped her lover's silk-covered breast with her free hand, tweaking her nipple to wring out a greater sensation.

It was over very quickly. Isis fell away from Tricksie and slumped against the alley wall, breathing heavily. 'Champagne, goddamit!' she muttered, her eyes closed, her wet mouth smiling with satisfaction and devilment. 'I must look a complete monster.'

She did, after a fashion, but a glorious one. Skirt pushed up, thighs and belly exposed, sexy pussy split by her pleasuring G-string. Her camisole was crumpled and half out of her waistband, and her chic little hat was tilted at a dizzy, demented angle.

'You look gorgeous,' said Tricksie, reaching to straighten the jaunty *chapeau* as if she were Isis's mother, or a nurse or governess. Of their own volition, her fingers slid lower, ruffling the glossy hair that streamed from beneath the hat and trickling it across her hand like fluid.

'And this is beautiful ... Unbelievable ...' She couldn't stop touching it, stroking it, fondling the satiny rippling mass as if it had an independent life of its own.

'I suppose I'm entitled to *one* attractive feature,' Isis said wryly, locking Tricksie's breath in her lungs when she reached down to her disordered crotch and plucked the G-string damply from its groove. The action was so casually done it was art, and Tricksie knew that soon – very soon – she would have to make love to this woman again. And far more than once.

'Don't put yourself down,' Tricksie ordered, her heart pounding. She felt a sharp sense of loss when Isis smoothed down her elegant skirt and brought order to her camisole and jacket, but it faded as soon as it had formed. They'd hardly begun. 'Let's go to that room of yours and then I can show you how beautiful you are.'

'All right,' Isis said easily, her sensual smile quite startling on her peculiar asymmetric face. 'But promise me one thing, Tricksie ...'

'Anything,' Tricksie vowed, thinking of all the things

she could do and praying that one of them would be Isis's pleasure.

'Promise me you'll put *these* on – ' Isis dipped gracefully and picked up Tricksie's forgotten harem pants, ' – before we go any further. I don't want you to get arrested before I get you into bed.'

Tricksie reached for the pants ... but suddenly what had been near seemed infinitely distant. Isis's image receded like a cheap film effect, wavered, then phased diagonally across Tricksie's field of vision.

The words 'into bed' began to repeat and repeat and then continually overlap. Uncoordinated noise and colour meshed into a solid wall and became suddenly and scarily dazzling.

A tenth of a second later, and just as suddenly there was a total, silent, blessed darkness.

And then light ...

7

Intermezzo II

'Oh! Oh! Oooh!' cooed Isis, jamming her free fist into her mouth, then wriggling her way off the stool. She was vaguely aware of a red light flashing somewhere to her right, but it would just have to flash. It was all she could do to stand upright. Stand in a cool dark alley somewhere with her skirt round her waist, her thighs splayed and three fingers working in a wedge against her clitoris.

Scrunching her eyes tight, she clawed back the last seamy shreds of her time in the alley. She could see her own face and body, her scars, her own wild snarl of orgasm. She could hear her own screams and groans, but faintly now, fainter and fainter as light replaced gloom, and the antiseptic whiteness of the treatment room drove out the sleazy beautiful shadows that lurked in the backways of the city. Her hips flipped and jerked in one last hot fling, then stilled.

She'd come. Caressed to it by another woman. Even though that woman had seemed to be herself . . .

'Too weird!' Isis muttered, out – at last – from the adventure. Beneath her pressing fingers she was wet, but calm now. Sated. And so, presumably, was the wired and dreaming Josh.

Hence the red light and the words, 'event sequence over' flashing insistently on the main computer screen.

Look sharp, Ice! she told herself sternly. Her adventurer was stirring already, fretting in his bonds as his cuffed cock rolled on his belly, its plummy length sticky with drying semen.

111

She was pretty sticky herself . . .

'You've got one helluva mind, Josh Mortimer,' she whispered, tugging up her panties, then shuddering as they clung to the soft, slick flesh of her vulva. 'And you, oh Isis the great inventor, are a dirty, disgusting little wanker!' She grinned and patted the thin damp crotch of her knickers. 'Nearly as wet as in the alley.'

Josh had dreamed a fabulous dream. It had been deliciously horny and said more about what he felt for her than he could possibly express in words. She felt thrilled. She felt troubled. What if she and Tricksie *had* met that way? Had wild kinky sex in an alley not fifteen minutes after they'd first said 'hello' . . .

The reality had been less fraught, less messy, and taken a good deal longer. They'd spent several weeks circling like a pair of scared gazelles, trying to figure out whether they did actually want each other or not, and when they did eventually go to bed, it had been gentle, tentative and very beautiful. And also very conclusive.

In the real world Tricksie had been the instigator. Isis felt her sex shiver at thoughts of that first time. The first time those slim skilled fingers had touched her . . . How she'd looked down between her own thighs, in the dim light, and watched those scarlet-painted fingertips dance amongst the crimsons and mauves of her quim.

'Isis!'

Oh shit, Josh was awake!

Hurriedly smoothing down her smock, Isis whipped off her headset and turned her attentions to the naked, struggling man. As the eyemask came off, his long black lashes were fluttering crazily . . .

'I . . . Oh God! Was it really like that?'

She watched his pupils dilate, his vision clearing fast as he focused on her. He blinked several times, then came that weird, poignant moment when the fantasy persona was sloughed away like a snake's dead skin. She felt a pang of loss as Tricksie dissolved from both their minds.

'Not quite,' she murmured non-committally, trying not

112

to be too affected, either by the transition or my Josh's bared body.

Half-naked and wholly vulnerable, he was glorious. Sexed-out, gleaming with sweat, spunk in a lacquer-like film on his belly, his loins and his thighs.

There was something especially tempting about this moment; all men were delectable still strapped, but Josh was the only one who seriously threatened her professionalism.

He was the only one she wanted to leave in restraint . . . then masturbate to a fresh, furious rigidity that she could climb on top of and enjoy. She'd done it once, all those months ago, and the resonances would always be with her.

Cautiously, she set about freeing her prize from his bonds.

Josh said virtually nothing as she unhitched the various straps and sensors, then took up a soft moist cloth to clean him. The only sounds he made were a low moan when the sensor probe slid out of his bottom and what sounded like a reluctant sigh of pleasure as she delicately wiped his penis.

'What's wrong?' she said at last, unnerved by silence.

'That was an experiment, wasn't it?' he demanded, his brown eyes unusually hard. 'It finished too soon. You pulled the plug on me, didn't you?'

'What do you mean?'

Her hands shook as she handed him a blanket. Under normal circumstances she'd have wrapped the thing round him herself, enjoying the intimacy, but tonight she felt irrational fear. He would read guilt in her fingers if she touched him. Guilt, because she had reason to be guilty, it dawned on her now.

A damned good reason.

'You *know* what I mean.' He opened the blanket with an aggressive flick and swirled it around his shoulders and torso like a cape.

And she did know. Precisely. When the red light had flashed, she could have cancelled it and let the adventure proceed to its natural conclusion – herself and Tricksie going on to the hotel room and making full lesbian love to an exquisite mutual climax. As they'd done, eventually, in the real world.

But she hadn't. She'd aborted his trip before he'd got to the 'best bit', simply to test out a theory.

The trouble was . . . she wouldn't get her results until he dreamed.

But will he want to tell me about his dreams now? she wondered glumly, later. He mightn't even want to speak to me.

She was alone now, getting ready for bed, but she could still hear the cold ring of anger in Josh's accusing voice.

She couldn't blame him though. It was the second time she'd experimented on him. A fact Josh had pointed out to her, nay, shouted out to her, as he'd stormed out of the treatment room half-naked.

She'd tried to explain her reasons to him, but he'd slammed the bathroom door in her face, then left fifteen minutes later, still muttering darkly about 'packing the whole thing in' . . .

'Not that you tried all that hard to tell him,' she observed to herself as she curled up in her chair in front of her small flame-effect fire, and nursed her favourite bedtime drink – hot milk liberally laced with brandy. The chair was her 'naughty' chair, but she had no big plans for it right now.

Alone tonight, and preoccupied, she'd chosen a practical nightie. There was no one to see her in virginal white winceyette that covered her from throat to toe, pin-tucked, prissy, relentlessly unsexy. Wearing it, she should have felt placid and unstirred. Yet as she drained her warming drink and put aside the cup, she suddenly didn't feel that way at all.

There was something ominous about Josh when he was mad. Something threatening, dangerous, sublimely erotic, a quality that reached out and stroked an answering chord in her. She turned soft to his hardness, yielding to his strength. Submissive to his maleness, his dominance.

It was uncharacteristic but, feeling like this, she felt the fantasies stir in her. Strong fantasies. Crude fantasies. Exposure and humiliation. Being buggered, being taken roughly and painfully . . .

In the flickering theatre of the flames, she saw Josh rise up, majestic in his anger, from the stark white of the couch he'd dreamed on.

It was what she deserved. What she wanted. She rummaged in the voluminous billowing whiteness of her pretty, old-fashioned night-dress.

'You bitch! You cheated me!'

His cock swung heavily as he lunged at her, waving like a thick red bar between the tails of his floating black shirt. His erection was bloated, furious, its tip as dark and livid as the rage that burned in his eyes.

'I'm sorry . . . Forgive me,' she returned meekly, enjoying the slight pain as he grasped her upper arm and shook her like a naughty child.

Back in her tiny cozy living room, Isis smiled slightly, recognizing that incongruous streak of humility. Her real self would have told him calmly to 'get stretched', but within the fantasy she grovelled. And her body loved it.

Parting her swollen nether lips, she touched herself lightly, stroking up a little of her moisture and pasting it slowly onto the tip of her clitoris.

'Oh Josh,' she murmured, rubbing gently. 'Oh Josh, please forgive me,' she begged, back in her dream of contrition. 'I'm sorry . . . Please punish me . . . I'll do anything!'

'Bare your breasts, then kneel down and suck me!' He was already parting his thighs in readiness, tilting his lean hips, thrusting forward his sex.

Isis had never seen him bigger. She shivered, imagining her mouth bulging with his flesh, his enormousness holding open her lips and making her drool and dribble helplessly as he plunged in again and again, each thrust going half-way down her throat.

'Do it, cheating bitch!'

Fumbling, she obeyed, and buttons went flying from her lab coat. Her lace bra defied her, and she whimpered as Josh dashed away her fingers and wrenched apart the cups himself.

'That's it! That's better. Now hold your breasts in your hands. Play with your nipples. Pinch them while I'm in you.'

Almost before she could touch herself, his wine-dark glans was butting its way between her lips. She took her nipples in her fingers, belatedly obeying him as he pounded her mouth with his stiffness and made her gag and splutter as her eyes filled with tears. His fingers went wild in her hair, digging, grabbing at her scalp, tilting her head, angling and adjusting so his cock could go deeper into her throat. He was fucking her mouth now, using her as basely as she'd wanted. As she'd needed. As against her conditioning, she'd longed for . . .

She was a nothing more than a receptacle for his pleasure, a warm hole to work in, a mouth to flood with his spunk. He was treating her as a thing now. Using her, debasing her . . . and her sex was leaping and raving for more of it.

In the dream she swelled and pouted and dripped; and in reality, the same, her clitoris fluttering beneath her fingertips in a first sharp climax. In the firelight, her pumping hips danced, and she moaned Josh's name, shouted and jerked, then fell back exhausted to a plateau . . . ready for the next mad rise.

Still throbbing, Isis merged dream and reality, scrabbling open the bodice of her nightdress to reach in and pluck at her nipples. She pulled them, twirled them like berries in her fingers as dream-Josh pillaged her mouth, stretching the corners of her soft pink lips as she gasped and drooled and gulped.

Focusing her eyes in the flames, she saw not the red and yellow of fire but the soft fuzzy blur of silk-black pubic hair and a flat brown belly pushing hard against her sweating face.

Expecting jism on her tongue any second, she sobbed weakly when Josh pulled out abruptly, took his cock in his fingers and waved it tauntingly before her eyes. Her own saliva shamed her on its red veined length . . .

'No, sucking slut!' he hissed. 'Not this time. Not in your cheating mouth. You'd like it too much.'

Isis waited, fearful and silent, still holding her fruity, swollen nipples.

'Take your panties off,' he ordered quietly, standing like a lord above her, slowly stroking his erection. She obeyed, then stood, bare-arsed, holding them nervously between finger and thumb.

'Show me.'

Isis held them up, spreading the juice-dampened crotch for his perusal.

'Horny bitch!' he said, reaching out without warning and grabbing her crotch. He squeezed her, once and roughly, and she fluttered like a bird in his grip – her flesh pleading for more, and harder.

'Now put them in your mouth.'

Isis froze – both in and out of the dream – boggling at his gross instruction.

'Do it!' he shouted, and when she put the sodden garment tentatively to her lips, he took hold of it and pushed it right into her mouth.

Her taste was rich and raunchy. Saliva pooled beneath her tongue and her sex softly wept. Thick juices flowed afresh, overflowing the engorged folds and rolling in a loose silvery stream down her thighs. She felt blood rushing wildly around her body, puffing up her quim even more and making her face burn furiously with shame.

With a faint smile, Josh stroked her bulging cheeks, a gesture so tender it seemed strangely out of character for this particular moment.

'And now you're going to put on a performance for me,' he purred, pushing in the cloth a little further. 'Lift your smock. Tuck it up at the waist. That's good,' he murmured when her damp pubic curls were displayed.

Tears of mortification and unbearable lust trickled from

Isis's eyes as she stood before him: her panties in her mouth, her breasts bare, her moisture bright and shining on her thighs.

'Beautiful . . . Now turn around, face the couch and put one leg up on it.'

Confused, she obeyed, then bubbled behind her gag as he reached around between her thighs, pulled her sex-lips rudely apart, then pressed her, split and dripping, hard against the edge of the couch. She mewled with shame when a finger snaked into her wet groove to make sure her clit was erect, out of its hood and lodged directly on the stitched ridge where the white leather panels made an angle.

'That's it, my little cheat,' he said into her ear, pressing his erection against the back of her thigh and stroking the cheeks of her bottom with his fingers, 'Now frig yourself off on that edge. Do it baby, I want to see and hear you come . . . Now!'

She wanted to scream 'I can't!' but the obstruction in her mouth wouldn't let her.

'Do it!'

She shook her head, then moaned. She'd hardly moved, but it had still rocked her sex against the stitching.

'Okay then . . . I'll have to help you.' His voice was menacing, barely audible. 'Hold the cheeks of your arse open.'

'No!' she tried to say through the muffling thing that silenced her. But her vagina was gently throbbing now, and the answer down there was 'yes'.

'You owe me, Isis,' he said grimly, 'you cheated me . . . Remember?'

Sobbing, her crotch rioting, Isis struggled to obey, her own weight crushing her breasts as she slumped face down on the couch. Her clitoris was still perfectly positioned and jumping against the leather. Working through layer after layer of shame, she plucked apart the rounds of her buttocks and waited – quivering – for the buggering thrust of his penis.

When the impalement came it wasn't his cock, but a dry,

painful, unlubricated finger; a violation ten times more demeaning.

Even so, she came hugely and cried out through her gag. The cruel digit bored ruthlessly into her bottom, forcing her even harder onto the abused bud of her clit and pinning her there like a mindless, gibbering doll. As her legs jerked wildly and her quim found a new dimension, the last thing Isis dreamed of was hot, satin semen jetting thickly down her naked thigh.

'Wow,' murmured Tricksie as she settled her silver-ringed hand over Isis's gloved one. They were in La Selene the next evening, sharing a drink between appointments. Isis had just described her fireside fantasy.

'That was wild, Ice,' the whore said, her eyes wide. 'I wish I'd been there now.' Tricksie had spent her night in magnificent elective solitude on one of her periodical crying jags for Diabolo. She never actually mentioned these little misery sprees to Isis, but there was always something over-smooth and faintly doll-like to her make-up on the day after she'd had one.

'I could've held you, love,' she went on softly, 'or maybe even helped with something?'

Her long red-nailed fingertip defined an obscure symbol on the back of Isis's black kid glove, and Isis felt a soft rippling answer between her legs.

'You would have had to take these off first!' she answered with a grin, flipping over her hand and flicking playfully at her friend's long, false, blood-red nails. You're a hopeless case, Trix, she thought fondly. The whore had on an elegant grey dress and matching suede courts, her hair was in a perfect upswept knot and her make-up, though comprehensive, was creamily muted . . . but her fiery painted talons screamed out pure, high voltage sex on every receivable channel.

'Of course, dearest.' Tricksie raised the operative finger to her lips and sucked it lewdly. 'And I wouldn't have been so rude with my fingers either.' She winked so slyly that Isis wondered if it were merely imaginery. 'Do I detect a hint of masochism sneaking into your fantasies, Ice? Only a pain freak would get off on a bone-dry finger in such a naughty place.'

'I don't think so . . . I don't know . . .' Isis examined her memories, excited again by the potent image of that shaming finger pushing relentlessly into her rectum. She'd played mild dominance games with Tricksie, but never done a full pro-active sado-masochism scene for real. Her dreams and adventures were full of it, though, and in them, pain games aroused her beyond measure. Whatever the role she took on; top or bottom, slave or domina, whichever way the lash flew, Isis knew her quim would ooze.

'I could help you work it out,' Tricksie offered, her eyes bright and coaxing, 'Whichever way you want to play . . .'

That was true. Tricksie was just as much a switch-hitter as Isis was, and she'd told many a tall tale, as they'd fondled each other in bed, of the wild roles she'd been called on to play in the course of her colourful 'career'.

'I might take you up on that sometime,' Isis said softly, as lewdness scored her brain from within, stunning her with unthinkable images again. Stainless steel and rubber. Stretched limbs. Gags. Moist pink flesh inspected, then abused with obscene intrusions.

'But not until I've got our friend Mister Mortimer sorted out. That man really gets to me, Trix . . . It's subversive. I feel out of control when he's around.'

'Yes, so it seems.' Tricksie's white grin said do-tell-all.

'I think the guy should have a health warning tattooed on him,' Isis went on resignedly. 'The only way I can stay on top is to pick a fight with him.'

'On top?' Tricksie waggled her finely etched brows. 'I seem to recall that was how you dished it out last time.'

'Trix! You know what I mean.'

'Face it, Ice. He's pretty, he's a stud, and you want him. What's the big deal? Have him!'

Tricksie's small, pointed tongue did a sweep of her soft red lips. 'I can't see the problem. You throw the switches for me when I'm tripping but it doesn't stop you having *me*!'

Touché. It was true, she did have Tricksie. Often. Maybe she was being silly over Josh? Sticking to letters of laws that both he and she were outside? She'd have to sort herself, and the situation, out somehow . . .

But not with Tricksie, just this moment. Across the room was a vaguely familiar face.

'Isn't that your next client, Trix?'

A slender, rather timid young man was sitting at the other end of the bar and trying studiously not to stare in their direction.

'Oh, you mean Mikey? He's keen. He's not due for ages yet,' Tricksie said casually, although Isis noted a hot sparkle in those beautiful emerald eyes.

'I hope you're behaving yourself with him,' she mock-cautioned. 'He looks extraordinarily young and innocent to me.'

'You're right about the "innocent" bit, but he's older than he looks,' Tricksie answered. 'He's one of the richest men in the city, and exceptionally shrewd. It's only when it comes to sex that he's a novice . . .'

'What sort of adventures does he choose?' Isis was curious now – intrigued by this wealthy but fey-looking young man, and his sexual involvement with her invention. She wondered, too, how he responded to Tricksie and her irresistible full-spectrum sex appeal.

'He lets me choose,' Tricksie said blithely. 'He asked me to "educate" him all about sex, so we're working our way through more or less everything.'

'But he doesn't have to adventure to get his education.' Isis reached out and touched Tricksie's dewy cheek. 'Does he?'

'I think he's trying things out in fantasy before he tries them for real.' Tricksie was a little wavery; the small caress had clearly affected her. Or was it the precious young Mikey? 'To be honest, I think he's a virgin.' She turned, dusted a tiny kiss on Isis's leather-covered palm, then swivelled back to look at the immaculate, unsullied Mikey. 'He's such a sweet thing.'

'Well, you'd better not keep him waiting then,' Isis said

briskly. 'And behave yourself!' she added as Tricksie rose and made ready to leave.

'Of course, I shall. The way you do with Josh.' With a wicked grin, Tricksie waggled her fingers in farewell, and then seemed to pour her sumptuous body across the room in the direction of her shy young client.

Her prey, more like, thought Isis, her mind in sudden turmoil. Images of Tricksie and the inexperienced Mikey joined her own of Josh and herself. Four bodies writhed in a moaning, thrusting tangle. It was an explosive, intoxicating brew.

I can't blame Trix for wanting to get involved, Isis reasoned. I'm hardly the best example of professional detachment, am I? And she's missing Diabolo, no matter how hard she tries to hide it.

She had a sudden urge for several extremely strong drinks and a few hours alone. To sort her head out.

But as it was, she sipped unenthusiastically at her Astrapure, powerless as her thoughts ran in concentric solutionless circles . . .

'I'm sorry.'

The familiar voice, from just inches away, made her start wildly. And blush like fire.

When she turned towards Josh, she felt sure he must know she was thinking about him. Thoughts that weren't platonic. She could almost believe he could see what she'd seen. That it would be in her eyes, both sound and cosmetically lensed; tiny twin images of their nude bodies screwing furiously. Close-ups of his prick reaming her slit in a rhythm both violent and divine.

'I'm sorry,' Josh repeated, slipping onto the stool that Tricksie had vacated.

'What for?' Isis asked without thinking, then dropped her gaze to her gloves so she didn't have to look at him. Lost in her erotic day-dreams, she had forgotten how badly they'd parted.

'For being a mean-spirited, ungrateful bastard. And for forgetting that my favourite mad professor always, but always delivers the goods.'

Raising her eyes to his face, she smiled, then couldn't help her usual knee-jerk reaction ... A quick pan down to take in the rest of him.

As always, Josh looked great. Positively fatal in fact, with a repentant, boyish grin on his brown and handsome face.

Clothes-wise he pleased her too. Chosen from what she suspected was an extensive collection of pure silk shirts, tonight's was in a fine soft cream, topped with a black leather waistcoat. His jeans were gloriously distressed denim and clung to his well-formed masculine crotch in a way that made her lace-covered and very feminine one go crazy. She could feel herself pouting and swelling, but suddenly the significance of his *words* got through to her too.

'Did you dream?' she asked redundantly, knowing he must have. Why else would he apologise?

'Yes,' he said hoarsely. 'You could say that ...' He shifted his weight on the stool, clearly uncomfortable, and Isis couldn't help but imagine his erection stirring in his jeans. 'Look, do you think it'd be okay if I had a drink? I think I need one.'

When white wine was brought and poured, Isis prompted the deeply thinking man at her side. 'Well then? You said you had a dream. Tell me about it and I'll know if it was the right one.'

Josh drank deeply, studied his dusky fingers around the glass, and began to speak.

'It was like an extension of the adventure. I was ... I was Tricksie again and I was with you.' He glanced up, his eyes full of heat. A heat that went straight through her skirt, straight through her slip, straight through the panties beneath.

'We were in a room. A hotel room.' He paused, glanced around, seemed to check for listeners. 'You kissed me. I couldn't move. Your tongue was in my mouth and I felt hot. I was melting all over. Especially ... Esp ... God, this is nuts! How the bloody hell do I describe having a pussy?'

123

'Try,' Isis encouraged softly, trying to hide the way she loved him being forced to blush.

'Okay.' He squared his shoulders, took a small sip of wine, then fixed his eyes on somewhere in the middle distance. 'I was in bed waiting for you. Thinking about your body and all the things I like about it. I wanted to touch you . . . Touch your quim, then open my legs wide and press my own quim against it . . . I was imagining how wet you'd be and touching my own wetness at the same time.'

It was Isis's turn to wriggle now. And be wet. She was trickling in her panties, running as heavily as if Josh had reached out and stroked her. His voice was deep and dark and charged; he might as well have been using it on her sex directly, each word a solid thing. A finger. A tongue. A penis.

'And then you were there.' He turned, and gave her a single quick, searing glance. 'Almost naked. As good as . . . In some thin, silky thing I could see straight through. And I could smell your perfume.' His nostrils flared, and Isis nearly swooned. Godammit, even his nose was sexy.

'You got into bed and started m . . . making love to me. My breasts were in your hands and you squeezed them and kissed them and rubbed your face between them. The way a cat would. Then you were licking and sucking . . . It drove me crazy.'

You're driving *me* crazy, thought Isis wildly, struggling to sit still. Josh's detailed description was inverting itself as she listened. Twisting about but not, she realised, a true mirror image. He was describing things *she'd* done to Tricksie, but what she felt was herself being made love to. Being caressed and stimulated by a strange, formless amalgam of Tricksie, herself . . . and even a bizarre feminised version of Josh.

'Crazy,' she whispered, but Josh didn't falter in his narrative. He was somewhere else, aroused.

'But that wasn't enough. I wanted you to touch my cunt. I opened my thighs and pressed my sex against you. I . . . I was crying for you to rub me or something. I wanted your fingers inside me, but you wouldn't do it. Not then . . . You just teased me. You got naked, but you still wouldn't touch me. You made me lie back, hold myself open, and just show myself to you. I was so wet I felt ashamed, the juice was pouring out of me.'

Same here, Isis said silently, her own sex on fire. She wanted to do what he was describing. To climb up onto the very bar they were sitting at, haul up her slim leather skirt and let him pull down her panties and look at her.

'You made me come then,' he whispered. 'You put this finger – ' he raised up his strong brown hand, middle finger flexed, 'you put it right on my clitoris and rubbed till I had an orgasm.'

At that they both shuddered. Which was more eerie? A calm, quiet, utterly convincing male voice describing what it was like to have a clitoris; or the sharp, hard pulse in her own real clitoris, a spasm of pleasure from a caress that was only imaginary? It was weird but she prayed he wouldn't stop.

'And when I'd come, and I was panting, you opened your robe and started masturbating.'

Did he know she was throbbing? She suspected he did.

'You looked all pink and pretty down there. Just like – ' He paused, and gave her a long steady look. 'Well, you know what it looks like, don't you?' He smiled, and before Isis could stop him or even flinch, he'd reached out and drawn his forefinger across the marred skin of her cheek.

Isis's sex fluttered instantly and she felt an overwhelming urge to turn and bite his fingers passionately. She was in a fever from his words and all it had taken was that one small touch to make her come. She could feel her cheeks staining, both perfect and flawed, and she knew she was an open book.

'You did that on purpose, you swine!' she hissed, gasping.

'What?'

'You know!'

Josh laughed, a sound as erotic in its own way as his words had been.

125

'You asked for it. Doubly. You asked. And you caused the goddam dream in the first place.'

Well sussed.

'Yes, I did,' she replied, clawing back some poise. 'You're my most responsive dreamer ever. I wanted to see if I could trigger you, make you finish the adventure on your own. I can do it to myself, but I didn't know if anyone else could. It doesn't quite work with Tricksie . . . Although she does get enhanced day-dreams the way we do.'

'Tell me how it works then.' Josh's voice was genuine and serious. He reached out and patted her gloved hand, and Isis shuddered minutely, remembering how his fingers could give pleasure. Remembering a night when they'd ranged across her naked flesh and had her sobbing again and again and again.

'Well, it's founded on the imagination-enhancing characteristics of dreaming. As I said, you're probably my most responsive client – ' A movement behind Josh's left ear suddenly caught her eye. 'Holy shit! It's *her* again! And Ett too . . .'

'St Etienne? Oh God, is *she* here?'

Josh's tension was a palpable force, and she sensed him fighting not to turn around and stare. Stare at the two astounding women who had just walked arm-in-arm into the bar.

One of them was more likely to ping her own sex radar than his, given certain thoughts she'd had during the last couple of days. But it was obviously the other, her own cousin, St Etienne, who had put Josh on red alert. He'd only met the woman once – but in dream-time St Etienne had fucked him. Literally.

'Yes, it's cousin dearest, out in full drag with her latest girlfriend in tow.' She saw him look puzzled. 'A well-known redhead so trashy she makes Tricksie look like a Methodist librarian.'

He was still frowning, but seemed loath to look around and see who St Etienne's companion was.

'Think of a long, lean ginger pussy who tends to keep her own pets in chains,' cued Isis.

'Red Cat?' Josh asked, alarm and curiosity fighting an intriguing battle across the contours of his face.

'The very same,' Isis answered, smiling a small smile as he gave in and turned round.

There was plenty to look at.

St Etienne was her usual debonair self, and Isis felt her usual pangs of disquiet. Ett was beautiful in a wacky and androgynous sort of way, and it was impossible not to respond to her. Josh wasn't the only one with arousal problems right now; but at least he wasn't related to their cause.

Under normal circumstances, sweet St Ett would have been the complete conversation-stopping focus of the room in seconds. But tonight her gelled hair, her mannish gestures and her Italian designer man's suit in blue-grey silk seemed positively conservative when compared to the totem of strangeness at her side. And – even though Ett was easily as tall as most of the men in the room – she was dwarfed by the statuesque proportions of the woman who accompanied her.

Red Cat was well named. The famous rock singer was dressed predominantly in her favourite shades of scarlet and her long dreadlocked hair was so red it almost had a voice and shouted. Her face too was stunning. Her upslanted feline eyes stared out from her dead white complexion with a fierceness that arced across the room like a deadly feral beam.

She was trouble in letters of fifty-foot neon, but both sexes fell down like fools before her.

When the famous woman turned fully around, Isis had to stifle a giggle at Josh's reaction. He all but dribbled wine down his shirt-front at the sight of the red one's staggering outfit.

Beneath a gleaming red biker jacket, Red Cat seemed to have forgotten about any blouse, T-shirt or top of any kind. All she wore was a micro-fine black lace bra. Her large breasts jutted brazenly from her open coat, virtually naked in the sheer gauze-like silk. And even though her breath-takingly long legs were encased in a pair of neo-brutal red leather chaps there was virtually nothing beneath those . . . Only a minute pair of red leather bikini briefs kept her vulva from the eyes of La Selene's ogling patrons.

A tooled and studded belt, and stiletto ankle boots completed the mind-bending ensemble, but Isis doubted if Josh had noticed these fetishy accessories. His entire attention was focused on a single tiny triangle of supple crimson hide.

'She's shaved. She's just got to be,' he murmured – and Isis had to agree. The shape of Red Cat's sex was quite pronounced, a visible bifurcation beneath the fiery wafer-thin leather.

'Oh, she most certainly will be,' she said out of devilment. 'She's got real live slaves to perform all those services for her. It's a wonder she hasn't got "Nothing" cringing at her heels right now. On a leash.'

'Nothing? What do you mean, "Nothing"?'

Josh's face was a picture: curiosity and rampant lust, what a combination.

'The keyboardist in her band. She calls him "Nothing". He's her pleasure object. He's probably chained to the end of her bed even as we speak. Stark naked, with his cock in a vice.'

The picture of Josh's gaping face grew more revealing by the second. If Isis had been scared that he could read her eyes earlier, right now she could certainly see things in his. Chains. Clamped, swollen flesh. Tortures obscene and sublimely erotic . . .

'You're trying to imagine it, aren't you?' she asked him softly. 'Punishment. Humiliation. Penis bondage.'

He said nothing, and Isis could see he was struggling with something he didn't quite understand: his own pecul-iar fantasy yens. The submissive streak that was so wildly out of character for the big, strong Josh of the real world.

And as she watched him, she understood a startling new truth. To be Red Cat's plaything was *not* the something different he needed tonight ... To be the slave was too simple, no real challenge.

'Listen to me, Josh.' She reached out to touch his face. 'What you're thinking ... It's the easy way out. I know your fantasies. You're submissive. You always end up "taking it" instead of being the prime mover.' She cupped his cheek and turned him towards the erotic sexual animal that was Red Cat. 'The real adventure would be to dish it out, Josh. Bend someone else to *your* will. Impose. Kick ass. Dominate.' Discreetly, she pointed in the direction of the fearsome singer, who even as they stared seemed to reach out with her flaming feline aura and engulf them. 'It's no use just copping out and being her slave, Josh. If you want a real trip tonight, you've got to be *her*.'

Josh didn't agree, that was obvious.

On all his previous adventure nights, he'd been out and ready for wiring in five minutes, but this time he seemed to take ages. When he hadn't appeared after a quarter of an hour, Isis knocked on the bathroom door, entered, and found him still drying his cock on a towel. She told him to get a move on.

Josh frowned, but his firm red rod didn't fail him and Isis eyed it longingly.

'I'm really not so sure about this,' Josh muttered, his stiff flesh waving before him as Isis led the way into the treatment room. Leaping lightly onto the couch, he began a reasoned argument and Isis was forced to smother a smile. Logic didn't go too well with a semi-naked body and a rampant horn of an erection.

'Look, this is all supposed to be for my entertainment, isn't it? I should have the adventure *I* want. Right?' he challenged. 'Well I don't want to be that monstrous woman, Isis. She's a hot piece, but she's just too fucking weird!'

Isis regarded him narrowly for a few moments, hoping her condemning look would be the goad he needed.

This was probably the most sexually imaginative man she'd ever met. He wouldn't let her down ... Because

she was looking forward to being Red Cat. To being –
temporarily – a woman for whom the bizarre and the
perverted were simply an everyday norm.

'Are you listening?' Josh demanded when she didn't
answer.

'Yes.' Isis remained cool and resumed her silence as she
fitted a few of the straps and sensors, trying desperately
not to stare at his waving sex and wish she was sitting on it.

When she thought he'd stewed long enough, she turned
towards his strapped and gleaming body. 'And I'm beginning to wonder if you're a coward. I used to think you
were the boldest man I'd ever met. I did have some big
plans for you tonight . . . But now you seem singularly
lacking in bottle.'

'That's not fair!' Josh protested, and Isis could see the
inner debate on his lightly sweating face, and the ancient
anger of impuned machismo. It was the old, old alpha
male story – me Tarzan, you Jane – but Isis found it
deliciously arousing.

'I –'

Josh stopped short when she took hold of his cock and,
taking more time than she needed, slipped the transceiver
cuff over its rosy, dripping-wet tip.

'Hmm . . .' She turned and looked him squarely in the
eyes.

'I told you . . . I don't want to be fucking Red Cat!' His
eyes were closed now, his jaw tensed and working.

'Why in heaven's name not? There are millions of men
who'd love a chance to *fuck* her.'

'I didn't mean that, you contrary bitch!' Isis was glad
his arms were strapped down now; an angry Josh was
capable of just about anything.

'Oh Joshua, Joshua, Joshua,' she murmured, loving the
sweet sexy intimacy of his full christian name. She'd called
him 'Joshua' before . . . While his prick was deep in her
body. 'Can't you see? This is another frontier. A real
"adventure". You've crossed the gender divide often
enough, but this is an orientation threshold too. You owe
it to yourself, Josh, really you do.'

'But I'm pretty dominant in real life . . .' He was teetering now, she saw, and her next words drove home the point.

'It's not the same. Not a bit. Believe me, I've tried it.'

That clinched it. The change in his face was startling. If *she'd* done it, *he* wanted it. Their empathy was still true blue.

'Okay, then, situation normal. You win.'

His slow grin, when it came, was twice as dangerous as his anger. Isis felt something go 'oof' in her loins; his smile as potent in her as his strong thrusting cock had been. 'Let's roll then, shall we?' he whispered, his licking of his lips a sexy assent.

Not quite 'on it', Isis set about her tasks . . .

A personality profile of the Cat was a simple matter for the 'Zone's computer; the singer's notorious life was public domain, and Isis had already inputted all the data she needed. It was all there. An openly sado-masochistic lifestyle, and pain-based relationships. An existence where it was quite natural to have a bound man at your mercy . . .

Isis looked down at Josh, and with as much tenderness as she could muster, settled him deep into the shaped leather of the couch. One keystroke and its lower half was splitting, easing apart the cheeks of his bottom for the entry of the anal/prostate transceiver.

How far were they into the fantasy already? she wondered dreamily, slathering his rear with the cool soft lubricant and positioning the probe against his anus. Two more keystrokes set it moving, and she turned and took his hand, squeezing it reassuringly as the dildo bored its slow, sure way into his rectum.

Josh's eyes, as he was being penetrated, were almost her undoing. They widened hugely, glittered with sweet humiliation, and she was one with him utterly. She wanted to be plugged in the selfsame way. To have her bottom stuffed and possessed . . . To be rammed, lusciously, by his long thick cock and be nothing more than an open, subjugated hole for his pleasure.

It took every last ounce of her inner discipline to finish

the programming, apply the rest of the sensors, then very carefully inject the final shot of dream-inducing hallucinogen into Josh's bare forearm.

Almost immediately his eyelids drooped and he moaned softly, wriggling his muscular bottom on the sturdy plastic mass inside it. Wires rustled as his cock waved and Isis felt her vulva shiver, struggling with an entrapment all of its own. She pressed the last few keys, covered Josh's eyes and then tugged her own headset into place.

Juices squished in her panties as she settled on her stool, and she knew that before long there would be more. With the bizarre events ahead, her underwear and her smock would both be soaked.

Keeping her voice low, she spoke into his ear. 'Are you ready, sweetheart? Do you feel the straps? The probe? Soon it'll be you doing the same to someone else. Making them surrender. Making them be nothing but yours. You'll be the Cat, my angel, and his life will be one perfect hell on earth... He'll be "Nothing" and you'll be everything... An empress. A goddess. You'll extinguish him...'

Isis felt her flesh respond to her own incantation; images formed in the sight within sight. A few flashes of Josh suffering blissfully at *her* hands: his body agonised, demeaned and exposed... Then the pictures phased seamlessly into others. Other bodies, other faces.

'I dunno,' she heard him murmur as he started his drug-hazed drift. 'It... It doesn't...'

'You mustn't worry,' she said, her voice strong to reach him as his senses went into overdrive and he became a person he wasn't. 'This is consensual domination and submission, my angel. It's done for pleasure... For affection...' Pressing the final key, she hitched her ride on his mind. 'There's no hate in it, Josh, only love. Just love... Remember that. Remember remember remember...'

8

Cat's-Paw

It was morning, and as a narrow beam of sunlight hit Red
Cat the domina's face, the heat of it kissed her awake.
Without opening her eyes, she stretched deeply and luxuriantly, offering her long body to the newness of the day
and welcoming the return of her strength. This moment
was a special kind of ritual for Red, something secret,
private and informal. Putting her fingers between her
thighs, she slid them into her sleep-warmed sex, then
brought them back to her lips and licked off their coating
of love-dew.

Sexy pussy, she thought smugly, lapping each digit in
turn, then smiling her slow feline smile. She touched the
wetness again, but didn't stir or rub it. There was time
enough for that when she'd woken up properly – and
surveyed all the good things that were hers.

Lying motionless, her hand still at her crotch, Red Cat
flicked open her eyes but didn't look around. She had
no need to, she knew exactly what this room of hers
contained . . . and a silence didn't always mean emptiness.

Stretching again, she looked downwards at her own
body. Sleep had bunched up her red silk chemise and
from the waist down she was completely exposed. Red
had no false modesty – in fact she didn't have any modesty
at all – and she applauded the excellent view. A board-
flat belly; a deep, indented navel; slim, athletic thighs that
were corded slightly with muscle. Her quim was bare
and immaculate, shaven and pouting. Moisture glittered

thickly in the groove, and her burrowing fingers were shiny.

There was a lot of her favourite colour down there too. The crimson of her skimpy shift. Blushing tea-rose pink where it had twisted against her skin while she slept. Succulent, dripping scarlet that shone in the chink between her legs. She shifted her thighs to expose more, and gasped. Silvery knife-like frissons jolted her loins, her arousal hot and deep though she was still only partially awake. She needed to urinate too, and she patted her clitoris, then hissed between her teeth as her mind filled with vague scraps of fantasy. Herself with another woman. That woman massaging her aching bladder in a cool dark place. Teasing, whispers and agonised moans. It was exciting, but strangely unfocused, and she filed it away for another time. There was no need to chase dreams and visions today.

A tiny sound brought her fully awake. It was one she'd been waiting for and hoping for, and the reason her quim was so sticky. Still not looking around, or rising from the warmth of her bed, she flexed her slender fingers and started to masturbate.

Being shaven was the perfect condition for a confirmed self-lover like Red Cat. With no hair between her legs, it was easy to get around and be precise. There was no straggling thatch to blunt her long hard strokes. And Red's pubes had been straggly ... Thick and bushy, her quim had been pretty in a way, but not the sleek uncompromising shape she'd wanted. It was perfection now, although she could feel stubble already as she ran two fingers in a vee down the edges of her thick outer labia. Someone would have to shave her today, she decided.

For a moment, she tried to remember what it had been like being hairy down there. Having a dense, furiously red thicket to match her dreadlocks – the heavy, tumbling fall of softly fuzzed strands that she'd been growing since the day she'd first understood herself. The day she'd discovered her secret and awesome nature, then reached out and possessed its great power. She'd been just a girl then, and even though she was only now reaching her prime, her magnificent dreads already reached down to her equally magnificent arse.

Shuffling for a better purchase, her movements made the bedsprings creak; and as they protested, there was another of those tell-tale sounds. Two in fact. A faint muffled groan and the mercurial tinkle of metal falling against metal. Both were barely audible, but if she'd been a light sleeper, the second would probably have woken her. She smiled and noted the 'offence' for later.

Bending her knees, she flung her legs wide open and admired the abandonment of her pale belly and elegant limbs. Her slit itself was vivid, trickling and tumescent, and impatient, she put both hands to work. With a finger pressing on her clitoris, she put two from her other hand inside her, probing for the secret, interior pleasure zone. When she found it and rubbed, a sharp white spasm arced from one place to the other, and she cried out exultantly.

Yes, oh bloody hell yes! It was gorgeous, but it felt deliciously like pain . . . a sensation she understood with some intimacy.

Yipping like a cur, she prodded within at her full, bursting bladder. Then prodded again, beating the bed with her heels when it all got too much and she climaxed in a long hard jolt.

It was sharp and bright and good, but left a need for more in its wake. The need to pee lingered too, a pleasure in its own right as the pressure still pushed out her clitoris. Greediness tempted her to rub again, but she drew back and refrained. There was the whole day for that if she needed it.

Shallowing her breath, she listened again. And sure enough, there were the tiny sounds.

The faint gobbling of saliva as it bubbled around an obstruction; a body rocking obsessively yet trying at the same time *not* to make a noise. Thinking of her own bladder, she could well understand his torments. Poor sweet thing, he'd cried like a baby when she'd made him drink all that water. Last night . . .

Leaping lightly to her feet, she smiled catishly at her own wince of discomfort. It would be much much worse for him, she thought, walking around to the foot of her bed and looking downwards.

A slender, naked and very beautiful young man was chained to the stainless steel footrail. He was heavily blindfolded and around his neck was a narrow collar of plain black leather. His hair was even blacker than the collar, and shaven to velvet against his scalp. A hideous ball-gag stretched open his soft red mouth, and his cock was fiercely erect, its bulging, fire-red length encased in an elaborate lacing of thin, tightly woven thongs.

Aware of her nearness, he moaned again, as if there was now no point in being stoic. Red Cat reached down and very gently removed his blindfold.

Huge nut-brown eyes blinked back at her; bottomless pools of suffering and kittenlike devotion. He flinched and let his eyes drift downwards, then gobbled again, double-damned and knowing it, for having looked at his mistress's body.

'You might as well look, Nothing,' she said softly, then thrust her sleep-scented crotch a little closer to his blushing face.

He lurched towards her, eyes squeezing shut at the misery of movement, but was balked immediately. His chain had only nine short inches of play. His wiry shoulders almost popped at the joints, and his arms, pinioned behind him at wrist and elbow, fought in vain for their freedom of movement.

'I said "look",' she said, her voice quieter, but sounding loud. 'I thought you were beginning to learn, Nothing, but I see I was wrong. We'd better give all this some thought today, hadn't we?'

The bound boy nodded, and Red noted the pleasing way his purple-capped penis bobbed and waved in time to it. She edged closer, and he remained still this time, tears glittering in his fine dark eyes and a single jewel of pre-come poised on the tip of his prick. Which was the saltiest?

136

Red wondered idly. Tears or jism? It would be nice to taste both and compare them, but now wasn't the moment.

Her swollen bladder gave a sudden throb and she frowned. She was starting to feel uncomfortable... Returning to her bedside table, she picked up a small handset and aimed it towards Nothing. The digital padlock on his collar flashed once and sprang open, then his thin securing chain dropped away and jingled as it fell against the footrail.

Red pointed towards a moulded chair of shiny red comfyplas that stood in the corner of the room, then pointed again to a spot some feet from where she stood, a rose-painted tile that was the floor's natural focus. Nothing got awkwardly to his feet, gulping around the bulbous rubber sphere in his mouth, and Red tried to imagine how his throbbing loins might feel. Worse than hers? Or better? What was the difference? Bad and good were just two halves of one whole if you thought about it...

Keeping her face an impassive mask, she watched Nothing struggle with the chair. Hugely hampered by the handcuffs, it took him quite some time to drag it to the rose, but eventually he got it there and nudged it into position with his nose. Conscious of a great pounding in her genitals, and that urine was seeping down her thigh, Red walked slowly across the room and settled on her red plastic throne.

A lift of her fingers brought Nothing slithering to his knees before her. He was shaking slightly, his eyes fixed on the tiled floor. Reaching out with the finger that had summoned him, she tilted up his chin and studied his brimming tears; then, still with the same finger, she circled his horribly stretched mouth. There were beads of sweat on his upper lip and saliva dribbling from his lower one. Giving him no warning, she slid her hands around the back of his head and unfastened the strap of his gag.

Drawing the monster slowly from his lips, she first made him kiss it, then flung it away across the room. Sticking her fingers into his mouth, she let him suck them like a ravenous infant. Her vagina pulsed anew with hunger, reminding her of *its* need to be fed, and sliding her bottom to the lip of the chair, she opened her legs and pointed again. Nothing edged forward to obey.

It was a move as familiar as well-worn boot, though for Nothing, far less comfortable. Red watched him distantly, letting no sign of her tangled feelings reach her face. It was easy to *look* detached, but below, her creature's pathetic struggles made her flesh convulse and drip. He'd love that, she knew, even bowed as he was beneath the burden of a hundred hardships . . .

Oh God, boy, you're so lovely, she thought behind the fastness of her dominating mask. In secret, she admired the way he licked his dry lips before putting them to her. The way his plump red tongue darted round the bow of his even redder mouth. Respectfully. Obediently. Beautifully.

'Get on with it,' she snapped, filling her voice with fury to hide the way he moved her.

The touch of his tongue, when it came, was divine. He'd given her magnificent head the very first night they'd ever met; but now, after months of intensive practice, he'd become a true virtuoso. His tongue flicked efficiently to all the best spots, and his pronounced lapping noises only added to her surging pleasure. Coiling to a point, the firm wet explorer stabbed hard at her clitoris and she made a gutteral sound of approval. Then it flattened, swooped and scooped, and drew lubrication out of her vagina and back to the very tip of her clit.

Stab, swipe, stab. Flick flick flick. He worked forwards and back, side to side; and Red fought a weight that was both mental and physical: the powerful urge to praise him, to say or more probably scream something that was utterly and completely preposterous.

With his arms shackled, there was little Nothing could do but lick her; and conscious of other compelling urges, Red pressed her fingers to the curve of her belly. Yowling as pressure knocked the root of her clitoris, she orgasmed like a wave and yellow-gold urine gushed visibly into Nothing's open mouth. Her sex pulsing wildly, she emptied her swollen bladder in a glorious, collapsing release, laughing inside as he struggled to drink her flow . . . even though more fluid would only increase his own agony.

Still coming, she dashed his face away and rubbed violently at her jumping clit. Grunting freely, she worked and worked and worked herself until all was calm and quiet between her legs, and her soul had returned to the world of her and him. Replete, with her features completely neutral, she looked down into the wet, wide-eyed face of the man who had so obediently served her.

His eyes were huge with distress, yet fired from within by a familiar radiance. His soft mouth glistened. Saliva, piss, her juices . . . perhaps even his own tears of ecstasy. A thought intrigued her. He was expressly forbidden to emit anything from his cock voluntarily, was this his fluids finding their own way out?

Red dismissed her fancies and stood up abruptly. 'Filth! How dare you look at me?' she snarled, knocking him off balance with hardness at a moment when most would have been soft. 'Get down. Face to the floor. Arse in the air.'

He obeyed awkwardly, his eyes more tearful than ever.

'Facing away from me,' she ordered, then, as he complied and safe in the knowledge he couldn't see her, she leant on the chair for support and placed her naked foot on the upthrust curve of his bottom. She knew he was suppressing his groans and biting his lips, but nevertheless, she wrung a bleat of outrage from him as her toes travelled rudely over his rear, then slid into the groove and pressed in hard against his anus. She considered forcing her big toe inside, and heard his harsh gasp as he instinctively second-guessed her.

Not yet, sweetheart, she told him silently, then kicked him fair and square on the butt, making sure the point of impact was exactly on his rose-brown hole.

He was sobbing helplessly as she walked from the room to her already running shower, and the thought that he might weep his way through the whole of his wait made her sex ache all over again.

In the shower, she couldn't stop thinking about him. As

her maid, Andrea, dried her, she imagined his smooth young body and what it must be going through. Frustration made him fabulous, and pain made him perfect . . .

While she cleaned her teeth, she thought of *his* teeth. And his lips and his long nimble tongue.

Most of all, as Andrea massaged scented lotion into her skin, and between her legs the slow, sly massage brought an inevitable orgasm, Red Cat thought fondly of a beautiful tortured toy – the leather-bound column of her victim's superb young cock.

She imagined it, bulging in its straps, as she lay recovering from her climax, her nude body white against the black leather massage table. She could hear Andrea fussing with towels and toiletries and suchlike, but all the time she was listening for moans from the the bedroom beyond. Not hearing them, she sat up and unwound the damp towel from around her unusual hair, testing its wetness between her squeezing fingers. Not so bad. A spell under the infra-red lamps would have it fluffed and ready in minutes, but she decided to let it dry *au naturel*.

'Andy, go into the bedroom, please,' she said quietly, reaching for a red silk robe and shrugging it round her shoulders. 'If it's made any mess, you have my permission to punish it, and then you may bring it in here for its ablutions.'

'Yes, ma'am,' murmured Andrea. Red caught a narrow smile on the girl's face as she left the room, and she wondered if she'd been *too* unkind this time. There was no love lost between Andrea and Nothing. Far from it. The blonde maid was insanely jealous of Red Cat's pretty slave boy and never missed even the thinnest chance to diminish him.

A black marble counter ran the length of the bathroom wall, and a selection of lingerie had been laid out of it for Red's perusal. Every item was costly, custom-made and exquisite, but without hesitation she chose a crimson satin G-string and slid it on under her robe. She'd been shaved and creamed after her shower and the sheer garment clung like a film to her doubly bared sex-lips. It seemed to make her feel more naked than ever, and as she pulled it up tightly between her bottom cheeks, she felt the string-like thong caress the crumpled bud of her anus.

Alive with reborn lust, she was on the point of fingering her quim when there was a sharp sound from the next room. The crack of skin against skin, closely followed by a storm of childlike weeping, then more ringing, merciless slaps. Her stilled finger surged eagerly under the red silk, wormed its way between her outer lips and hit the target just as the gulping voice broke and whimpered piteously. She rubbed quick and hard, and came off again just as Andrea dragged Nothing into the bathroom, yanking him along with a finger hooked cruelly through his collar.

Red pushed her ruined G-string firmly into her slit, then closed her kimono to deny both maid and slave her sex. Leaping lightly up onto the massage couch, she assumed the lotus position, intensely aware of her quim pouching forward beneath the thin red robe and a sodden strip of silk pulled tight between her still-throbbing folds. The stimulation was invisible, but strangely enough, Nothing's abused penis pointed straight towards it.

'Why was he punished?' she enquired of the smirking Andrea.

'He'd started to wet himself,' the blonde answered, her pretty face scrunching with disgust. 'He lost control . . . I saw him peeing.' Her small, button-perfect nose wrinkled on the word.

'Well, perhaps, now, we can all see that,' Red said calmly. Beneath the red robe, she felt her cunt flow over the imprisoned G-string. 'Bring him to the toilet,' she nodded to the lavatory, less than a yard from where she was posed, 'then unlace him.'

The blonde maid did as she was told, with glee on her doll-like face. There was abject misery on Nothing's more truly beautiful one, and Red smiled to herself. Humiliation before Andrea was stern, stern test of his mettle.

She saw him wince and gnaw his lip as the thin strappings were wrenched unceremoniously off his flesh. His cock was an angry burgundy-red, and the marks of his binding were livid darker stripes that criss-crossed the whole imposing length. He stayed silent beneath what must have been considerable pain, but sobbed out loud when Andrea pressed slyly against his belly and his drum-tight bladder beneath.

'Andy!' Red said sharply, shaken by an empathic throb. 'Kindly get on with it.' Then she watched, rapt, as the maid's pale fingers encompassed the fiery, quivering prick and pointed it roughly at the bowl of the toilet.

Nothing's eyes were beseeching. Not this! he seemed to beg. Red held his gaze and nodded.

The slight gesture was for Nothing alone, but Andrea took action. Jiggling his irritated organ, she did something quick and jerky behind him that Red couldn't see but had a pretty good idea of.

With a loud whinnying cry, Nothing ejaculated, his wasted semen jetting out into the plain white bowl. After a minute pause his penis leapt again, gave a couple of short spurts, then gushed forth a hard yellow stream that splattered like a hose against the gleaming porcelain.

As the urine flowed on and on, it was his eyes that Red watched, fighting her own sobs of pleasure as his thick black lashes fluttered down and fat tears oozed like diamonds onto the fawn-gold skin of his cheeks.

Joy and pain. A twin release in conditions that shamed him utterly . . .

Red felt her quim convulse again, and ignoring both maid and weeping slave, she slid off the couch and walked calmly out of the room, closing the door behind her.

In the bedroom, she threw herself onto the silk-sheeted bed, opened her legs as wide as she was able and masturbated furiously.

Rubbing without grace or artistry, she writhed and tumbled in the same spot where she'd orgasmed before . . . but with her finger poised for the final killer stroke, she stopped.

This is just being greedy, Red, she told herself sternly, then smiled a slow, wry smile. How on earth could she impose order on others when her own interior control was so hopeless?

Her sex still hot and needy, she closed her legs and sat up. The day had hardly begun and she was already consumed by mad energies. They were eating her up, devouring her, and yet in a strange way she also felt renewed. She was being eaten, yes, but only to be spat out again as something far fiercer and freer and stronger . . .

Each time it happened it was the same; her own outrageous cravings invigorated her, and her imagination lifted her to a high, pure realm where both art and discipline could thrive.

Ready for all challenges, she sprang up and began to dress with her quim still wet. The tissues between her legs were engorged, and neither sitting, standing, nor lying brought ease from it, but even so she knew the very lack of satiation was a goad to her; it was the cutting edge that she needed.

He and she were going to work this morning, after a fashion, but mindful of the day's true purpose she chose clothing that would suit its special requirements.

Lycra.

A brief breast-hugging top and cycling pants embraced her like a thin red skin. The shorts gripped her vulva like an insolent hand, aggravating her state of arousal and soaking up moisture in seconds. She felt the seam slip between her folds and rest against her clitoris. It reminded her of . . .

No, not yet! she thought, pulling them up tighter but plucking away the fabric from her groove. Smiling again, she wondered what the inventive Andrea was up to now. What she was doing to Nothing, how severely, and what with.

That girl had a million demeaning tricks up her sleeve, but that was the beauty of being able to hand him over to a subordinate. It reduced him even further, bent his will by showing him his own unworthiness. As if to prove the point, another skin-to-skin smack rang out; audible even through the closed door, as was the high clear cry of a man in acute, unexpected pain.

'Andy? What's happening in there?' Red called out to them imperiously. 'I'm ready and waiting!' She wasn't, but it took just a second to slip on her aerobic ankle boots, and tie her damp hair back with a thong, one of the thin leather strips that had coiled around Nothing's stiff cock.

A sidelong glance in the mirror assured her that she was stunning even without her famous and elaborate make-up. Cosmetic tattooing of her lips and around her eyes meant her catlike features were always defined, and her skin – pampered by Andrea's ministrations – was a pure milk-white ivory all over without benefit of artificial aid. Red knew she could be a devil-goddess nude and straight from the shower if she wanted. She very often did.

The door flew open and Nothing was propelled into the room, by a well-placed foot, Red suspected from his ignominious stumble. Their eyes met for a second – plenty long enough for her to decree that both the stumble and the look itself were noted and would be dealt with. He lowered his eyes again, as the conventions laid down, and Red's lacquered fingertips tingled. He looked so choice. So ripe. So ready.

Andrea had dowsed him in ice-water and his cock was cowering close to his body, its generous girth crimped against his pubes. Red nodded faintly as she gave him another black mark, and one to Andrea too. Presentation was everything in this, and a stiff cock essential. It was up to Andrea to maintain her charge's rigidity.

Red had to admit, though, that apart from his flaccidity, Nothing was a joy to behold. Water droplets glittered like rhinestones on his suede scalp and his fine body gleamed with health despite its night of privation. He was still naked, apart from his collar, but there was a also a rather fetching red hand-shape adorning his long muscular thigh – a good slap well delivered on a skin that marked like magic. Maybe she could be lenient with Andrea after all?

'Come along! We haven't got all day.' Red swept from the room, knowing full well that they *did* have all day.

She sensed servant and slave following behind her at the prescribed distance, and she wondered if Nothing would risk watching her bottom as she walked. She increased the lilt of her hips and contemplated an on-a-sixpence spin to catch him out. No, it was too obvious.

The music room was studiedly gothic, dark as a classic horror flick until the computer arrays came on. Even then, the technology itself gave the room a 'Doctor Frankenstein' ambience. Red wasn't sure who was the monster today, but she still loved the atmosphere. It was the perfect backdrop for anarchy, she thought, and turning, found both the naked man and the sleazily clothed woman waiting silently for her word of command.

Andy's getting too fond of that costume, Red decided, subtly annoyed by the sullen blonde and her tacky black nylon micro-skirt. It's time you were put back in your place, young lady, she threatened silently. But not today. Andrea was only the best supporting actress in this dream . . .

'I don't need you any more for now, Andy.' Red kept her face haughty, but grinned inside at Andrea's look of disappointment. Honesty and single-mindedness were the girl's most sterling qualities. She loved to terrorise Nothing and made no secret of it. 'But before you go, one thing.'

'Yes, ma'am?'

Out of the corner of her eye Red noticed Nothing's instant tension.

'For God's sake make him worth looking at.' She nodded in the direction of his cock. It was perking a little now, but still not as impressive as it ought to be.

'By what means, ma'am?' the blonde enquired, her voice squeaky with excitement.

'Good grief, girl, use your initiative. I couldn't care less as long as he's presentable. I've got a guest coming shortly and I'll want him at full stand when she arrives,' she finished, almost creaming at the look of pure horror on Nothing's golden face.

Yes, little one, you hadn't bargained for that, had you?

Should she tell him who it was? And would that make things better . . . or worse?

Andrea went about her work with gusto. Red saw Nothing's long fingers clench as the maid slid onto her knees, and then, as if handling a particularly tasty delicacy, fed his thickening cock into her heavily lipsticked mouth. Red liked this feeding image, especially when Andrea's head started nodding rhythmically and her sticky pink lips slobbered around Nothing's almost instant expansion.

Moving closer, Red stood behind the gobbling maid and stared into her slave's brown eyes. His mouth was twitching and he tried to look away – to the side rather than down at his own immolation – but Red tapped the corner of her own long slanted eye and wordlessly commanded his gaze.

What are you feeling? she asked without speaking, knowing beyond doubt that he 'heard' her. She knew also that he wanted what was happening to him as much as he hated it. That he loved the shame, the surrender, the submission. That he flew like a bird on the ache and ache for denied release, and the far more befuddling desire for the greater, more complicated shame ahead of him.

She could see the fight on his face; his struggle against a stimulation so spitefully inflicted. He was being sucked on and slavered over by a woman who despised and resented him, and Red could see his spirit being bowed by the weight of callous arousal, and the knowledge that there was no hope whatsoever of it being resolved. At least not for a long, long time.

She could see him begging for it to stop, pleading that it go on and on and on and on . . .

Joy and pain, long may they reign.

'Enough now. Show me his condition.'

Andrea pulled back, then rose to her feet, wiping her mouth on her frilly white apron. Her lips still glistened as she slid her pale fingers under the dark, straining bar of Nothing's penis, and offered it like a cut of lean meat for her mistress's inspection.

'Good enough, I suppose,' Red murmured thoughtfully,

146

'but work him with your fingers for a minute, and then you can go.' It was difficult not to laugh as Andrea dutifully checked her dainty chronometer before taking hold of her victim's swaying sex. Red turned away and fiddled with the mixing console. Mistresses could be seen to be grimly amused, but giggling insanely was a no-no.

Red had no timepiece, but after what she estimated was the minute, she turned to review the results of Andrea's labours. Nothing stood like a statue, his limbs as rigid as his cherry-red prick and his handsome jaw tight with agony. There was no doubt about it, Andrea was good at what she did.

Red dismissed her cordially. The girl would get another crack at Nothing later, but right now Red wanted him all to herself.

'Well then? Get on with it,' she said crisply, careful that her voice didn't betray her.

They got on with it. Nothing was preparing orchestrations for their new album and in this, paradoxically, he was the master. The maestro. Red was a talented, purely instinctive performer who could control her audience totally and belt out a song without really knowing – in a purely technical sense – how she did it. She could hear music in her head but found notation tedious, and the theory of arrangement stifling. The skilled, artistic transformation of her ideas into finished songs was Nothing's sphere of excellence.

And that was what created the excitement. Sooner or later, as the superior musician, he'd slip up and tell his mistress what to do . . . And give Red just the point of order she needed – if one *was* needed – to subject him to heavy discipline. She could already barely contain herself, and as Nothing powered up the system and she sat down and doodled on the main keyboard, it was all she could do not to reach into her shorts and stroke herself.

She didn't have long to wait.

Within the first few moments there was a minor infringement. Nothing's cock brushed against her arm as he reached out to key in one of the sequencers. Red said

147

nothing, but her warning glance had him shrinking back, his face crimson, his eyes cast down.

The music came together surprisingly well – a cohesive sound built from Red's improvised but melodic vocals, and Nothing's synthesised approximations of the various instrumental lines the whole band would play when they eventually assembled in the studio.

But for all the genuine musical progress they made, the whole exercise was – at its heart – just a shadowplay. A convention. A context for a brighter and more dangerous game.

The flashpoint arrived – inevitably – when the accomplished, academic musician attempted to correct the naturally gifted but basically untrained and untrainable singer . . .

'But Red, you can't – '

There was a long crystalline silence.

Red stared into the middle distance as her black libido rose up and bayed to be fed. It was ravenous, untameable, and it bawled and howled like a living thing inside her. The thin lycra of her costume was suddenly two sizes too tight, and her whole body seemed to pulsate like an enormous, tumid sex. Sparks danced in her hair, and she wanted to spit white fire at the world and wank until her fingers seized up in exhaustion . . .

'You might want to think again about that, my angel,' she said quietly, thrilling to her power and her softly phrased threat. Nothing hung his head, then slid gracefully to his knees at her side. Red remained quite still where she was, seated on the old fashioned dark wood music stool.

'Forgive me, Mistress,' he whispered, and knowing he couldn't see it, Red smiled with elation. He was locked into his role now, and the temptation to caress herself was more urgent than ever before.

But to control him was also to control herself . . . Pleasure must simmer like a shaman's potion, get thicker and richer and darker. And then, and only then, be enjoyed at the moment when release was essential and unstoppable.

'I think not, slave,' she replied after a long, long pause, ascending to the entirety of her own role. 'You forget yourself. It's time to impress upon you the lowliness of your status ... Reacquaint you with the taste of obedience.'

'Forgive me, Mistress,' he repeated, eyes still searching the floor.

Red pounced on an opening.

'Were you given permission to speak, I wonder?' she mused aloud. 'Perhaps I should stop up your insolent mouth?' She could see him shaking now, see gooseflesh on his skin. She almost climaxed at the sight of it.

Rising to her feet, leaving Nothing hunched by the stool, Red crossed to the bulky, lovingly polished sideboard in whose drawer – the previous day – she'd secreted a number of 'props'. She took out a ball-gag similar to the one he'd spent the night in, and then, making an elaborate show of enjoying herself, rubbed it slowly back and forth between her legs. Not hard enough to induce a climax, but more than enough to coat the rubber with the flavour of her sex.

Red watched Nothing's eyes widen, then his jaws start working as she buckled the thing into place. The rubber was specially treated to be neutral, so the only taste in his mouth would be hers ... He was forbidden to touch himself – unless ordered to the contrary – and she shivered with pleasure as his fingers flexed convulsively at his sides and his stiff prick wept clear fluid.

'Now, slave,' she went on, knowing what the taste of her juices was doing – it turned *her* on, so Nothing must be going insane – 'Now, slave, let's consider her true humility might be learned.' Glancing around, her gaze lit mischievously on another of her carefully placed 'props'. 'Right, over that stool. Immediately!'

Staggering as if he were drunk, Nothing hurried to obey, draping himself over the solidly built music stool. The pose was uncomfortable because the stool was designed for sitting on, not lying over. He could neither bend his legs nor straighten them, and as his arms and upper body hung forward at an awkward angle, his erection pointed down towards the carpet. For Red's purposes, his naked rear was perfectly exposed and presented.

'Hmm . . .' She placed her hand on his bare bottom, fingers delicately curling, touching the crack but not quite stroking it. 'Not bad . . . A passable display. But it lacks a certain something. We need to *amuse* my guest.'

She made much of pausing, of considering. She'd already decided what the final touch was, but Nothing needed time to speculate and be frightened.

Returning to the sideboard, she pulled an unused black candle from one of the room's many antique candelabra, then walked slowly back to stand beside her trembling slave.

'Yes,' she murmured, drawing the smooth wax cylinder tauntingly up the crack of his arse. When she pushed slightly on the small rosy hole, he bounced on the stool and whimpered into his gag like a baby.

'Be still and be silent,' she warned, deliberately withdrawing the candle for a moment to give him hope. 'Open yourself.'

Swivelling on his platform of shame, Nothing pleaded up at her with his great brown eyes.

'I said be still. Open your bottom with your fingers, and do it now or you'll get a spanking. I'm sure St Etienne will love it if there's a red backside on display, but I'll be very angry if you force me into it.'

Another whimper.

'Silence! Open your hole or I'll thrash it for you!'

His whole body shaking furiously, Nothing reached back with both hands and thumbed open the portal of his anus. As the tiny orifice winked and fluttered, Red moved forward, spat on the thin tip of the candle, then gently pushed it in.

The honeyed flesh beneath her fingers pulsed slowly in reflex, and Red could well imagine the unthinkable

150

sensations that were roiling inside his rectum. What the nerve-ends were signalling to his brain . . .

'Don't be such great big baby,' she chided, 'It's only one tiny candle . . . Before this day's over you'll be begging for *just* a candle.'

He sobbed, and deciding to overlook the sound, Red massaged his buttocks soothingly.

'Easy, little one. Relax and you might start to like it. You look very pretty with a candle stuck in your bottom . . .' His sobs deepened. 'I might even suggest that she waggle it about for you.'

This was all a stroke of pure devilment on Red's part. St Etienne was her dearest and most like-minded friend, and in the real world, a woman who Nothing was powerfully attracted to. He'd admitted several times that he'd like to go to bed with her, and to exhibit him to her like this was a twist so delicious it almost made Red giddy.

As if on cue, the internal communicator beeped.

'Your guest, ma'am,' announced Andrea's disembodied voice.

'Very good, Andy, ask her to come up. She knows the way.' She placed her hand gently on Nothing's bottom and fondled him slowly. 'And then will you go and prepare the special room. I'll be using it later.'

Heated flesh tembled beneath her fingers. But was it in fear? Or anticipation? Red felt both, and the mix made her hot sex quicken. She placed her finger on the long protruding shank of the candle, swirled it lightly, and heard a tiny moan from behind the gag. 'So much to do today, my angel,' she murmured softly into his ear.

The door opened, and Red smiled in welcome, delighted as ever by the face and figure of her striking and unusual friend.

Addicted to wearing men's clothing, St Etienne was as bewildering to the eye as she was beautiful. She wore her hair in a severe slicked back bob, her make-up was seriously strange, and her mannerisms were as camp as a drag queen's. It was almost impossible for the uninitiated to work out where she was coming from, and today she appeared to be on some kind of militaristic kick on top of everything else.

Dressed in a natty set of *haute couture* fatigues, she sidled over to Red and stood close beside her, looking downwards. She seemed entirely unfazed by the sight of a naked man stretched across a piano stool with a candle sticking out of his arse.

'My darling Cat, how utterly charming,' she drawled, patting her sleekly gelled hair, a gesture that Red found both affected and curiously appealing, 'but you shouldn't have bothered just for me.'

'Oh . . . it's nothing,' murmured Red, her laugh low and husky.

'That's true,' observed St Etienne, licking her delicately sculpted lips, 'but Lord, doesn't he have a beautiful arse on him! And as for you, my dear . . .' She turned to Red, her eyes sparkling, her mouth moist and slack. 'You look good enough to eat.'

St Etienne was one of life's most acute sexual observers and had a keener nose for a potential fuck than anyone Red had ever met. Right now, she was staring hard at Red's crotch, her perfectly plucked eyebrows quirked in amusement.

'No panties under lycra? Oh, sweetheart, how naughty!' Her eyes flicked to Nothing's impaled arse, then back to Red's well-stained shorts. 'It's just like being in a candy store here. I simply don't know where to start first.'

Red stared back at her. St Etienne was eccentric but bewitching . . . and beneath that army drag – or any of the other peculiar outfits she was wont to wear – there was a glorious female body that screwed like a wild animal with lovers of either sex and in any known quantity. She was the succulent sinful frosting on the feast of Nothing's great shame. Red felt hungry now – beyond her own power to suppress it – and with a sigh of resignation she thrust the heel of her hand against her quim.

'That bad, huh?' St Etienne murmured. 'Though it's hardly surprising . . .' She glanced at Nothing's twitching, naked cheeks. 'Mind if I help myself?'

'Be my guest.' Still clutching at her loins Red staggered across to one of the leather-covered wing chairs.

With a perfect view of her friend and the 'amusement', she settled back into the chair's deep, dark comfort and felt her flesh shiver wetly. Overdoing it as usual, St Etienne cracked her fingers like a burlesque masseuse, laid both hands squarely on Nothing's smooth bottom, then began, slowly, to manipulate . . .

'God, what a fabulous bum,' she crooned, mounding the firm, blushing flesh and pulling it this way and that. 'And this is *so* yummy.' She flicked the candle.

Nothing was in terrible trouble now. He groaned as the candle bobbed in his body, the tortured sound stifled by his gag. Tears dripped continuously from his eyes and the curve of his back was pink with shame. Strings of juice were dangling from his penis like sap.

Inside her lycra Red was just as sticky from watching him. Bloated with blood, her labia ached and throbbed, and her fingertips slipped and slid as she rubbed at the stuff of her shorts.

Leaving Nothing to St Etienne's strange whims, Red Cat gave herself up solely to pleasure. *He* couldn't see her now, so it was all right to lose her cool, kick off her boots, peel off her shorts, and open her legs up wide and drape them over the chair arms. The upholstery felt like Nothing's velvety scalp, and the empty air tingled on her clitoris. Within seconds she was bucking and heaving.

Orgasm took her almost before she was ready. Two hard strokes and she was arching, coming, crying out; gouging the chair arm with her free hand while the other went to work with a will. Massaging and swirling, she sustained the first note of her climax and played it out as a high, clear chord.

Yet even as she came, her brain still listened and monitored.

She heard the sound of a slap. A bubbling gasp. Muffled words. 'Oh no, you don't, buster! That's not for you to see!'

Then more slaps, repeating in a fast steady sequence.

There was a rustling and a tussling, and finally, when she opened her weighted eyelids, Red saw St Etienne crouched at Nothing's side, spanking his naked bottom with her bare hand – and a fair degree of force for someone so apparently effete. The black candle lay discarded on the floor beside them.

'Just warming him up for you, my love!'

St Etienne's eyes were wild, and her face, usually dead pale, was flushed with desire and exertion.

Nothing was blushing too. Everywhere. On his face and limbs and torso the pink had turned to rose, and the cheeks of his arse were already a screaming, singing scarlet. He was taut as a wire, and Red felt a shudder of sympathy.

St Eitenne's narrow hand was poised for another smack, but suddenly she straightened up and left Nothing clenched and trembling, his hot body still braced for a blow.

'Jigger this for a game of soldiers!' she exclaimed, dashing an imaginary speck off her camouflage trousers. 'He's had quite enough fun! And so have you, Mizz Greedy! It's time *I* had some jollies!' Patting her smooth hair, she seemed to be looking around for something, but then she dipped gracefully, fielded the candle with one hand and reached between Nothing's legs with the other to scoop up some juice from his prick.

'We'll just butter our little friend here, shall we?' she said conversationally, smearing fluid on the candle-point, 'and pop him right back where he belongs!' Nudging aside one well-beaten cheek, she slid the dead black cylinder into its living mauve-brown niche.

Red threw back her head and laughed. 'You're priceless, Ett! Do you know that?' She made a 'come and get it' gesture to her oddball, off-the-wall friend, 'Come here, you disgraceful rogue. I'll give you "jollies"!' And with that she let her fingers drop artfully to her cunt.

St. Etienne's soldierly pants were at half-mast in two ticks . . . and away across the room, his mouth and bottom plugged, Nothing continued his sobbing.

* * *

Still hearing him, but now only as a memory, Red paused in her final preparations. His muffled sobs had been the soundtrack to a long, fine debauch at the hands – and the ultra-nimble tongue – of St Etienne. The fact that Nothing had heard every giggle and sigh, and every suck and slurp and liquid squelch, had only added to the piquancy of their pleasure.

St Etienne, bless her, had no qualms, no inhibitions and no limits; no act was too low to sink to, and no state too altered to strive for. Yet in a naked, sweating 'dare' game, Red had matched her orgasm for orgasm. They'd wrenched bliss out of each other's bodies by main force, and tried, for the sheer hell of it, to see who could make the most noise when she came. Red stifled a groan right now; she was still tender where those unrelenting fingers had worked and worked her . . .

The commotion had had a motive, of course, a purpose Red had never lost sight of, even while she was writhing and squealing and having her clitoris chewed by St Etienne.

Such a cacophony of climaxing flesh had made it impossible for Nothing not to lift up his head and look at them. And as Red had unwound herself from St Etienne, and the last of their panting entanglements, she'd looked across and met his bugging, anguished eyes, then panned lower to where his fingers were wrapped round his prick and semen was pooling on the carpet.

'Shall I smack him again?' St Etienne had enquired, wriggling into her mottled trousers with a grimace. Services you right! thought Red now, knowing she wasn't the only one who was sore.

'No . . . Thanks, love, but I think he knows what's coming to him. When I've had a rest after *you*, that is . . . Come on, Madame Scamp, let's have lunch!' She'd ruffled St Etienne's still-unsullied hairstyle then, and gotten a howl of mock rage in reply, followed by a deep and searching kiss.

But St Etienne was long gone now. Lunch had been

eaten, more love made, and Red had finally got her rest. Now the real game could start.

Nothing had been left with Andrea for the last few hours. He would have been fed too, from his bowl, but Red chose not to think of what else he might have gone through. She'd given the girl *carte blanche* – the only condition that he still be fit for tonight. Andrea was probably still tormenting him right now, even as she groomed and prepared him for the coming ritual.

His appointment in the special room . . .

The rite demanded a great deal of both of them, and Red too was preparing with all due pomp, clothing her body in visual majesty while the sweat and juice of sex was still pungent on her smooth white skin.

Breathing in, she pulled on the abbreviated metal corset that was part of her most spectacular stage costume. Made of wafer-thin denatured steel, it sat on her curves like a vapour but gripped like a savage caress when the micro-buckles locked and the lightweight material regained its rigid character.

Finishing just above her belly-button, it compressed her tiny waist and forced her large breasts to bulge up and out, and her internal organs to mass in her pelvis. Blood and heat were a bomb between her legs and she could climax at any moment. Her sex was dripping profusely, her vulva wet and puffed as she pulled on a G-string made of thin crimson latex. It was red on Red all over tonight; even the steel of her relentless corset had a scarlet lacquer overspray.

Her thighboots were red too, and just as viciously sexual. Five-inch heels created fierce tension all down the length of her legs. It felt as if thin wires had been run between her calves and her clitoris, and every step was a breath-taking jag. Her clinging G-string was matched by gloves that went well past the elbow, and even though she was fully and fearsomely painted, the upper part of her face was covered by a jewel-trimmed cat mask. Round her throat was a ruby-studded ceremonial collar, and her

156

slim, beloved whip was the only other accessory she needed.

Omnipotent in her finery, she paused with her gloved hand on the handle of the door to the special room. Andrea would be gone by now, and Nothing would be waiting. On display.

This is it, Red! she told herself, steadying her breathing and the runaway beat of her heart. He's all yours now . . . It's time to take him to the limit.

The special room had concealed lighting, one mirrored wall and three white tiled ones. The floor was vulcanised black rubber.

Inside it, Nothing was also clad in rubber. Thin dark rubber. At least parts of him were . . .

Andrea had prepared him perfectly. Fastened by wrists and ankles to the four corners of a square steel frame, he hung in the exact centre of the room; trussed like a bird, but with all the crucial portions of his anatomy available. Black latex mitts enclosed his tethered hands and his head was sheathed in the same grim fabric with holes for his eyes, nose and mouth. His lips were stretched in a wide open 'O' around a horrid inflatable gag, and his eyes were closed as if he were conserving his strength and sleeping in the cradle of his chains.

The main garment that covered him was a one piece play-suit of skin-tight rubber; short-sleeved and high-necked at the top, the lower half shaped like cycle pants. Cutaways exposed his bottom and crotch, and his bare feet were pale and vulnerable.

His genitals were vulnerable too, but not bare. Andrea had crammed him into a small meshed-metal pouch and secured it in place with a digitally locking clip. The handset for this, his other fetters and the raising and lowering of the entire frame, lay on a stainless steel trolley that stood against the shiny white wall.

There were still some finishing touches to be added. The final refinements. The last subtle brushstrokes that only the artist herself could add . . .

Silent on the sound-absorbing rubber, Red approached

the assembly from behind, knowing that Nothing was aware of her. His buttocks were taut and he swayed slightly in the frame; and then, when she walked around to the front of him, his long lashes fluttered and lifted.

Breathing smoothly now, Red stayed silent and menacing as she stood before him and looked into his wide, whitened eyes.

She knew he could hear through his rubber hood, but she didn't say anything. She let her actions speak. Pushing a hand into her G-string, she rode on a long, hot spasm, then offered its result to Nothing – her gloved fingers, coated and reeking, pressed against the flare of his nostrils. Very precisely, she smeared her juice into the small area of exposed skin, and as his pupils dilated hauntingly, she felt him breathe in her definitive fragrance.

'Testing time, my angel.' She stroked his lips where they strained around the gag, then touched rubber to rubber – her gloves against the swollen ball that sealed his mouth. 'But first . . . We've got to finish the rest of *this*.' She tapped the gag again and fearfulness glittered in his eyes. He'd seen what was on her trolley . . . His buttocks quivered as she wheeled it into place behind him, and he started struggling in his chains when she dipped her fingers in a pot of clear gel and began slathering it heavily on his anus.

His grunts and thrashes grew louder and wilder as the anointing continued, and turned frenzied when she picked up nine small pellets of fast-dissolving glycerine and pushed them one by one into his rectum.

One hard slap stilled him, and as the back of his knee sizzled, she finished his packing with a flanged rubber butt-plug that was as black as the candle of earlier but far far broader . . .

Narrow leather straps secured the insult in place, and within seconds the glycerine was working.

First his buttocks quivered, then they jostled, and then he was mincing and waggling in mid-air and throwing himself through space to the very limit that his bonds would allow. When Red sidled around to the front of him

158

and stroked his rubber-masked face, his eyes were almost starting from their sockets.

'Don't worry, my sweet,' she whispered. 'You'll soon forget *this*.' Reaching around behind him, she stroked his jiggling bottom. He was crying now, and she licked up his tears and pressed a single, delicate kiss on the corner of his cruelly stretched mouth.

All that remained then was to lose the trolley, wind a supportive strapping around her wrist, and pick up her slim, black multi-tailed whip – her evil and awesome 'cat'. As she advanced upon her waiting slave, she gave the instrument of his correction a smooth, sighting swish . . .

Thirty seconds later, several discreet phenomena occurred in rapid succession.

Nine thin woven leather cords sang and cracked across space, then impacted on bare human skin. Nine thin white marks turned into nine thin red weals on that same targeted area. A man screamed high and sweetly in the confines of a woman's hypercharged brain. And Red Cat the domina had an orgasm.

Three hours later she'd had more orgasms than she could count, the last one with her cunt crushed across Nothing's ravaged, pulsating backside.

The heat of him has made her scream too, and only then, with her own sex finally at peace, had she released her slave from his torments – the metal cage that had tortured his cock, and the glycerine that had churned in his arse. While he'd still been in shock, she'd thrust her rubber-clad fingers inside him, taken a sure, gentle hold of his penis, and quickly and lovingly brought him off.

After freeing him, she'd left him alone. Alone with his thoughts and his dignity. Alone with his muck, his sweat, his semen and his tears . . . Alone with a hot running shower to clean everything away but the glorious marks of his whipping.

And now, her own shower over, she lay naked, relaxed and scented in the haven of her silk-sheeted bed. Drifting, she listened idly to the familiar sounds of the night – birds and breezes, distant traffic, scraps of music. All these pleased and soothed her, but it was only certain other sounds that brought her widely and exquisitely awake . . .

She opened her eyes, sat up, and looked towards the doorway.

Nude and beautiful, Nothing stood on the threshold, and for the first time in twenty-four hours, he was free of bondage and his handsome face wore a smile.

'Ready?' he enquired, his soft voice composed but still ever so slightly respectful.

'Ready,' Red answered, her heart swelling.

Raising one slender hand she snapped her fingers . . . just as the man who had been Nothing snapped his.

'Darling,' she purred, smothering him with kisses as he slipped into bed beside her.

'Oh, my lovely, lovely Cat,' he whispered, then hissed through his teeth as her caress brushed the cheeks of his bottom.

'I'm sorry, my love.'

'Don't be. I'm not.'

Snuggling carefully against his long, warm body, Red Cat stretched like the beast she was named for and fit her own shape affectionately to his.

Then she sighed contently and let sleep and the arms of the man she adored draw her safely unto their own . . .

9

Intermezzo III

She brought him up slowly, the measured return to consciousness for her own benefit at least as much his. The trip had been too deep and too strange, in spite of its gentle ending, and to launch him stone-cold back into the real world was asking for trouble. He was still 'under', a half-naked sleep-walker, when she led him into the lounge and settled him on the sofa like a drowsy child who had got up in the night for a drink of water.

It was much easier to fuss around him while he was still out; do all those cozy solicitous things like smoothing back his hair, wrapping a blanket around him, taking his temperature and pulse ... Then kissing his cheek, and sneaking the blanket off again and looking at his body. Oh dear.

It had been frighteningly good being Red. Multi-orgasmic for her as the 'watcher' and a whole different world from the mild dominance scenes she'd played with Tricksie. A whole different world.

She'd always secretly loved ordering the male Pleasure-zone customers about. But strapping on a steel corset and whipping a man's bottom to a bruised and swollen ruin? That was something else altogether. Not to mention the other strange pleasures they'd shared. Rubber. Black candles up the bum. What she'd done with, and had done to her by St Etienne. And that was yet another dodgy can of worms she'd opened. Suddenly she needed a drink. Or perhaps several.

It's a good job he's the last tonight, she thought, sipping

a small neat scotch as she waited for Josh to wake up. But that fact itself was a huge temptation. It would be only too easy to ask him to stay over ...

It was his vulnerability that was doing it. With echoes of Red Cat still rampaging through her, having Josh at her mercy felt dangerously like déjà vu. Trouble was, she was flipping the roles too. When Josh woke up he'd remember being a dominant, not a submissive slave.

He was beginning to stir already, and as the blanket slipped, Isis felt a weird pang of need.

By rights, it should be erections that got her going, but seeing Josh's cock looking all soft and sweet and used, she felt a great desire to kneel down and kiss it. To lick him and fondle him with her tongue ... Dreaming back over the months, she remembered his taste, and the way he stiffened so quickly and got so big. It was a commonplace miracle, it happened to men every day, but she would never stop finding it amazing.

She'd cleaned him after his ejaculations, but she knew if she gave in now and sucked him, he'd still taste of semen, of fresh male sweat. Of beautiful, beautiful Josh ...

Oh boy, that night! Only a few hours but what things they'd done. She remembered *le soixante neuf*, well executed for once, the big fat flavour of him in her mouth while he brought her to the peak with his tongue. She'd been able to split her faculties in two, concentrate on both her pleasure *and* his. She'd not thought about it at the time, but afterwards, having two sets of memories had seemed utterly bizarre. It was down to the 'Zone, she supposed.

And it could all happen again in a few minutes if she wanted it. Josh had amazing recuperative powers and she'd no doubt he could rise to the occasion. He was a down-to-earth sort of man, with a practical mind and a solid workmanlike body, but as a lover, he had the stuff of fantasy about him ...

Why not go for it, Ice? she asked herself. You want him. He wants you. It's going to happen eventually.

Yet she had the strangest feeling that if she went back on her word, he'd think less of her. What was that saying about women and inconstancy? If she offered sex now, he'd be getting what he wanted, yes, but somehow *she'd* be letting the side down.

As his eyelids started fluttering, she put aside her glass and sat down on the end of the couch – waiting for what, she wasn't quite sure.

'Oh God,' he muttered, struggling to sit up, his long frame shaking. 'Oh my dear God . . .'

In a flash, Isis was beside him, her nurturing instincts taking over. What did it all matter? Sex and deals and principles. Sliding her arm around his shoulder, she pulled him close to her body.

'It wasn't me,' he mumbled into her white smock. 'It was incredible . . . but it just wasn't me.'

Isis raised his face so she could look into his eyes, finding tenderness suddenly sexy. 'What's wrong? Didn't it work? You were "her", weren't you?'

'Yeah . . .' He straightened up, seeming vaguely embarrassed. 'I was definitely her at the time, but just now . . . waking up . . . It all seemed wrong again. I dunno . . . I can't explain. It was all incredible stuff but I think I should've been him . . . been "Nothing".'

'Perhaps so,' Isis said quietly, 'but the challenge was to try a switch, Josh.'

His muscular shoulders bunched in the circle of her arm. Against her will, she glanced down at his cock and saw it rousing.

'I'm not a wimp in real life,' he answered, his sudden lack of expression more assertive than anger would have been. Isis felt her heart beat crazily, and sex gush hot in her loins.

No, this man wasn't weak at all. He'd proved that comprehensively, both on the treatment couch and afterwards in the warmth of her bed. All she'd had to do was capitulate once, and he'd taken the lead in everything. He'd chosen their sex acts. Made her do things. Assumed – without consulting her – that he was in charge. She'd accepted it because *then* she'd wanted it. But now, with the Cat still at work in her mindset, her needs had drastically changed.

'No, of course you're not a wimp, Josh,' she said crisply, her skin prickling with heat beneath her smock. 'And neither am I.'

It got the desired effect. But they were back on thin ice. And Josh was erect.

Heat flared in his brown eyes, and not for the first time, she knew he'd instantly and eerily 'read' her. No, he wasn't a real life submissive, but would he act that way to please her?

He was well up now, his prick jutting proud from the silky nest of his pubes. It would be so easy to forget all deals and trips, and just slip off her panties and slip onto him. Or even nudge them aside – they were soaking anyway – and get him in her body while she was still fully dressed. It had been too long since she'd had straight sex with a strong straight man. Someone who could fill her up with authority, yet fuck her as an equal. A warm, caring equal. Her last fuck as such had been a peculiar, frantic session with the errant Diabolo. A wild ecstatic bang, but with precious little sense of anything but raw physical sensation. The Moon Devil was a superb technical lover, but emotionally a deadzone. It was debatable whether even Tricksie had made meaningful contact . . .

'It's not actually going to happen, is it?' Josh enquired softly, snapping open her musings.

It could have happened. Almost. But Josh himself had brought Isis back to her senses. 'There's still one more adventure,' she offered, hiding her confusion. Her irrational disappointment.

'Okay, I'll buy that. But if you won't let me bonk you, at least let me tell you what it'll be like when you do.'

'I beg your pardon?'

A shiver ran down Isis's spine and ended in the cleft of her sex. Josh's eyes twinkled and she felt it, there in her fluttering moistness, like a charged and scintillating ray.

'I'll describe my ideal fuck. With you.' He leaned back

against the sofa, arching his body luxuriantly and lifting his hips for emphasis. 'And while I'll telling you about it, you can deal with *this* for me.' Without warning he whipped out a long sinuous hand, grabbed one of hers, and closed it around his erection.

Isis tried to pull away, panicking. It wasn't that she didn't like holding his cock. She did. But the feel of him undermined her. Having him in her hand was like having him in her quim. She tried to wriggle her fingers, but Josh held her fast.

'No! Be fair to me, Isis. Just hold me, that's all I ask.' He squeezed, caressing himself *through* her. 'For now . . .'

She stopped resisting. When he throbbed in her fingers like velvet, she didn't want to . . .

'Okay then. Talk to me.'

Josh licked his lips, rested his head back against the chair. As his eyelids closed, he smiled – supremely confident – and took away his hand.

'You're waiting for me in a bedroom somewhere. Your flat, I think. You're hot for me. You want my cock in you. You've been playing with your little girlie, with Tricksie. And she's made you come . . . But you want more. You want meat inside you.'

Oh yes, Josh, I do, she told him silently, flexing her thumb and finger, sliding, working. This thing in her hand, this beautiful thing, it had once felt so godlike inside her.

'You're lying on the bed . . .' His voice checked slightly. 'Wearing something flimsy. A teddy. Camiknickers or whatever they're called. It's – ' His eyes flicked open for a second, although Isis had the strangest feeling he wasn't seeing the here and now version of her. 'It's blue. Dark, smoky, blue. High-cut legs, lace here.' He ran a hand across his chest. 'You've been tossing about on the bed. You're on fire and you can't keep still. The teddy's twisted up between your legs and I can see the hair . . . It's the prettiest thing I've ever seen. Gold and red and brown. Tortoiseshell. And sticky-wet, where she's been playing with you. The crotch of your knickers is wet too. Dark. Soaking dark. I can see it . . .'

Isis shifted uneasily, fantasy real between her legs. She was sopping, running, her real pants clammy against her hot, swelling lips.

'You're not quite awake, but you're horny. You start playing with yourself, touching your breasts through the lace, pinching your hard little teats. One by one. Pinch. Pinch. Together, with both hands, nipping hard and hurting yourself. And your hips are moving in time, your legs opening wide. I can see more and more. Everything. I want you so much I could die.'

Eloquent. Impassioned. True? Isis didn't know, but the hard, red column in her hand said probably. He was steely between her fingers, his hips moving as hers did in his dream. Her dream.

'I sit down on the bed beside you but your eyes stay closed.' Josh's own eyes stayed closed too, but his hands moved caressingly on his thighs, saying 'stroke me, woman, stroke me'.

She did.

'I know you want me to look at you ... *Really* look at you. You splay your legs wider and I reach between and pop the little buttons. The crotch of your teddy is sodden, wet through with your juices. You smell wonderful; strong but fabulous. Rich. Like a she-cat. Like the spices of the Orient. You smell as if you've come. A lot.'

Oh God, I'm going to come now! thought Isis wildly. Her vagina sucked like a tiny mouth, her fingers closed, and Josh groaned and bucked in her grip.

'I'm sorry,' she muttered, loosening her hold, afraid she'd hurt him.

'Don't be. I like it.' His eyes opened again, but this time he was aware, looking at her, smiling. 'Squeeze me, Isis. Rub me. Please.' Once again, his pelvis rose up to meet her.

Carefully, measuredly, she began to wank him. Josh went on with his story.

'I push up the stuff of your teddy. Up to the waist, so I can see your belly and your lovely soft hair ... Your skin's so white. So moist. You're sweating now. I can see

166

it. You're burning up inside because you want me. I don't touch you yet, though. Not between the legs . . . I stroke my fingertips across your stomach. I put one in your belly button and – '

Isis moaned, loving the image, feeling the impudent finger in her navel as clearly as if he'd actually touched her.

'You moan,' said Josh with a soft laugh. 'Then you ask me to stroke you. To caress your quim with my fingers. You say 'please', but you've teased me so much I decide that it's my turn. I take your hand and kiss it, tasting your juices where you've touched yourself. Then I rub the lace of your teddy across the tips of your breasts. Sweet stiff tips . . . You lift your crotch off the bed to try and entice me. You're dying for me to diddle you.'

For her part, Isis was watching Josh's face. Studying his closed eyes and wondering if she dare slip her hand beneath her smock.

'Why don't you?' He grinned, his eyes still closed.

'You devil! Keep your mind on your story.'

'You want me to touch you . . .' His voice was so creamy and taunting. He was stating facts now, not telling tales. 'I decide to have mercy . . . put you out of your misery.'

'Chauvinist shit!'

Josh seemed unfazed, but his cock throbbed in her fingers like a rocket on stand-by. Primed. Loaded. Ready for glory.

'You want me,' he repeated, her seigneur driving home his will. 'You're very wet. I touch you and you make that little sound of yours . . . That grunt and a purr thing you do when you're losing it.'

She knew that sound; her teeth were deep in her lower lip to keep it inside her mouth now. Her quim was sweating its nectar, the tissues heavy and needful. If Josh made one bold move, she was lost. It would be full hard-driving sex. Cock in cunt; raw lust in heavenly motion.

But he went on talking.

'I rub you, tickle your clit, press you. You're so wet my fingers slip about. You take my hand and guide my touch, put me where it's best. I rub you hard then and you come on me. It's beautiful, a great gooey gush. I get two fingers inside you and I feel your spasm, but I keep my thumb on your clitty where it matters ... I work you and work you until you're coming continuously. And then, when you're really out of it, I tip you on your back, spread your legs and push myself into you.'

Josh matched deeds to words and guided her hand as in the story she'd guided his. But he didn't follow through. There was no throwing her down on the carpet caveman-style, just the race of their woven hands on his prick.

She was being used. She was an improvised mastur-bation aid, but she didn't give a damn. He'd eulogised her dream-wetness but now he was the slippery one. Pre-come was streaming from him, coating their laced fingers and surrounding his own flesh in a sleek satiny tube. Isis worked him harder and harder, feeling crazy transferences from his sex to hers ... Sensations. Fluids. Flames of pleasure. Arousal hard and killing.

'And I come in you!' he shouted, his voice snapping as his stiffness pulsed in her hand – and her cunt, his echo, rippled softly. 'Oh God, yes! Oh, yes yes yes!'

His semen was very hot, very thick and very copious. A pearlescent satin cream that spattered her hand, her wrist and his belly. The heavy droplets captivated her, looked rich, opulent and tempting. Without thinking, she released his softening penis and raised her hand to her lips, pointing out her tongue to lick up the gift of his seed.

She lapped up every scrap of it, savouring its strange blandness, the faint whisper of salt, the vague ammoniac traces. She lapped up his semen, his all, then glanced furtively along his thighs where some more of it still lay gleaming.

Josh gasped, and she realised in one great rush of heat exactly what she'd done.

He was watching her closely, his eyes heavy-lidded, and when he licked his lips, she blushed furiously. He was in shagged out post-orgasmic euphoria, but he was *still* teas-ing her.

168

'I –' Where had old 'Red Cat' gone all of a sudden?

'Don't worry, I've had what *I* wanted.' He grinned and squirmed on the sofa, visibly savouring his afterglow. 'In my book that was sex, Isis. I came. You made me. *We* had sex.'

'We didn't. Not exactly...' She was splitting hairs and she knew it.

'Maybe you're right,' he conceded, then sent Isis leaping away as his hand tried to worm up her skirt, 'Let me touch you, Isis. Now. For real. Let me give you what you gave me.'

The temptation was huge, but she stayed put, just out of reach, wishing her stubbornness in hell.

With a resigned sigh, Josh lay back, his cock flopping on his thigh as he settled amongst the cushions, his smile weary but mellow and satisfied.

'All right, my delicious doctor, I'm happy with that. I can wait.' His eyes fluttered closed again. He'd come, and like most men who'd come, he was going to sleep. 'But the big question is... can *you* wait?'

'Well, I think you're nuts,' said Tricksie cheerfully. She was lying in Isis's bed, wearing Isis's wrap, drinking Isis's wine and flicking the pages of one of Isis's books. Isis hadn't specifically asked her to stay the night, but it hadn't been necessary. Tricksie had a sure sweet knack of knowing when she was desperately needed.

And not having Josh had left Isis needing more than her own deft fingers.

'You're absolutely right of course,' she said. 'I was cutting off my nose to spite my face.' She sighed. 'I should've got astride that erection while it was there... Not just tossed it off for *his* benefit.'

'Spoken like a true sexual *bon vivant*.' Tricksie's green eyes were bright with mischief. 'I hope that means you'll rectify the situation next time...' She shuddered expressively. 'Because there was talk of "sharing"...'

'I dunno, Trix. Really, I don't.'

And she didn't.

A threesome? She'd done it in her 'Zone dreams, of course, but not for real. She and Tricksie had both been involved with Diabolo at the same time, but they'd made love together. Never been three in a bed.

'It's fun, Ice. You'd love it.'

Tricksie's voice was coaxing, cajoling, and Isis knew that she too was thinking about the 'event' of three rather than simply a three-way relationship. She sat down on the bed at her friend's side, reaching for their shared wine and taking a sip, savouring the crisp cool fruitiness, but knowing that nothing but sex could quench her heat.

Why had masturbating Josh unsettled her so much? It wasn't as if she hadn't done it before. She'd handled his prick often enough in the course of Pleasurezone procedures. She'd even brought him off before.

But this time things had been different. She'd been wanting him at the time, really turned on for him in body and mind, and she'd let him control her. She tried out the word 'manipulate' and knew it was the right one. Even though she'd been the one who'd been doing the touching.

'You know something? This is absolutely fantastic,' Tricksie said suddenly, interrupting Isis's ponderings.

Isis looked puzzled at the glass in her hand, then realised her friend wasn't talking about wine.

Tricksie was sprawled back against the pillows, her white breasts spilling from the open gape of her wrap as she pored over her book, a slim, elegantly bound collector's volume she'd picked up to read while Isis was showering.

Isis agreed about the book, it was a favourite of hers, totally pervy, and a product of St Etienne's prolific, offbeat and breath-takingly degenerate mind.

It was no wonder Tricksie was gasping and going 'ooh' all over the place. Isis had read *At the Academy of Madam Woo* at least half a dozen times and she'd always ended up stroking herself. It would probably have that effect now if she read over Tricksie's shoulder, especially given the view from there, but nevertheless she slid onto the bed, snuggled up and tried to pick up the book's outrageous pornographic thread.

Words leapt out at her. Precocious words with wicked weight ... 'lash', 'weal', 'pain', 'bottom' ... and less obviously 'governess'. A fast reader, Isis cruised the page, feeling the loaded prose sink in and do its deliquescing work even though she'd read it all before.

At the Academy of Madam Woo was a true modern classic – a historically accurate and lusciously explicit novel of Edwardian schoolroom flagellation. The plot and the verbiage were controlled but red hot, to say the least, and the effects it produced were immediate. It was difficult to understand why her cousin's elegant descriptions of thrashed red backsides and exquisite humiliation were so compelling, but every time she read them Isis felt a strong, almost lemming-like urge to find someone who would smack her bottom for her. The orientation, it being told through the victim's eyes rather than the punisher's, was the complete reverse of the Red Cat adventure – but the sense of identification was no less explosive.

She wondered what effect it was having on Tricksie. It was certainly doing something because Trix was already shifting her long thighs uneasily, her free hand searching for her hot spot.

'I've done smacking. It's fun,' she said as she turned a page, casually flipping open her robe.

'Did you smack ... or were you smacked?' Isis asked, her eyes following the traverse of Tricksie's white fingers as they slid nonchalantly across her belly, then dove into her lustrous red thatch.

'I've tried both ... Ooh ... Ooh ... Yes!' She was rubbing now, freely and unashamedly, as relaxed about masturbating in Isis's presence as she would have been on her own. Within seconds she was pumping her loins, gnawing her lips and grunting and gapsing in an obvious, uninhibited orgasm.

Isis had never wanted her more.

'Remind me to thank Ett for that when I next see her,'

Tricksie said blithely, removing her glistening fingers from their hideaway and licking them one by one.

'She might want payment in kind,' murmured Isis, imagining her lover's sweet taste.

'Would that bother you?' Tricksie's voice was suddenly serious. 'St Etienne's so crazy, so bizarre . . . She's a real turn on, you know.'

'You'd have to get in the queue behind a helluva lot of people . . . Including Josh and me,' said Isis, enjoying the shock on Tricksie's beautiful face.

'But – ' She paused, and Isis could see all the possible combinations being run through a sexual computer.

'Together?' Tricksie said at last, 'And anyway, wouldn't it be illegal or something? Her being your cousin and all.'

'I'm not sure how things like that apply to same-sex relationships. It's a bit of a grey area. And not a problem for Ett and I. She is my only living relative, but we're not actually close in blood.'

'Oh . . .'

'I always imagine her as the heroine of this book.' Isis picked up the abandoned *Madam Woo* from where the jerking Tricksie had dropped it.

'You mean Louise?' Tricksie cocked her head on one side, her wine-red curls gorgeous on her bared white shoulders. 'I don't see that . . . Ett wouldn't keep dropping her drawers and taking it. It's not her style at all.'

'Oh no, she's Madam Woo. that's obvious.' It was easy to exchange Ett's sleeked back hair for a governess bun, and her cross-dressed, pin-striped chic for the sober elegance of the archetypal Edwardian schoolma'am. It was also easy, seductively so, to imagine bending over before her and exposing your trembling bottom to her for discipline. A rogue image flitted through Isis's mind. Ett in khaki, spanking a naked young man in a collar . . .

Returning her cousin to her institutional black silk frock, Isis had a sudden sparkling idea that made her laugh out loud.

'I've just found Josh's last adventure,' she told the puzzled Tricksie, then smiled and went on to explain.

'Yeah, I see what you mean.'

Tricksie had snuggled close as she'd listened, and her bare boob was pressed against Isis's arm. Its firmness and heat were distracting, but Isis still warmed to her theme.

'He enjoys submission. He said he'd rather take CP than dish it out. And he *loves* adventuring as a girl ... He's a natural for Louise.' She flicked pages furiously, not having to look too hard for the juicy bits. 'I wonder if Ett would lend me the disk for this? We could load it straight into the 'Zone and there'd hardly be anything else to write. We could run it as an adventure straight away.'

'Do you think she'd let us?'

'I'm sure she will.' The difference between literary dream-weaving, and Isis's electronic version was in essence marginal, and St Etienne had frequently intimated she'd like to get involved with the Pleasurezone. Cousin Ice's 'boutique d'amour' as she was wont to call it.

'And would I be in it?' Tricksie's glance was sideways, sultry and unmistakable, her hunger evident in the hardness of the nipple against Isis's arm.

'Pick a role, sweetheart.'

Isis leaned into the sweet firm curve of Tricksie's breast, turning pages, but no longer seeing the words. Adventureland, her own creation, was a miracle, but there was much to be said for living in the real world sometimes. A world where beautiful women pressed their bodies against you, and their flesh said how much they wanted you. She flicked another page, then turned to meet emeralds glowing with lechery in a pale and exquisite face. 'But I already know who you *ought* to be.'

'Me too,' whispered Tricksie, her breath hot on Isis's neck. Tapering, red-painted fingertips stole into a different robe this time, and Isis felt their sexy sneakiness slide between her towelling lapels, then home in on her tingling breast-tips like heat-seeking missiles.

'But if I'm Flossie, typecast as a trollop as usual, who are you, my darling doctor?' The question was punctuated with delicate tweaks, naughty little tugs and demonic tantalising twirls.

'Young Belinda, of course,' panted Isis, her stomach trembling, her breath light and butterflies doing a tango in her sex.

Tricksie seemed to think about this for a few moments, her fingers pinching and stroking, pinching and stroking until Isis was at screaming point and her running cunt was wetting the towelling beneath her.

'But don't Belinda and Flossie play games with each other at night?' Both hands were on her now, one hastily stripping aside the robe, the other burrowing purposefully between her helplessly opening legs.

Isis nodded, then leapt and arched as a whore's skilled fingers found her.

'Doesn't Flossie get into Belinda's bed and touch her pussy?'

Isis nodded again, moaning as Tricksie palpated her fluttering clit.

'Doesn't Flossie tickle Belinda's naughty little clittie and make her come again and again and again?'

'Yes! Oh God, you bitch, yes!' Isis shouted as a finger pressed hard and a star exploded in her cleft – the orgasm so sure and quick and overpowering that she nearly wet herself with pleasure.

'Good,' said Tricksie creamily, pulling Isis fully into her arms and starting to kiss her neck. 'Because I've just read a smashing bit on page one hundred and twenty-three that I think we should re-enact.'

'What is it?' asked Isis, shocked by sex and the slurred, throaty sound of her own voice. Tricksie was a drug . . . and she'd just mainlined on her. 'Tell me, you minx!'

'I'd rather show you.' Tricksie's voice was distorted too, muffled as her lips nibbled a path down Isis's belly to her ideal and inevitable destination.

There was no more reading that night.

'You mean your cousin wrote this?'

Isis smiled in satisfaction. She'd just given Josh *At the Acadmey of Madam Woo* and it was already having the same effect on him that it had on her. Well, an equivalent one. Even as she watched, he licked his lips and wriggled almost imperceptibly on his stool.

Pretending to turn her attention to her mineral water, she took a sly glance at him out of the corner of her eye. He shifted again, and a few seconds after he'd turned another page, his eyes widened: pupils dilating and darkening in an obvious sexual response. He'd be hard in his trousers now, his brain filled with images of exposed bottoms and girls being thrashed and fingered. Of shame, humiliation and sublime, crypto-mystic submission. He'd be putting himself in the place of the poor spanked pupils of Madam Woo – the young women who whimpered and sobbed for her to stop, but prayed with all their hearts that she go on and on and on.

Isis had endured all their torments with them whilst reading the book, and knew with no doubt at all that any minute now, Josh would demand the same scenarios for his adventure.

'Well then, Josh, do you fancy getting your bottom smacked tonight?' she said into the charged quiet between them. 'A session with your "governess"?'

'I – ' Josh began, then stopped. There was no need for him to speak, the answer was in his burning eyes, the slight flush on his high, sharp cheek-bones . . . the bulge in his tight, black jeans.

He'd enjoyed his time as Red Cat – the data and his orgasm had proved that – but equally his profile indicated he'd get even greater pleasure from a 'victim' role, from receiving the pain rather than inflicting it. The role of a naughty, punished schoolgirl would be perfect for him. Especially at the hands of such a 'teacher' as Isis had in mind for him.

'Face facts, Josh,' she said gently. 'You've admitted it yourself. The best trips for you are the ones where you "take it" from women. Rio, Queen Nef, St Etienne. They've all called the shots, haven't they?' She saw him nod, slowly, admittingly. 'Now it's Madam Woo's turn.' Together they looked down at the book, and Josh's fingers flicked back to the introductory pages.

As a luxury collector's edition the novel had been furnished with one or two fine art illustrations. The frontispiece was a pen and ink sketch of a sombrely beautiful woman flexing a long rattan cane between her elegant fingers. The face was rather indistinct, but to Isis it was disturbingly familiar.

'What are you grinning at?'

Isis hadn't realised she was smiling, but at Josh's question she looked up and faced him.

'I was just thinking how typical of Ett it was to cast herself in the starring role.'

'I was sort of assuming you'd be Madam Woo.' Josh looked vaguely disappointed.

'Oh no,' said Isis quickly, feeling selfish, guilty, and suddenly very hot and bothered.

In bed last night, she'd fantasised compulsively while Tricksie had caressed her. With a finger moving delicately on her clitoris, she'd sent her consciousness winging to Madam Woo's menacing schoolroom and the harsh but fabulous regime that held sway there. And the fantasy had become more vivid than ever when Tricksie had really got down to business.

Isis had writhed and cried in both worlds. In the dream, Madam Woo had pulled down her rebellious pupil's knickers, exposed her shameful wetness to the whole class, then beaten her naked white bottom with a leather-soled slipper.

In the real world of sex, Tricksie had had the very devil in her. She'd made Isis lie on her back with her knees bent, holding her thighs wide open with her hands. Ready ...

Isis had squealed in glorious outrage when Tricksie had stuffed her. With a dildo in each orifice, she'd yelped and sobbed in climax after climax as nimble, knowledgeable fingers had abused her aching clit. Nipping it, rocking it, wrenching it to and fro in a rough primeval rhythm that had made her sweat and writhe and cry. The spasms had synched perfectly with the blows of Madam Woo's cruel but imaginary slipper.

The sensations last night had been so huge and sweet

that she wanted to regain them through the medium of adventure; and to this end, when she'd programmed *Madam Woo* for Josh, she'd cast the players exactly as she had while Tricksie had been making her come.

So Madam Woo was still St Etienne. St Etienne – stern, immaculate and sensational. The trip would be so good it would blow Josh away, and Isis felt entitled to be selfish.

'Oh no,' she repeated. 'I think we should stick with the one who created the role, don't you?' She cocked her head on one side, confident that if Josh was already getting into *his* role he'd accept what she said without question.

'Yeah, okay . . . Whatever you say.'

It was as if she'd already put him half under. He was hers, in the palm of her hand, it was intoxicating.

But it's only for now, Ice, she told herself firmly. When the trip starts it'll all be different. You'll be him, and he'll be a girl . . . And Madam Woo's going to thrash the living daylights out of both of you!

'Would you like me to get you a real date with St Etienne sometime?' she enquired, her voice as nonchalant as she could make it.

She was slightly ashamed of her tactics, but she couldn't help herself. Teasing Josh was irresistible at times like these. She'd waited until he was strapped to the couch with all the probes in place and only then started zapping him with questions.

'I dunno . . . No. Yes. How the hell should I know, Isis? I can't think straight when I'm like this.'

Hardly surprising, she conceded, grinning wolfishly out of his line of sight. She couldn't think too sharply with a probe in her bottom either. She caught his eyes, and found them surprisingly bright and penetrating, given that his cock was so stiff in its tether.

'How would you feel about that?' He was grinning himself now, as if he'd sussed her ambiguous feelings for her divine but peculiar cousin.

She turned the idea over in her mind and found it intriguing. Especially if she could watch what they did . . .

Or more probably what St Etienne did to him. Ett *never* let a man take control!

'Oh, I think it might be a fun idea to get you two together for real, don't you?' she enquired sweetly, reaching between his legs to make a fairly unnecessary adjustment to the position of his testicles. She made her fingers light and deft, but Josh still trembled violently as if he feared for what she had in her grip.

'Why . . . why do you say that?' he croaked as her fingers skimmed up the underside of his prick.

'I've seen the read-outs of how you react to her in adventures. And the thing is, Josh, she's far more outrageous in real life than she is in dreamtime. She was fabulous with Nothing. I'd just love to see her work on you. The living *her*, that is . . .' Her fingers flicked around his cockhead, adjusting the cuff slightly, then touching him, just once, right on the tiny open eye.

'You mean you'd watch?' Josh was blushing wildly now – everywhere – and Isis was irresistibly reminded of Nothing.

'Why not? Now I've followed the progress of you "at it" with all and sundry via *this*,' she gestured towards the screens, the read-outs and the monitoring headset. 'And I've had you myself. It'd be interesting to see you with someone else now . . . Purely for research purposes, of course.'

She was joking, but in a strange way it was also true.

'Jesus, Isis, you're the most fantastic woman I've ever met . . . But sometimes I could smack you senseless!' Josh muttered, then swore profusely as the hypodermic of hallucinogen went unexpectedly into his forearm. He'd been so incensed he'd never even noticed her pick it up . . .

'Now, don't be a kiddie. You know it didn't hurt,' she soothed, making the final programming adjustments, settling onto her stool and putting on the headset. 'And if there's any smacking to be done, you'd better get used to being on the receiving end.'

Josh blinked furiously as the drug began to take a hold. Already partially in phase with him, Isis sensed the drifting of his consciousness and slid the softly lined mask over his eyes. 'Think of Madam Woo now, Josh my sweetheart. Think how nice it'll be to let *her* smack *you*. You'll be good and brave for her, won't you?'

'I dunno ... Mebbe ...'

With the last sequence keyed in and running, Isis closed her eyes for a moment and a surprising alluring image formed in the blackness. A woman with severely styled hair and a seriously serious outfit. A thin rattan cane swished slowly in the grip of her long elegant fingers ...

'Go to sleep now, my dear,' Isis whispered, opening her eyes, running quickly over the figures on the screen, then turning to the bound and wired man at her side. 'It's school tomorrow, and you've got to be bright and alert. It's your very first day at the Academy ...'

10

The Academy of Madam Woo

'Louise Sutherland, you're day-dreaming again!'

Louise snapped to attention, every nerve in her body a-quiver as the beautiful dark-clad woman strode purposefully towards her.

'What is it, Louise,' Mrs Woolstencraft enquired coolly, 'that is so very much more interesting to you than our simple French translation? Enlighten us, if you please?'

Oh God, thought Louise, if I do tell her, she'll kill me!

Yes, if the truth came out Louise knew she'd be in worse trouble than she already was. Madam Woo would tan her hide if she found out the subject of her pupil's delicious but foolhardy fantasising. And that, in a way, Louise supposed, would be poetically fitting.

She'd been fantasising about bottoms. Women's bottoms to be specific. Girl's bottoms. Maid's bottoms. Even the magnificent arse of the governess herself. What she could see of it, beneath that long flowing skirt.

A woman's derrière was actually the reason she'd ended up in this peculiar establishment in the middle of what should have been her summer holidays.

But it wasn't all her fault. Maud had been asking for it for months. Batting her eyelashes at Louise. Finding reasons to brush up against her. Especially with those plump little titties of hers. And the times she'd shown her drawers when she'd just happened to be standing on a stool dusting a high shelf.

Louise remembered the moment it had all come to a head. She'd been reading in the library – reading her father's erotic books, something else she wasn't supposed to be doing – and Maud was laying the fire. The titillating literature had already caused a degree of hot commotion in her own underwear, but the sight of the maid's bottom so saucily displayed when her skirt pulled tight . . . Well, that had been the moment Louise's hormones went berserk.

Maud hadn't complained, though, when her rump and her deep warm cleft had been explored through the layers of her frock and petticoat. And when she'd slipped up her skirt, peeled down her lacy bloomers and let Louise thrust her hand inside, she'd moaned softly and writhed on the invading fingers.

'Ooh, Miss Louise, you shouldn't,' she'd whimpered as Louise had pawed her dribbling cunny; and she'd been grunting like a little dog, sitting blissfully on her young mistress's hand and rubbing her clitty with her own finger, when Mama had walked in, screamed in abject horror and promptly fainted clean away from a double shock. The sight of her daughter doing something utterly unspeakable . . . and to make matters worse, doing it to a member of her very own sex.

Maud had been banished to Aunt Augusta's now, and she, Louise, had agreed – to help poor Mama get over the vapours – to present herself at this dour Academy in order to 'improve her character'. It was only because she loved Mama and felt so guilty that she'd submitted without complaint. After all she was a grown woman now! At seventeen going on eighteen she was far too old to be consigned to what amounted to a 'dame school'.

'Louise, I'm waiting,' the dame in question repeated. Although the slender, elegant and surprisingly young Mrs Woolstencraft – or Madam Woo as Belinda, a fellow 'prisoner' had dubbed her – was the very least damelike figure imaginable. Her large penetrating eyes froze Louise like a mouth on a pin, and her beautiful bosom in its serious white blouse and sombre black brocade waistcoat was almost as mouthwatering as her perfect, though more or less hidden backside.

'Bottoms!'

'I beg your pardon?'

I've gone completely mad! thought Louise, her heart racing, and to her astonishment and horror, her cunny getting extremely hot. Being here in this schoolroom was like being clamped in a pot on a stove; it had cooked her brains to porridge. Why else had she told Madam Woo *exactly* what was on her mind?

'I think, Louise, that you'd better expand on that answer,' the governess murmured smoothly, patting her sleekly coiffed hair, 'or I'll have to think you were being intentionally vulgar.'

'I was thinking about my ... er ... About my ... um ... transgressions and that bottoms always seem to be at the bottom of them ...' Boggling at her own stupidity, Louise waited for the axe – or something – to fall, then breathed again as an explosive, spluttering giggle from across the room temporarily diverted Madam Woo's attention.

'Belinda Gascoigne, this is your last warning,' she said to the impish figure sitting at the other school desk. 'If you persist in behaving like a hoyden I shall be forced to chastise you. Again. You're eighteen now, Belinda. A grown woman. You should know much, much better than this.' She turned then and behind their governess's back, Louise saw Belinda's pretty but unfortunately disfigured face crinkle in a broad, wicked grin. Not for the first time, she wondered just what her partner-in-crime's face would have looked like without that horrid birthmark. Knowing as she did it that she'd suffer, she laughed out loud as Belinda made a rude and graphic grabbing gesture and winked broadly out of Madam Woo's line of sight.

In the next breath, Louise was on her feet with her right ear in the vice of Madam Woo's slender but powerful fingers ...

'Stand perfectly still, Louise. I shall deal with you in a moment.' The vice opened, and the cool gaze drifted downwards. Steely eyes narrowed threateningly when they lit upon Louise's thighs, and their slow scissoring action – quite evident even through layers of school skirt, petticoat and bloomers. 'And I've nothing to say about *that* phenomenon.' She nodded, dismissing Louise's flesh, and its helpless carnal itch as loathsome. 'Except that I hope to see it subsided by the time I've finished with Miss Gascoigne!'

With that she spun on her daintily booted heel, strode to her own desk, and rang hard on the small schoolroom bell.

'I think we'll need Flossie's assistance for this, don't you, Belinda?' she said almost pleasantly as she advanced upon her victim, looking determined but slightly flushed.

Louise trembled, knowing what was coming and wondering why the prospect of it made the tingle in her cunny burn hotter than ever. She really shouldn't be getting those nice, sexy, squidgy feelings now ... This was what was delicately termed a 'correctional' establishment, and judging by the pallor of Belinda's unmarked cheek, they were about to be faced with the full meaning of that awe-inspiring definition.

There was a swift rap on the door, and it swung open immediately to admit a buxom and rather handsome red-haired young woman clad in the black dress and white pinafore and cap of a maid. Louise sent up a silent prayer that the newcomer – Flossie – wouldn't still be here when she got *her* forthcoming punishment. Especially not after last night ...

'Now then, Flossie,' Madam Woo said briskly. 'Miss Belinda has tried my patience once too often this morning, and I find that I need your assistance. And the use of your invaluable pins.'

'Of course, Madam,' murmured Flossie, sashaying forward and, to Louise's mind, blatantly flaunting her magnificent bosom at her. The thin black stuff of her frock did nothing to hide the sweet rounded breasts that Flossie had suddenly and wantonly exposed to Louise while she was getting her ready for bed last night. To make matters worse now the maid also flashed a sly wink in Louise's direction.

'Louise!' said Madam Woo, not looking round and presumably not winking. 'I'd like you to watch closely. You may find this informative. Flossie, kindly put Belinda into position over the desk and turn up her dress.'

'But, madam –' began Belinda, resisting Flossie's strong-arm hold. She stilled, though, when Madam Woo snatched hold of her pretty brown-blonde ringlets and marched her over to the desk by them.

'I've put up with quite enough defiance, young lady. For that you'll be punished with your bottom bared.'

Her loins churning madly, Louise noticed a special emphasis laid on that most topical of words and she watched, rapt and with her mouth fallen open, as Flossie pressed Belinda face down over the desk and drew up first her pretty flounced skirt, and then her delicately lacy petticoat.

Oh lor, it's actually going to happen! she thought wildly, biting her lip and wondering if she could manage to watch any further without disgracing herself and getting her knickers all sticky. In the furrow between her legs, everything went quivery and her little bud fairly jumped at the pure stretched whiteness of Belinda's thin, girlish bloomers. The fabric of them was so sheer it was almost a lawn or a muslin, and the firm globes of a truly pretty bottom were already clearly on show. Louise could see the dark shadowed blur of a hairy feminine cleft. She could see – she'd swear to it! – a faint trace of dampness on the fine white cloth wedged right at the apex of Belinda's long slim thighs.

'The pins, please, Flossie!' said Madam Woo, and the maid went about her work, securing the skirt and petticoat in place. Moving closer, Madam Woo pressed her hand to the crown of Belinda's right arse-cheek, and to Louise's almost demented excitement, squeezed it slowly and gently, 'I'm afraid this will hurt you quite a lot, Belinda my dear,' she whispered, leaning over, her lips close to her trembling victim's ear. 'In fact it will hurt you a very great deal indeed. But you know how much better you will be for it, don't you?'

Beneath the thin white fabric the waiting bottom seemed to pulse . . . but stubborn Belinda remained silent.

Madam Woo squeezed again, the action slow and voluptuous. 'Don't you, Belinda?' she persisted, her voice low and strangely urgent, a timbre that was shockingly familiar to Louise. It was how Maud had sounded when she was being fingered between her legs.

'Yes, Madam,' Belinda's voice was clear and brave this time, but she gulped as the squeezing fingers strayed ever so slightly towards her cleft.

Sweet Jesus, what's she doing? thought Louise, battling to control her breathing and the turmoil in her aching crotch. Oh Lord, she's almost diddling her!

Madam Woo spun away then, her bright eyes catching Louise's challengingly for a second, then shuttering immediately. There were two small spots of colour high on her elegant cheek-bones, and Louise could have sworn there was moisture on her upper lip. 'Untruss her,' she commanded to Flossie, and with a smile of pure salacious glee the maid slowly and quite theatrically obeyed.

Taking a precise hold on Belinda's knicker elastic, Flossie tweeked the garment downwards inch by inch ... and Louise thought she was going to faint, have an orgasm or wet herself – possibly all three at once – as twin perfect mounds of young feminine bottom-flesh were at first partially and teasingly, and then fully and blatantly exposed to her. The pretty lace-trimmed bloomers finished up around Belinda's quaking knees, and then, as if to shame her right to the core, Flossie deliberately nudged the prone girl's legs as wide apart as they would go within the bounds of the containing elastic.

Belinda sobbed loudly, before a single blow had even been struck.

And Louise sobbed too, in humiliated bliss, as her cunny fluttered and betrayed her. The feeling was so forbidden and sweet that she had to clutch herself, and Madam Woo whirled around like a dancer and caught her in the very act of doing so.

'And *that*,' the governess said quietly, looking at Louise's crumpled skirts and the fingers that just couldn't keep from squeezing, 'that will make things all the worse for you, my girl.' Her voice was chilled velvet as she returned her attention to Belinda, but her dark eyes still gleamed with that odd, feverish light.

Louise was having trouble standing up, but with a supreme effort of will, she locked her knees and managed to stay aloft. She'd never had a come in the vertical position before; except perhaps with that crazy girl at Mrs Fortescue's party, but that didn't really count because her hips had bucked so hard when that clever little miss had sucked her that they'd both fallen over in a panting heap. All the other times she'd been fairly safely positioned: either draped across the partner's body somehow, or snuggled up in bed with her hand up her night-dress.

By the time she'd regained control of her wavering legs, other matters were already at crisis point. Flossie was leaning bodily over Belinda's stretched form, and Madam Woo had taken a thick, bifurcated leather strap from her cupboard and was hefting it experimentally.

Louise had been blushing but she felt the blood drop from her face and disappear to God alone knew where.

Oh no, oh no, she was going to tawse the poor thing!

'Now, Belinda my sweet,' Madam murmured, her voice soft as a lover's, 'I'm going to beat your naked bottom with this strap.' She laid the strip of leather almost reverently across the bare white mounds and Louise saw the pale flesh quiver.

Louise's own flesh quivered too, her sticky little quim jumping as the stern dark-clad woman placed her hand beside the thick leather band and caressed – there was no other word for it – the very skin she was about to wound. Belinda jiggled in Flossie's hold, her thighs moving lewdly and opening even wider. Louise bit her lip, but couldn't look away.

She could see it. See everything. The swollen wet folds of the struggling girl's cunt.

She could see her holes, her lips, the soft curly hair. She could see her pulsating. Moisture glistening on the redness . . . It was as if she were waiting for a lover to take her, to stroke her and touch her; not for a thick slab of leather to beat her white bum into flame!

'Be still, you lewd girl,' commanded Madam Woo softly. Louise nearly came again as Madam touched her charge's moist place and her fingers lingered for a full half second. Belinda's bottom rose yearningly as her tormentor's hand withdrew.

'Prepare yourself.' Madam Woo stepped back, narrowed her fine eyes, sighting her target, then in a movement of supple lightning grace sent the leather arcing through the air to connect – loudly – with Belinda's proffered bottom. Belinda made a mewling noise – just as loud – and threw herself wildly forward in Flossie's unremitting hold.

Louise felt sick, aroused and mesmerised. That sweet, snowy bum seemed to resonate visibly under the cruel impact and within seconds grow redder and redder. But there was hardly time to keep track of the changes as more blows were already falling with steady, almost metronomic precision.

The 'crack! crack! crack!' of the tawse seemed to burn itself into Louise's brain, as did the sight of the jouncing, palpitating buttocks growing brighter and brighter and fierier and fierier . . .

Belinda was not a stoic sufferer. Whimpering and blubbering, she waved her legs wildly and waggled her bottom outrageously under the blows. 'Belinda, behave! Or you'll get more!' only seemed to make her struggle harder. And in the few seconds of respite, while Madam Woo flexed her wrist, Louise could clearly see a thick gelid liquid oozing between the punished girl's thighs. What's more, and she could hardly believe what she was seeing, Flossie seemed to have let her charge shuffle up and balance her crotch right on the edge desk, and Belinda was unashamedly working the front of her body on that very same edge!

When the next blow fell – with eye-watering ferocity – Belinda gave a huge gobbling cry, her legs flailed, and the whole of her abused body seemed to leap and convulse.

'You wicked, wicked girl!' cried Madam Woo, her voice

sounding choked, excited. 'I've warned you about this.' Louise watched her, fascinated, as her hand strayed to the front of her long black skirt and she seemed about to caress *herself* too! 'Now I shall have to cane you as well! Flossie, kindly get the straps.'

The maid let go, but Belinda remained stretched across the desk, her lower body moving gently and her cunny still wide open and dripping heavily.

She's had a climax! thought Louise numbly. Belinda had come because Madam Woo had beaten her ... What kind of girl would do that? Suddenly though, she didn't care what kind of girl Belinda was; she only wanted to touch that cherry-red bottom. Smack it a little, perhaps? Then put her fingers into that perfectly exposed slit and bring its owner to another groaning shaking orgasm.

It took every last scrap of her self-control not to rush to Belinda and frig her, regardless of the baleful presence of Madam Woo, who Louise now realised was watching *her* just as closely as she was her victim.

'Take heed, Louise,' she said coolly as she went to her cupboard again, opened it and perused contents Louise couldn't see from where she stood. 'Belinda is an unusual and rather dirty little girl. I think you'll find that when I punish you, you won't find it quite so arousing. It will hurt, Louise!' She drew out a thinnish cane, and swished it assessingly. 'You won't gain a perverted pleasure from it as Belinda does. It will just cause you extreme pain and make you cry. Do you understand me?'

Louise nodded, wondering furiously why just the idea of that pain was having the same weird effect on her that it obviously had on Belinda. Her cunny was all twitchy again, and felt disgustingly gooey inside her already christened drawers. The cane swished again and she had a sudden quite weakening yearning to feel it flash across *her* naked bottom instead of Belinda's.

By now, Flossie had pulled off Belinda's bloomers completely and was strapping the girl's ankles to the legs of the desk. The poor creature was perfectly positioned now: for heavy punishment, for examination ... or something even more wicked! Louise stared at the delicate little rose-brown bud of Belinda's bottom hole and she longed from the pit of her soul to be able to guide her finger into it. Belinda would resist of course, but oh how she'd wriggle and sigh when the naughty, skewering digit went to work.

'This time I'm really going to hurt you, Belinda,' Madam Woo said quietly, leaning over the secured girl and stroking her tangled hair. 'It will hurt a lot and it won't give you pleasure. You mustn't scream, but I think we can make that a little easier for you ...' She reached behind her, waggling her fingers, and with no word of instruction, Flossie handed her Belinda's discarded bloomers. These the mistress wadded into a ball then pressed – partially – into their former wearer's mouth. White cotton and lace trailed obscenely from Belinda's widely stretched lips, and Louise wondered deliriously if the mortified girl could taste her own taste on the gusset ...

As Flossie resumed her hold on Belinda, Madam Woo spun away and took her position. There was something almost exultant in her stance, and Louise felt both thrilled and horrified. That dark, menacing beauty was as arousing as the sight of Belinda's reddened and peach-like bum – it was a different feeling but in its own way at least as strong ...

God, how she loves this! Louise thought in wonder, watching the pain-goddess closely as the cane went whistling through the air. And when the wicked thing struck and Belinda bucked in silent agony, an almost beatific smile crossed Madam Woo's ice-pale countenance.

White lines became vicious red as Belinda's bottom took a sustained, unremitting going-over with the cane. The tethered girl kicked, and squealed into the gag, and as her own head filled with the muffled sounds of anguish, Louise boggled at the insane and ludicrous images that joined them.

The wounded bottom before her became Madam Woo's: enticingly naked, fizzing red and framed in both the voluminous folds of her elegant black skirt and the exquisite ruffles of the most luxurious of pure silk panta-

loons. Louise saw – and felt – the stick in her hand . . .
Then saw herself massaging those lush, maltreated buttocks, her fingers exploring their heat, their softness and
their pain.

When Belinda's arse was reduced to a mass of weals,
Madam Woo paused in her endeavours and moved from
her arm's length position to an intimate closeness to her
victim. Her pale fingers moved lightly over the crimson
mounds, as if assessing the precision of her own cruelty.

'How beautifully you mark,' she murmured to the sobbing girl. The caress brought a renewed spate of writhing,
as if the intimacy, the fastidious thoroughness of the touching, was at least as distressing as the beating that had
preceded it. The faster Belinda wriggled, though, the
slower and more lingering the stroking of the fingers
became. As they slid dangerously near to the exposed
privates, Louise saw Madam Woo breathe deeply as if
trying to contain some great emotion, some overpowering
need.

'Flossie, kindly unstrap her,' the governess ordered
softly, seeming to gather herself. Stepping away from her
spectacular handiwork, she turned, 'Louise . . . Please go
to your room and wait there until lunch-time. And don't
look so relieved.' Her eyes narrowed. 'I'll be dealing with
you later. Right now, Belinda must confess her sins and
be forgiven. And after that I shall take a short rest. Did
you hear what I said, Louise? You seem to be dreaming
again.'

'Yes, Madam.' Louise made her way disconsolately to
the door. It was incredible really, but if she didn't know
better, she'd have almost believed she was disappointed
at not being punished immediately. In front of Belinda
and Flossie . . .

As she paused at the door, her heart seemed to clog
her throat. Madam Woo was cuddling Belinda in her arms
and talking to the girl in exquisitely gentle tones. Belinda
was still sobbing and hiccuping, but the glow in her eyes,
and the penitential smile on her curiously marked face
made Louise long to take her place. To endure the same

pain and humiliation – to take much more and for far longer – just to enjoy such perfect tenderness.

The last thing Louise saw as the door swung to was Belinda closing her eyes in agony and bliss as Madam Woo's long white fingers returned to their work on her bottom . . .

Waiting in her room was appalling. Why did she feel so let down? Why had the sights in the schoolroom aroused her to such a hair-trigger state of excitement?

She kept seeing Belinda's jiggling bottom again, and as she did so the urge to touch herself was astoundingly powerful. She had a vision of diddling herself . . . Then of standing behind Belinda's sublimely punished arse and rubbing her own body against it. She wanted to open her cunny and press it to that puffed red flesh. She wanted to work herself up on those plump sizzling buttocks and feel the heat of them on the sensitive membranes of her sex.

She was only next door . . .

Louise knew her urges were absurd and highly punishable – they were the reason she was here in the first place – but almost before she realised what she was doing, she was out in the corridor and turning Belinda's door handle.

The girl lay face down upon her bed, sobbing quietly into her pillow as her uncovered bottom seemed to pulse and beat with an independent life of its own. The delicate downy flesh was a brilliant, uniform scarlet, laced with a network of fiercer weals where the cane had added its agonising insult to the tawse's existing injury.

Louise had never seen a more thrilling sight in her life. The injuries themselves affected her in a way she barely understood; her own behind was twitching like fury as if it longed for the bite of the very same rod.

And what lay around the wounds, and beneath, had a charm and sweetness too. The pretty turned back petticoats; Belinda's really rather shapely legs; her dainty feet in their short white socks. The puffed up beauty of her luscious pouting cunny.

'Who's there?' the sufferer called out, her voice still quavery.

'It's me. Louise.'

Belinda shuffled on the bed, moving awkwardly in her pain. Louise noticed that the girl was holding a tiny lace handkerchief to her tearful face with one hand and that the other was lost in the folds of her clothing somewhere. She took a step forward, and saw Belinda's thighs quiver and part a little more. The bared cunt gaped invitingly.

'I'm sorry,' Louise muttered, choked by this display of everything that stirred her most. 'I'd better go.'

'No! Don't go!' Belinda scrubbed at her eyes with her scrap of a hankie, then pushed it away across the pillow. When she turned, wincing as she struggled to look over her shoulder, Louise was astonished to see she was smiling. Winsomely. 'Please stay, Louise. You can soothe me, if you like.'

'What do you mean "soothe"?' Louise stammered, drawn irresistibly to the prostrate form on the bed, to the apple-red buttocks and the wet, glistening quim. Madam Woo dressed her charges in the short socks and petticoats of little girls, but the pungent odour emanating from that open furrow told Louise that Belinda was unequivocally a grown and eroticised woman. The hussy was lying there with her cunt hanging out because she'd *known* Louise would come to her. And it was obvious now where that hidden hand was.

When Belinda arched her back and raised her abused behind, her dainty middle finger could clearly be seen . . . beating hard on her swollen clitoris.

'My bum's so hot, Louise,' the masturbatrix purred, her voice wheedling and sultry. 'Please cool it for me . . . It's burning up. Please help me.'

'What shall I do?' It came out as a pathetic trembling croak. 'Shall I get a flannel or something?'

'Oh no, Louise . . . A flannel is all nasty and rough. It'll hurt my bottom even more.' The flesh in question waggled, the undulation utterly lewd and the desperate frigging beneath it even more so. 'You must be ever so, ever so

192

gentle, Louise. You'll have to kiss my bottom to make it better . . . You'll have to lick it.'

'I . . . I . . .'

'Don't you want to kiss my bum, Louise? I thought you *wanted* to make me feel better . . .' The flaming cheeks clenched invitingly, and as Belinda hissed with the obvious pain, her arsehole winked obscenely.

Not stopping to think or analyse exactly what she was doing, Louise climbed onto the bed, knelt between Belinda's outspread legs and lowered her mouth to the temptingly offered bottom. The girl winced and cried out as lips made contact with her cane-seared flesh and Louise pulled back, shaking violently.

'No! Please! Don't stop! I like it!' Belinda shouted, rearing herself up higher. Louise obeyed her, as implicitly as she would have Madam Woo herself, her loins itching and aching, and enthralled that something so bad, so forbidden and so painful should be so good for both kisser and kissed.

Belinda's skin was hotter than Louise would have believed possible; heat rose up in a wave as blood surged furiously through mistreated tissues. Louise could feel ridges where the cane had bedded in. Her own sex pulsed as she laved her tongue across the sweetly savaged bottom beneath her.

Belinda moved voluptuously under the treatment, cooing in her throat as Louise licked eagerly. The tongue-strokes were light, but they must be hurting. Nevertheless, Belinda gave off all the signs of being in seventh heaven. Her fingers were working furiously somewhere just beneath Louise's chin, and the musky juices of her seeping fanny would have made an ascetic yearn . . . Louise was no ascetic, as her presence at Madam Woo's attested, and the smell of Belinda's sexy flow was driving her out of her mind.

'Oh, Louise, that's lovely,' Belinda cried out happily, lifting her hungry, bitchy little body as Louise's tongue dipped into the crack. 'Please . . . Please! Oh, Louise, Louise, do it! Do it! Do it!' Reaching around she cupped

193

one mound of her own sorry flesh, and though she yelped loudly, she worked her bottom-cheek mercilessly in time to Louise's snuffling attentions. And trapped beneath her body, her fingers were rubbing and rubbing and rubbing . . .

Louise pressed her own crotch to the mattress, working herself furiously against it in a bizarre emulation of sex. Making love to the bed beneath her felt as good in a way as the real thing. She was licking like a little doggie at the sweetest of womanflesh . . . but in her mind, *she* too was being licked and rubbed.

'I'd stop that immediately if I were you.'

Louise heard each perfectly articulated word quite distinctly, yet the whole sentence made no sense to her at all.

'Louise, get up. You're in quite enough trouble already as it is, but if you don't get up this instant, my girl, you'll certainly regret it.'

Louise struggled to sit up and achieve some dignity, a task that was more or less impossible with Belinda trying to do the same underneath her.

Madam Woo had changed her clothes – and when Louise finally dared to look at her, she knew she'd never seen a figure more grimly beautiful than their slender, forbidding governess.

A prim, high-necked silk dress in deepest black was moulded to her trim figure in a way that was diametrically at odds with its nominal severity. A narrow encrustation of white lace at wrist and throat seemed so unexpectedly sensual that it made Louise's heart ache. Not to mention certain less chaste of her organs . . .

'Belinda. Stand in the corner with your hands on your head – facing the wall – and wait. Let your dress drop, if you will. Exposing your bottom obviously gives you far more pleasure than it ought to.'

With this, Madam Woo snared the dithering Belinda by one soft ringlet and marched her over to the wall. 'I'll be spanking you again in a few moments, young lady, and believe me, this time you won't like it one bit.'

A knock rang out in the charged atmosphere.

'Enter,' said Madam Woo softly.

Flossie had a new frock too, and her crisp satiny 'best' uniform was even more becoming than her plain one, mainly due to its extreme thinness and the clinging nature of the fabric. The black dress was superficially as neat as a pin, but on a closer look, Louise noticed a vague dishevelledness. Flossie had clearly been recently involved in some sort of hectic activity. Hectic and highly pleasurable. Her naughty eyes were sparking like jewels, and there was a bright rosy flush in her bonny cheeks.

Come to think of it, Madam Woo had more colour than usual too. Just a hazy touch of pink but it was there. A crystal image formed ... and Louise welcomed total insanity.

Maid and mistress. Lushness and finesse. Mischief and discipline. The combinations formed deliciously in Louise's befuddled brain ...

Madame Woo's a lezzie too, she thought wildly. That's why she likes touching Belinda up. She's a dyke and she has it off with Flossie when the thrashing gets her all excited.

'Now, Miss Sutherland,' Madam Woo fixed Louise with a lovely but basilisk glare. 'As it's clearly unwise to keep you two salacious young women together, I want you to go and stand outside my sitting room, and wait there until I've finished dealing with Miss Gascoigne. Flossie, go with Louise and make the usual preparations. Do you have your pins with you?'

'Yes, Madam,' Flossie answered glibly, her pretty face alight with glee.

Damn that fat bitch! She loves all this! thought Louise, feeling utterly powerless. She didn't know whether to loathe Flossie ... or adore her as much as Madam. She was a merciless tease, yet there was something so earthy and so unavoidably sexy about her that it was impossible not to desire her. Rashly, Louise glanced at that thin but sober frock and saw the nipples beneath standing out like church-organ stops. Oh no no no ... Of course, she didn't loathe Flossie. The girl was vulgar and quite wicked but those scrumptious breasts made up for everything. Oh God, those delectable titties! Will I see them again? Louise wondered blearily, beginning the endless march to the door.

'Louise,' Madam Woo said sharply just as she got there. 'While you're waiting, I'd like you to consider the bad habits you so monotonously display. The acts and thoughts that keep you from being the wholesome young woman you should be. Will you do that for me, Louise?' Her tone softened slightly as Louise turned and nodded.

'Yes, Mrs Woolstencraft,' she said, her voice respectfully low.

Oh yes, yes, yes, Madam Woo! she screamed in her sex-crazy mind. I'll think about them all right . . . But, oh God, it would be so much easier if I could *stop* thinking about them.

And then the door was closed and Flossie was frog-marching her down the corridor.

'Come along, Miss Louise,' she said, her voice rich with amusement.

Madam Woo's sitting room was on the same landing but around the corner, and as they reached its door, a faint 'clapping' sound, followed by a thin squeal of anguish, came floating from the bedroom behind them.

'She's best with her hands,' Flossie said lightly as the sounds rang out again – then repeated and repeated with painful regularity.

'How do you know?'

'Now, now, Miss Louise, you know better than to ask naughty questions,' Flossie came back pertly as she manhandled Louise up against the wall.

'Does she smack *you*?' Louise persisted, then tried to struggle away as she felt hands burrowing in her skirts. 'Hey, get off!'

'Louise! Behave yourself.'

Suddenly Flossie's teasing tone was strangely absent, and in its place was the same steely softness that Madam Woo used to such chilling effect. Louise felt a great, sensual shiver rise up from her toes and gather in the cradle of her loins. Her hands lost strength and purpose, and dropped to hang loosely at her sides.

'That's better,' murmured Flossie, scything through petticoats with practiced ease. How many other girls had she humbled like this? Made ready for her dark-eyed mistress? 'And yes, she has,' she finished, her voice changing yet again – to soft breathlessness.

'What?' Louise was shattered. Both by the answer and by the fact that Flossie had hold of her bloomers and was pulling them down. Down, down and further down till they were bunched ignominiously around her ankles.

'She smacks my bottom. That's what you wanted to hear, wasn't it?' Flossie grinned and pressed her hand to the heat of Louise's bare thigh.

'I . . . er . . . I don't know. I thought you were her . . . her accomplice.' It was impossible to choose words accurately when Flossie was squeezing and pinching and getting closer and closer.

'Accomplice? That's an odd thing to call me,' she observed, her fingers brushing soft hair now.

'But you're her maid, aren't you?' Louise choked. With a couple of quick jerks, her thighs were roughly parted.

'Well, this *is* a maid's frock, Louise . . .'

Breath was hot on her thighs now and for one glorious moment, Louise thought Flossie would plunge right in and lick her. Make her all wet and creamy so Madam Woo would be more displeased than ever.

Suck me! Suck me! she wailed inside, caring not one jot that Flossie was evading her questions. All she wanted now was the feel of that soft red mouth.

Flossie's tongue-tip appeared tantalisingly between her pretty encarmined lips, but alas went no further. Gracefully, she rose to her feet and looked Louise in the eye instead of the fanny.

'Yes, Louise, she smacks me.' Perversely, she'd returned to the earlier question. 'She puts me over her lap, takes down my knickers, then spanks my bottom with her bare white hand . . .' Her voice regained its dreamy quality, and

197

in that softness was a fine, beautiful modulation that bore no resemblance at all to her usual saucy 'salt of the earth domestic' speech. 'She tans me until I'm in burning agony. Sets fire to every square inch of my cheeks. Just the way she's doing to Belinda now.'

As if on cue, a harsh wail pierced the private space between them, followed by an extended fusillade of echoing slaps and the sound of uncontrollable and piteous weeping.

'She'll touch her now,' said Flossie, her hands returning suddenly to their former haunts. 'She can't resist it. From the pit of hell to the vault of heaven ... and all done with the same beautiful fingers.'

'Does she touch you?' Louise's voice cracked as another set of beautiful fingers caressed her aching slit. Fingers that were soft and well-kept. Fingers that, if they *were* a maid's, certainly never blackleaded a grate or scrubbed a floor.

'Oh yes, Louise, yes!'

Flossie's bright eyes were unfocused now, as if she weren't in this corridor with her hand up another girl's dress, but was stretched and displayed across her mistress's lap, her bottom quaking in readiness. There were no squeals now, just silky full-throated sobs of an dramatically different character.

Flossie's tongue appeared again, and skimmed her parted lips. 'Oh yes, Louise, she touches me. And much better than a man, I can tell you.' One finger bored deeper for emphasis and Lousie groaned. The effort not to shout and writhe and come was almost tearing her apart.

'Have you seen those hands, Louise?' Flossie demanded passionately, her own hands a gorgeous torment. 'So long, so elegant ... Fingers so soft and yet so powerful. She just has to touch my clitty once and I come.' She swallowed and her eyelids fluttered as if word had been deed. 'But once is never enough for her ... She won't ever stop until she breaks your soul into pieces.'

'Oh! Oh God!' To Louise's rapture it was happening to her too. Heavy spasms wrenched her clitoris, her groove, her vagina. She closed her eyes as pleasure pulsed thickly through the whole of her loins and she surrendered completely to the moment. She was vaguely aware of small movements against her twitching flesh; and then, as before, her only remaining consciousness was needed to keep her upright.

After a long blissful stupor, normal thought returned and she looked down to see a swathe of snowy white cotton being drawn from between her legs.

Dear Lord, she's quick, Louise thought admiringly. Almost before the orgasm was over, Flossie had whipped out her hankie and was wiping her victim clean.

'Mustn't make a mess, must we, Louise?' Flossie's sauciness was back in full flower. 'Madam Woo wouldn't like to find a girl who's all naughty and sticky waiting for her, would she?' Deftly, she wiped and mopped; inflicting an almost heartbreaking pleasure as she did so. 'That's much, much better, isn't it?' She pressed lightly. 'She'd have been so cross if she'd arrived and found you all juicy and puffy. Remember what she said about lewdness of thought and deed?'

Louise nodded, her shame doubling and trebling as her skirts were pinned up both fore and aft and she was left standing with her pale body completely exposed from the waist down.

'There, my sweet, all pinned up and ready.' Flossie grinned at her handiwork, then proceeded to drop to the floor and sit down against the opposite wall, her legs crossed like a fakir. Her rustling black skirt fanned about her, but with no warning at all, she plucked at its hem and hauled the whole affair up to her waist.

And now two naked sexes were exposed.

Despite her lyrical descriptions of how Madam Woo was wont to pull them down, Flossie wasn't wearing any bloomers. Her black skirt and stockings, her pale skinned belly and thighs, and her vivid scarlet motte made a fabulously sensual tableau.

Life surged back into Louise's temporarily quiescent membranes – while her eyes embraced the beautiful display before her. She could see the thick glossy luxuriance of Flossie's bush, the soft, fine curliness of the hair. 'Flossie' by name and flossie by nature, she thought, feeling giddy. Her flesh twittered in tribute as the maid unbuttoned the front of her prim dress and exposed her bosom too. Again, she was completely naked beneath the plain black bodice.

'You like these, don't you?' Flossie cupped a breast in each hand, pushed inwards, and lifted, creating a most extraordinary and toothsome cleavage. She'd done this last night, the wicked tease, and as before, Louise longed for the chance to suck them.

But last night, she'd only seen breasts . . .

'Hands on head,' Flossie rapped out, as Louise's fingers flexed and fluttered. 'Madam Woo expressively forbids her young ladies to diddle themselves.' Her smile widened archly. 'Funny thing though . . . She's never said anything about her maids.'

Long, immaculate and entirely unservantlike fingers were suddenly wedged between Flossie's plump thighs; with one hand she held open her hair-covered labia, while the other sought the nexus of her pleasure. Her big breasts hung like fruits, ripe and pale against the dark folds of her bodice. Her fingers rummaged busily between her slowly shifting thighs.

'But . . . But what if she finds you?' Louise stuttered, her own crotch screaming for such expert attention.

'She'll be a while yet,' gasped Flossie, her hips lifting spasmodically, her boot heels dragging on the parquet. 'She won't be finished with young Belinda for ages . . . Oh! Oh, God!' Her pretty face contorted, pagan and masklike, as a long sigh of pleasure hissed between her drawn-back lips.

Two fingers were moving like a piston in her slit, as the middle finger of her other hand worked hard and long on her clitty. Louise was half in ecstasy, half in agony just watching. Not to mention wholly in need of another orgasm herself.

She could hardly believe the sights she'd seen today.

200

First Belinda diddling, now Flossie. And if what Flossie had told her was true, Madam Woo had been at it too.

And that would really be something to see.

As if on cue, a creaking door around the corner at the other end of the corridor, announced that Flossie's predictions were incorrect. Madam Woo had finished with Belinda. Either that or Louise had been watching Flossie's spectacular little sex show for far longer than she realised.

The next performance was equally miraculous too – albeit in a somewhat different way. Rising to her feet with a swift, sudden grace, Flossie let her dress fall over her streaming fanny, while her fingers were already at her front and buttoning fast. The strides along the corridor were brisk, but it was easy to see Flossie would be fully decent with plenty of time to spare. When Madam Woo turned the corner, her maid was demure as a nun and calmly smoothing down her frilly apron. Only her pink-ened cheeks suggested she'd been up to mischief in her mistress's absence.

Madam Woo's narrow-eyed stare, however, suggested that *she* was aware of both the mischief and its erotic character. Her dark gaze flicked first to Flossie's blushes and then to Louise and her spontaneously weaving hips.

'I see those bad habits have got the better of you again, Louise.' Her voice sounded pained, but knowing what she did now, Louise suspected it was an act. Madam Woo actually wanted her charges to be sexually excited. And in this instance, she wanted her, Louise, to think and act in the lewdest possible manner. So there was an excuse to punish her. To touch her body . . . To hurt and shame and arouse her, and in doing so, bring pleasure to the arouser. The punisher.

This act of punishing was Madam Woo's sexual foreplay, Louise realised, and in spite of the impending pain – maybe even *because* of it – she could hardly wait for it to begin. With all the braggadocio she could muster, she flaunted her hips forward; glad that her juices were gleam-ing on her upper thighs again and intoxicated by her own smell and its heaviness in the still air of the corridor.

Insolently she raised her eyes to meet Madam Woo's intent ones. But not before she'd caught Flossie's admiring, approving wink.

'That will be all, Flossie,' the mistress said somewhat coolly. 'You may attend Belinda now, she's in some distress and her bottom needs bathing.'

'Yes, Madam,' Flossie said meekly, and just as she was turning to go, Madam Woo's hand shot out with a lethal cobra-like swiftness and grabbed the maids' thin skirt. With a flick of the wrist, she whipped it up and bared one cheek of Flossie's opulent bottom. Her other hand swung out in a wide arc and fetched a ringing slap on the naked white flesh.

The chubby round marked immediately, and Madam Woo ran her fingers over her own perfect rose-pink handprint before passing them slowly into Flossie's accommodating crack.

A long shudder ripped through the maid's body and Louise felt her own slit twitch sympathetically. Her quim seemed to love the way Flossie tilted her hips and opened her thighs – the action a rude invitation to her tormentress. Explore me, it said. Abuse me. Outrage me. Madam Woo went in with a vengeance and Flossie cooed softly with pleasure.

'I thought so,' the mistress finally murmured, holding up the glistening evidence to her own nose, and then to Flossie's. 'And in future, Floss, remember to straighten your cap, as well as your frock, after you've been abusing yourself.' She let the black skirt fall and right itself, then with her own hands adjusted Flossie's starched white bonnet which had slipped ever so slighly askew. 'I'll deal with this matter – ' to Louise's shocked delight, she grabbed Flossie's crotch again, through the thin shiny cloth, and squeezed her crudely, 'later. Now go and see to Belinda, and make sure there isn't anything else I have to punish you for.'

'Yes, Madam.' Flossie was even pinker now, her face as flushed as the buttock that had been punished, but she seemed to skip like a lamb with joy as she made off down the corridor in pursuit of her tasks.

'Flossie is an excellent maid,' observed Madam Woo dryly, returning her attention to Louise and the 'problems' exposed by her pinned up dress, 'but she's also a greedy, carnal girl, and easily distracted from her duties.' As she spoke she moved up close; so close in fact that her gown brushed Louise's groin, the satin a butterfly caress as she stared accusingly into her charge's eyes, 'And on this occasion, Louise, it seems that you're the one guilty of distracting her, doesn't it?'

'Yes, Madam,' Louise murmured, her voice small but her anticipation large and thrilling.

Madam Woo reached past her, sliding heavy silk skirts across her bare thighs and belly in a manouevre Louise could only interpret as deliberate, then opened the door to the sitting room. 'In you go,' the governess said crisply, seemingly indifferent to the bizarrely displayed body beside her and Louise's struggles with the bloomers that hobbled her by the ankles.

It was a pretty room, very feminine, and filled with a lot of pleasant but rather fussy furniture arranged in conventional groups. There was a *chaise longue*, an otto-man, a pouffe, and an incongruously bulky oaken cup-board squatting ominously in the furthest corner.

Simple items, but each now assumed it own element of menace. Any one of them, apart from the cupboard, could well be the platform for some abject humbling. Even the cupboard . . . She had a sudden vision of herself suspended naked across the front of it, her behind scored with the fierce red marks of a beating as she ground her aching fanny slowly against the gleaming nut-brown wood.

'Stand there.' Madam Woo indicated a spot a foot or so from the chaise, and as Louise obediently took her place, the governess sat down gracefully in front of her. Louise could look down now, seeing the top of that perfectly groomed head, and yet she was still at a mighty disadvantage. For a slightly built women of moderate height, Madam Woo had a marvellous ability to 'loom' –

and she could even do it sitting down. Atavistic terror made Louise's thighs shiver, and without thinking, she pressed her hand to her crotch.

'Oh Louise, Louise . . . You don't have much control, do you?' Soft fingers brushed Louise's knuckles, and she let out an involuntary moan.

'You must learn, Louise.' The fingers moved slowly, tantalisingly. 'This, Louise . . . This part of you is wayward and selfish. You must learn to master your urges, not gratify them like a greedy child. And you'll be punished until you can control yourself. Punished severely. Do you understand me, Louise?'

The slight pressure increased, taunting so delicately that Louise broke down and sobbed. Never in her young life had need been so strong, so urgent. She wanted something, anything to assuage it. She imagined lurching forward, opening her legs wide, and smashing her heated membranes against the silk of that pristine black gown. Splitting her aching sex over that slender thigh, and rubbing and rubbing and rubbing till an orgasm released her at last. In an effort at control, she opened her tightly shut eyes and studied the sheeny dark stuff that covered Madam's long, graceful, yet always hidden legs. There was some kind of design to the cloth, she noticed, a brocade effect, birds or something, and even though it was the same coal black as Flossie's flimsy gown, the mistress's was infinitely more luxurious.

And beneath? Did Madam Woo wear drawers? Or was she naked beneath her austerity? Lush and sexy, with all her severity just a piquant facade.

Stop it, Louise, she ordered herself, feeling sanity flee her. There were hands at her crotch, Madam Woo's and her own, but it was another sweet quim she imagined. For the hundredth time since she'd arrived here, she filled her mind with a succulent vision. Her governess's naked womanhood, bare and ready for whatever stimulation that lady chose to award it. Her own hand? Flossie's? The maid's soft, pink mouth? In an instant, Louise saw them on the bed: Madam with her legs gaping open, her servant bending forward to kiss the place between them.

'Louise? Are you listening to me?'

Snapping back to reality, Louise felt herself suspended between a pair of irresistable poles – Madam Woo's perfect dove-white hands. One settled lightly on her cheek, the other remained at her sex. Louise felt her own fingers being nudged aside and one long, coolish digit wiggling its way through the hair to the heat within. As it reached its target, her swollen, slippery clitty, her face was gently tilted so her eyes might meet Madam Woo's. Reluctant yet yearning, she met those eyes. And found them dark but bright, the pupils hugely dilated.

Unable to speak, Louise nodded; as stirred by the touch at her blushing cheeks as she was by the caressing of her clit.

'Good,' Madam Woo said quietly, her voice calm though her eyes were manic. She seemed almost unaware of what she was doing between her charge's quaking thighs. 'Are you ready to be punished now, Louise?'

'Yes,' Louise croaked, her quim throbbing precariously. 'Oh yes! Yes, please!'

'Very well, then.' Madam was utterly decisive, her hands withdrew. 'Go to the cupboard and bring me the apron you'll find hanging inside.' She nodded to the large oaken cabinet. 'Well, what are you waiting for?' she said tartly in the face of Louise's hesitation.

Even walking was hellish now. Louise waddled across the room, her sex all puffed and bloated, her labia swollen with what seemed like a ton of blood. Each brush of her thighs was torture, even the movement of air between them a discreet stimulation. She expected to come any second, to spontaneously disgrace herself by groaning aloud. As she opened the cupboard door, she wondered just exactly *how* she was going to be beaten.

Reaching for the apron – a heavy rubber monstrosity – her blood froze at the sight in the cupboard before her; an array of fearsome instruments that hung on a custom-made rack.

Canes, long and short, slender and chunky, smooth and knobbly. Belts, straps and tawses; some thin, some massively thick and brutal. Whips various, and paddles. Not to mention a merciless selection of restraints to hold a miscreant in place while she suffered.

'Just bring the apron, Louise. We'll begin with a spanking.'

Almost faint with relief, Louise obeyed. Madam Woo smiled as she took the apron and tied it neatly around her sylphine waist, but there was a mocking light in her eyes. Taking a moment or two, she settled herself squarely on the chaise, then parted her rubber-covered thighs and placed her heels flat on the carpet.

'Come on now, Louise. It's time. Across my lap, if you please,' she said pleasantly, flexing her fingers as she spoke. Louise felt cold terror curl in her gut . . .

What had Flossie said? 'She's best with her hands'. What did 'best' mean? More effective or less? Just how much pain could that slender hand inflict?

'Louise!'

With an ignominious lack of grace, Louise laid herself across the rubber. As she settled in place a great lump formed in her throat and even though she hadn't been touched yet, her eyes filled with tears and her throat tightened with a great roiling of emotion. Sobs shook her body and she sank into a deep sweet well of surrender. A hand settled lightly on the small of her back just beneath her pinned up skirts, and another rested first on her bottom, then moved between her thighs to edge them further apart. Fingers danced delicately into the crack, first feathering her anus, then rising to touch her bottom cheeks, pressing firmly and prodding, as if testing the resilience of the target flesh.

'Please,' Louise whimpered, not really knowing what it was she was pleading for. She scrubbed at her streaming eyes with one hand as the other hung loosely against rubber and patterned silk.

'Don't cry, my sweet little Louise,' Madam Woo cooed in her ear. The governess was leaning over now, her satin-covered breasts almost brushing Louise's back. Her hands continued to explore and touch, appraising the flesh that she'd soon be marking and hurting. The search transmitted itself exquisitely to Louise's naked sex, and she squirmed in a vain attempt to rub against the rubber beneath her.

'There, there, Louise. Be a brave girl for me, won't you? A brave, clean girl. I'm going to hurt you in a minute. A lot. But if you're a good girl, if you're strong and quiet and pure, I'll be very pleased with you. Do you understand?'

'Yes, Madam,' Louise blubbed, the gentle words and the fingers palpating her bottom making it harder and harder for her to control herself.

'Ready now, Louise. I want you to count out each smack as it falls.'

The hand ceased its fondling and in her mind's eye Louise saw it arise like Nemesis and pause.

She's taking aim, Louise thought wildly, her body knotting with tension. The muscles of her arse went rigid with anticipation . . . then suddenly the first blow fell.

'Agh!' Louise's body arched under the impact, and her brain went white and blank. The pain was stunning. Breath-taking. Terrible. She'd been expecting something manageable. Sharp, but titillating. Almost pleasant . . . Instead the right cheek of her arse was a solid slab of fire, the pain so huge she couldn't even remember its beginning. Fresh tears flooded her eyes.

'One,' the wounder prompted lightly, her body subtly shifting as her hand went up for another blow.

'One,' Louise mouthed, all volume torn away by shock.

Slap! Her left cheek dissolved into flame and she moaned out a broken 'Two . . .'

Slap!

Slap!

Slap!

The blows went on and on and somehow Louise managed to count. Count with a mind consumed by the same infernal fire that scorched her buttocks. She was numb to all other thought as the slaps fell without pause and her bottom seemed about to burst its skin and disintegrate in formless agony. She was distantly aware that Madam Woo was talking to her in soft, encouraging tones, and that the exertion of the spanking had warmed that black-clad body and was sending spirals of perfume wafting through the raging red halls of her victim's torment.

The numbers intoned solemnly in Louise's head, but astounded her by coming out as pig-like squeals. Her behind seemed to have melted under the inexorable blows, and in a moment of strange pin-sharp euphoria, she rose up out of her quivering carcass and looked down upon the scene. Her own bottom pulsed below her as a swollen, shapeless pulp... A slender white hand descended and descended and descended... and the wretched body beneath it bounced and writhed as if palsied.

How could Madam Woo do this? How could a human hand inflict such an inhuman suffering? Surely she must have flayed her own skin too by now?

Louise realised to her surprise that she was thinking again – and that she wasn't counting. The spanking had finished, but her bottom was blazing so consistently and intensely that she simply hadn't noticed the lack of slaps.

A fresh bout of sobbing engulfed her, and as contact with parts of her body other than her buttocks was reestablished, she felt the fierce ache of her sex where it pressed against the slick rubber apron. Her legs had opened wide during the spanking and as she shifted slightly, seeking ease for her swollen clitty, she cried out aloud at the new blast of pain in her bottom.

'Easy, Louise. That's all for now,' her persecutor murmured.

But it wasn't. The need was as unbearable as the suffering. Grinding her teeth, Louise wriggled again, then whimpered like an infant when her loins burned as hot as her backside, and a great wash of pleasure disgorged itself clean through her cunt. To her befuddled mind and her cruelly smacked body, an orgasm felt the same as being beaten.

* * *

The smacking had been only the beginning. Louise's afternoon became a long round of delirious punishments, and soon a mere spanking by hand seemed lenient.

Looking back, she realised that her own responses had almost certainly been the cause of her undoing. Her ruttishness and her frequent pain-inspired orgasms had let loose a voracious demon in the slim dark-clad body of Madam Woo. With each paroxysm they ascended another step of the ladder, and through her own terrorised haze, Louise slowly realised that she wasn't the only woman coming and coming and coming. With the acuity of one in extreme pain, she studied her punisher intently. Madam Woo's eyes were like hot coals and her cheeks bore that tell-tale flush that came from far more than wielding a rod, a strap or a whip.

And yet there had been a devil loosed in Louise too. While part of her screamed for the ordeal to end, another darker facet had exulted in each and every stroke or blow or cut. By the time evening began to fall she was offering up her buttocks willingly. Waving her hips crudely, pushing her bottom into the path of whatever fell ... holding the cheeks apart with her own fingers so she could be struck right in the crack, where the pain bloomed more keenly.

She'd been spread across the pouffe to take the cane. Stretched over the back of the chaise for a long, vicious tawsing. Knelt on it, face buried in a cushion while Madam ran her fingernails over the weals and stripes. At the end, she'd been returned to the black, silken lap for another spanking, a virtuoso performance so fine and extended it was almost a benediction.

Then it was over. With a long, shockingly sensual kiss Madam Woo had dismissed her. She'd granted Louise some small degree of dignity by letting down her pinned up skirts, but she hadn't returned her bloomers.

Blessed privacy. Back in her room, Louise had lain face down on the bed, her bottom pulsing so intensely she could almost hear it. After a while she'd got up, eaten the cold supper she'd been left, and after that, and with a good deal of pain and wincing, she'd made her awkward preparations for bed.

She supposed she'd have to lie on her front, but when it came to it, a maniac impulse made her turn onto her back. A thin but softly padded quilt had been thoughtfully provided, but even so, fire roared through her injured bottom cheeks and she hissed aloud as she adjusted position.

What's wrong with me? she asked herself. Sliding her night-dress from beneath her, she ground her burning backside against the cool satin quilt and cried out in pain. Hot fluid started oozing between her thighs and the ache there seemed to sweeten and grow, enhanced by the effects of her wriggling.

Louise didn't properly understand the psychodynamics of pain, but in this mad place – the Academy of Madam Woo – it seemed to drive all the residents sex crazy. As she turned out her night-light, she imagined all the ladies of the house – both young and older – quietly and determinedly frigging themselves to a standstill.

If they were alone, that was ... As her fingers strayed lovingly into her stickiness, her imagination produced a feast of sapphic images.

Flossie servicing her mistress with fingers and tongue. Belinda being caressed by a penitent Madam Woo. Madam herself creeping into the servant's quarters and tonguing her maid to a climax. Belinda with her fingers ...

'You don't have to do that for yourself, you know,' said one soft, mirth-filled voice as another one giggled prettily close by.

Louise opened her eyes in a panic, and struggling to see in the dark, located two white-clad shapes hovering in the shadows. Her door obviously didn't creak like the one to Belinda's room, and she'd been so lost in her masturbatory reveries that she'd never even noticed her visitors arrive.

Her hand fell away from her body as the twin wraiths drifted to the side of the bed.

'I heard you crying this afternoon,' said Flossie gently.

The maid looked quite different in her night-dress, but just as delectable. Especially with her magnificent red hair streaming loose and unbound across her shoulders. 'That was some going-over she gave you. I bet your bum's killing you, isn't it?' she enquired, her voice soft and sympathetic.

'Yes,' Louise said honestly. It didn't feel so bad, though, when the second night-dressed beauty picked up the hand that Louise had just had in her quim and kissed it passionately.

'You're very brave, Louise,' Belinda said quietly, then paused to suck Louise's fingers. 'She can really lay it on, can't she? It sounded as if you were getting everything.'

'How could you tell?' Louise would have felt alarmed and suspicious, but somebody's hand went deftly and gently between her legs, and its clever actions left little room in her head for any negative emotions.

'We were outside the door,' Belinda said cheerfully, easing Louise's night-dress right up to her neck, then starting to kiss her breasts and suck naughtily on one of her nipples.

'Both of us,' chimed in Flossie. 'And now we've both come to soothe you.' Her eyes twinkled in the darkness – just a split second before she bent over Louise and opened her quim with a tongue that was long, sexy and mobile . . . and twice as naughty as Belinda's.

Louise writhed beneath their double onslaught, enraptured as the pain in her bottom mixed exotically with the pleasure at her crotch and chest. Both girls used their mouths like professionals, and to look down her body and see Belinda's shiny ringlets dancing as she switched from one nipple to the other, and then look beyond at Flossie's luxuriant red locks cascading across her loins, was probably the most beautiful sight Louise had ever seen.

As if by some silent agreement, both her seductresses started working harder. Flossie seemed intent on drawing Louise's entire sex into her mouth, and Belinda coated both of her tingling breasts with a web of the wettest, sweetest kisses imaginable.

Louise bucked like a hare on the bed, fire blossoming

in her abused buttocks at the very instant she convulsed against Flossie's lips and coated them heavily with love-juice. A martyr to ecstasy, she sighed her thanks to both her lovers and closed her eyes in a transport of bliss.

Only to open them again when a voice from somewhere nearby said a low, quiet, 'Good night, my dears. Sleep tight.'

The last thing Louise saw – before pleasure took her senses completely – was Madam Woo standing in the doorway, her dark eyes wide and glittering.

She was smiling . . .

11

The Game's Up . . .

Isis felt strange. Emerging from dreamland, she clapped her hands to her smock-clad bottom and wondered why it didn't hurt. It seemed impossible that it wasn't stinging and smarting. Josh was already stirring, his long limbs sliding uneasily, but she decided to take a risk. To touch herself. Pushing up her smock, she slid her hands down the back of her knickers.

Explore, Press. Squeeze the cheeks. Nothing. No pain. No heat. No red-hot glowing tenderness that flowed like lava through her sex.

It was almost a shame. The dream, Josh's dream, had been incredible. Incredibly painful; incredibly sensual. Like her fantasies last night with Tricksie, only more so. She'd never been punished in the real world, and she'd had more than most people's share of pain, but suddenly she began to wonder.

Sliding a finger between her legs, she discovered she was wet. And not just moist. Her whole sex was awash. Drenched. Swimming. It could've been what she – no, correction – what Josh in the guise of Louise had shared with Belinda and Flossie; but somehow Isis knew that the pain had been the true driving factor. The mover and shaker. The initiator.

What would it be like to be smacked for real? she wondered, still kneading herself. To have a red, fiery bottom without even resorting to the 'Zone'? Ideas surged outrageously through her mind. Maybe she could . . .

'It serves you bloody well right,' said Josh, his words sudden, but his voice soft with humour.

Isis jumped a mile, fumbled, and her panties nearly slid around her knees. She whirled around and glared at him, conscious of blushing like a rose, half furious and half thrilled at being caught, compromised, with her hands inside her panties.

'Why do you do that?' she demanded, smoothing down her smock and trying to ignore the insistent need beneath it.

'Do what?' Josh enquired lazily, shuffling his limbs and body, then moaning. Isis watched him tense, lift, then sink back down on the probe. His eyes fluttered closed and his cock twitched slightly, its head pink and glistening in the cuff.

'Pretend to be still unconscious and catch me. Catch me – ' Goddam the bastard! Why was he the only man on earth who could do this? Every other male client was putty in her hands. Almost literally. But Josh Mortimer made her tremble and blush and stutter like a bashful schoolgirl.

The thought of schoolgirls only made things worse. Being one. Touching one. It was still far too close to home.

'Why can't you just wake up and be grateful like everyone else? Why are you always trying to catch me out?'

'Would I do that?' He was still wriggling, still rising.

'Yes, you devil!' She reached out and took his pulse, shaking off the hand that twisted in its restraint and tried to grab her wrist.

His rate was fast, faster than it should have been for the recovery phase. It felt more like a man who was on the up-curve. She concentrated firmly on his wrist, then on his brow as she did a quick check of his temperature. She didn't dare look at his cock.

'Hey!' His voice was a purr, all chocolaty and cajoling. It was crunch-time and she knew what he wanted. 'Come on, Doctor Delicious . . . Why are you stalling? The game's up now, you know.'

Amazingly for a man who'd just come over and over

214

again in his dream, Josh was already erect again. His penis had reared up, still wet with the juices of his previous pleasure, the semen on his thighs a silvery, decadent lure.

Suddenly Isis felt scared. She did want him. She'd wanted him for a long time, but an old, old shadow hung over her. She'd come a long way with it, *believed* she'd conquered it, but her fingers still flew to her cheek.

'Let me up,' said Josh fiercely, his brown eyes hot, his gaze locking with hers. 'It doesn't matter! Let me loose and I'll show you! For God's sake, woman, look at my cock!'

She did. It was huge now, as stiff and inflamed as if he'd been celibate a week, rather than fresh from a long string of orgasms. 'If I thought you were repulsive, would *that* happen?' He bucked his hips, waving his flesh at her. 'Jesus, Isis, I'm dying for you. You're beautiful . . .'

Beautiful? Oh no. Her fingers traced her damaged face, her mind travelling back to the early days of horror after the accident.

'Isis! Set me free! Do it now!'

He was strapped and bound but the command in his voice was total. She felt her sex quiver its answer.

This is it, Ice, she told herself. Snap out of it. What does your bloody face matter? The man wants you, he's gorgeous, he's good and kind, for God's sake just have him. You'll always be scarred, but men like this don't come around too often.

Her fingers shook as she struggled with straps that were usually child's-play. His body was superb, long and brown and made for sex; worked out but not brutally muscled. Strong, but natural and real and beautiful. His cock was a great throbbing bar, and his handsome face bright with desire. She sighed with him as the transceiver withdrew from his bottom.

'Fucking thing,' he hissed. 'I shouldn't like it so much . . .' He was already reaching for her as the treatment couch closed up and became a solid one-piece bed-shape again.

'Come here, Ice, let me touch you.' He shook off his

215

thin silk shirt and pushed his hair out of his eyes. 'Please.'
His eyes were black with lust, huge, imploring.

Isis felt nervous again, but she began to unbutton her
smock; conscious that her bra-less state was too 'obvious'.
That her intentions would be as revealed as her body.

Josh responded with a long, low, classic wolf-whistle.
She remembered his hands on her firm breasts just a day
or so ago. That had been an accident, through cloth, and
unintentional – at first – on her part. But this was different,
a ritual, a strip for his pleasure. She sobbed when he
reached out and touched her.

Gently, reverently, he traced her curving shape. She'd
expected him to be hurried, desperate and greedy now
the game was over, but his caresses were measured and
frustratingly light.

'I kind of thought it might be different,' she whispered,
arching her back and pushing herself forward into his
hands. She was standing beside the couch, her clothes on
the floor around her, and he was kneeling with his cock
swaying out towards her.

'How so, sweetheart?' Josh was concentrating endearingly on her nipples, palpitating them delicately with his
fingertips, pausing to listen for her tiny sounds of response,
her moans as his nails scraped the dimpled rounds of her
aureoles.

'I . . . Oh God!' He'd dipped forward now, he was circling the tip of his tongue round a hard pink peak.

'You were saying?' His breath was agonisingly hot
against her sensitised teat.

'I thought we'd do it properly this time.' She slid her
fingers into his tousled black hair; he was taunting her,
teasing her, but there was no way she was letting him
stop. 'You know . . . A proper courtship. Dinner, soft
lights, music. All that stuff.' At that moment she couldn't
have cared less if she never ate again. The only sustenance
she required was the man, Josh, sucking rhythmically on
one nipple and pulling on the other in time to his sucks.
Isis felt her own hips take up the beat, driven by the tickle
that tormented her quim.

'Tomorrow night, we'll go out to the finest restaurant in the city and we'll have the best meal you've ever eaten. With candle-light, a dozen flunkies fussing around you and even a gypsy violinist if you want it.' Even as he spoke, Josh was slinging an arm around her waist, and like the swashbuckling hero he sometimes reminded her of, whisking her up onto the couch in front of him. The thing was narrowish but long; and with aplomb, he placed her in a sitting pose astride it, with her hips tilted and her sex wide open and available.

Moving lithely, he mirrored the position himself, dangling his long legs on either side with knees brushing hers. His cock pointed rudely at her breasts, and his balls snuggled dark and bloated against the pure white leather beneath him. His loins, ready for sex, were perfection to her eyes, and Isis wondered how she'd ever looked upon him impartially.

'You can have as many dinners as you like tomorrow, sweet Isis,' he murmured, running his hot brown eyes all over her, 'but tonight you're gonna have sex.'

With that, he leaned across and kissed her.

It was a strangely innocent kiss in such wicked circumstances, but its gentleness had an explosive edge. The angling of their bodies – to bring their mouths together – stretched her cunt and tugged hard on her swollen clitoris. In its hyper-sensitive state the steady pull was excruciating. She moaned beneath Josh's plaguing, nibbling lips as he rocked her slowly and deliberately. He was kissing her like an exploring adolescent, yet all the time using the cant of her own pelvis to masturbate her. Even as she came, shuddering violently, there was no doubt in her mind whatsoever that he knew exactly what he was doing to her.

As her lips tried to whimper, he breathed sweet encouragement between them. 'Yes, baby, yes! Let it come. That's it ... Let it come.'

And then he was pushing the words, his breath and what seemed like the essence of life into her mouth with his tongue. With a hand in her hair, cradling, and the other

217

on her hip, controlling, he blatantly fucked her mouth as he worked her on the tautness in her clit. She would have screamed now, if he hadn't taken her voice completely.

When he eased her backwards, supporting her by her shoulders, she felt liquid move beneath her as the arch between her legs relaxed, her labia softened, and tension on her clitoris ebbed. She put up a hand, smoothed her hair from her eyes but didn't open them, scared to reveal herself.

Josh was dangerous. Deadly dangerous. Once she let him, he went right through her barriers and unbuttoned all the tightly knit layers she'd built up through the years to protect herself. He laid bare the wide-eyed girl inside the cool analytical woman, the sex-crazy slut in the precise, academic doctor.

She loved it.

'Isis,' he murmured, and she felt his fingers beneath her thigh, easing up one leg to bend at the knee, drawing the focus of her body from the wet, glowing tissues of her quim. He was allowing her to think at last.

She drew up the other leg, slid into the lotus, let her hands drop limply over her bush. And opened her eyes.

It was a ripe moment for someone to say 'I love you' but neither of them did. The words would probably mean the end of something when she wanted it to be a beginning. They had to move forward. Keep growing. So she said, with a grin, 'But Josh, you still haven't fucked me.'

'The night is young, Doctor dearest . . .' His own smile was white and dazzling as he reached into her lap, took her hand, and placed it fairly and squarely on his cock.

The night was old, near gone, when Isis turned over, carefully, in the crowded space of her narrow single bed.

The care was for Josh, who slept soundly beside her, his body hot and moist from being so close to hers after so much hectic activity. It was also for herself. For a quim so tender after what had really been too much sex. *And* for her faintly tingling bottom where he'd spanked her at her own request.

It hadn't really hurt a lot, but afterwards he'd flipped her over immediately and applied his clever fingers for pleasure's sake rather than pain.

Isis knew she'd been greedy tonight and that she deserved her naughty little aches. Long after Josh, who had come so much in his adventure, had gotten beyond the ability to fuck, she'd still wanted to go on. And he, with the grace of his lips and his hands, had obliged her.

They had actually copulated, of course. Had intercourse. The long promised joining. And it had been simple and sweet and straight when it happened. He'd just stroked her between the legs for a few moments, to refresh her juices, then risen over her like fate and slid in.

The missionary position, so ordinary after the bizarre complications of adventureland, and yet at that instant it had been appropriate and divinely special. In orgasm, she'd cried out his name and heard her own on his lips. And tasted both their tears.

Then, sometime later, in the afterglow, she'd popped her audacious question and felt ridiculously nervous as she waited for the answer.

Josh had laughed; but only in surprise.

'I'm honoured. If you think I can do it, I'll try. I've been wondering how I'd occupy my time.'

'Welcome aboard, Mister Mortimer,' she whispered now, brushing a long strand of his hair from across his sleeping face. 'The ladies are just going to *love* you . . .'

He was a tempting sight, and as Isis was about to tweak down the single sheet and admire him even more, she heard a soft knock at the door.

'Nice timing, Trix,' she muttered, sliding out of bed and padding across the room to let in the only other person who knew her digital entry code.

Even in the darkness, Isis could feel Tricksie throwing off waves of excitement as they tip-toed into the flat's small lounge.

'What's happened?' she asked, feeling hugely excited herself. By her own exhibitionism. She could just as easily have picked up a robe when she'd answered Tricksie's knock, but here she was standing stark-naked and not long fucked before a woman she knew desired her. She should have been embarrassed displaying herself like this – straight from Josh and still smelling of him – but all she felt was arousal.

'Well?' she persisted, feeling blood surge in her body as Tricksie's wide eyes perused her.

'Oh bloody hell!' Tricksie dashed the heel of her hand to her brow in horror. 'I'd forgotten about you and Josh. Oh lor, Ice, I'm sorry! I just came rushing over. I didn't think. It never occurred to me that you'd be . . . Oh shit, I'd better go.'

'Don't worry, sweetheart,' Isis soothed, taking her friend's arm and leading her to the sofa. 'You didn't interrupt anything.' The two of them sat down, moving by unspoken agreement. 'We'd finished for the time being.'

'Oh God, he must be fantastic! You look fabulous, Ice. I've never *seen* a woman look as well fu – '

'Trix! Didn't you have something to tell me?'

'I've heard from Diabolo. He called me. He's fine. He's not dead or anything . . .'

Isis suddenly found herself in Tricksie's wildly hugging arms, the gabardine of a chic trenchcoat feeling strangely pleasant against her naked skin. She was just wondering if there was anything beneath the coat, then Tricksie's words sank in.

Diabolo. That stone-souled conniving bastard!

'Where is he then?' she asked softly, not pulling away, the left hand of her lust coiling slowly but surely in her belly. Tricksie smelt gorgeous too: half of sleep, half of sex, as if she'd been masturbating when the Moon Devil had called her.

'He's in France somewhere . . . He wouldn't say exactly and he'd locked out the origin code.' Isis felt Tricksie's arms tighten as she spoke, and sensed an acute sexual radar tuning in to her own new desire. 'And he's not coming back for a while,' Tricksie paused then, as if saying that had hurt her. Isis snuggled closer, kissing her neck reassuringly. 'But he looks great and he seemed . . .

220

Umm . . . Well, I know this'll sound unlikely, Ice, but he was nice.'

'I'll believe that when I see it,' Isis said as mildly as she could manage. 'I don't suppose he said anything about Pleasurezone, did he? After all, he was supposed to be working for me.'

'No, he didn't. I'm sorry . . . I suppose I should've asked him.' Tricksie's answer was matter-of-fact, but at the same time she was pulling at the tie-belt of her trenchcoat. When it was undone, and just as matter-of-factly, she shrugged the thing off and let it drop onto the settee, a crumpled beige heap around her completely naked body.

'Never mind,' said Isis, fighting for her own composure now. Would she ever get used to the magnificence before her? To such smooth-skinned animal fullness and its siren call to the side of her that loved her own gender. 'I put my proposition to Josh tonight and he's agreed. He's going to join us as a therapist.'

'What? Me and you and Josh?' Tricksie laid red-tipped fingers on Isis's arm, and then, as if unable to resist any longer, moved them to her breast. 'That's wonderful! And even if Diabolo does want in again, I'm sure we'll have enough trade.'

Isis melted. Tricksie's look was so earnest and winning, so childlike. But even as the words spilled from her lips, those fingertips were stroking and circling.

'We'll see,' she answered, linking her hands loosely at the back of Tricksie's neck and pulling her forward for a kiss, 'but in the meantime, I think we should all celebrate.' She pressed her lips against her friend's and probed gently with her tongue as lust sang like a drug in her veins. If someone had asked her a little earlier in the evening if she wanted to share Josh Mortimer, she might well have declined. But right now, with this special woman she could *admit* she loved and not worry about it, the idea of sharing a man was glorious.

'You mean . . . with *him*?' Tricksie said falteringly, nodding in the direction of the bedroom as their mouths parted. Isis nodded too, putting up her fingers to wipe away a tiny lipstick smudge from beside Tricksie's dawning smile.

'With *him*.' Isis slid her arm around Tricksie's bare waist and urging her to her feet.

Josh was still asleep, but stirred as they approached the bed.

'Oh love, he's so gorgeous,' mouthed Tricksie, rolling her eyes.

'Ain't that the truth,' agreed Isis, also in mime and meaning every word of it.

Josh did look wonderful. His skin was a caramel poem against the battered white sheets, his black hair was all over the place, and his long relaxed body had already stretched across the whole of the meagre bedspace. He looked good enough to eat, and Isis gave Tricksie a sly squeeze, then reached across to flick away the sheet that covered their banquet.

He was already partially erect.

Tricksie gasped and shuddered. Her sweet red mouth formed a small, perfect circle of wonder and *that* painted another incredible picture . . .

Tricksie Turing, possibly the city's most consummate fellatrice, enclosing that sublime male shaft and sucking its owner to ecstasy.

Isis felt strangely beneficent. She'd tasted Josh's fine body already tonight. She's been kissed and stroked and filled by him, enjoyed him and been enjoyed by him, had him every which way bar swinging from the ceiling. Now was the time to be generous, to give him as a gift. To her dearest friend in the world.

Josh stirred again, his hardening cock lurching to a full rise, and Isis felt her own flesh answer. In the hot furrow between her legs a moist flutter matched his stiffening. Blood flowed, tissues swelled and pouted, a low but imperious ache made its signal presence felt. Patience, she told her wayward, yearning body. Let Tricksie go first . . .

The lovely whore arched her finely plucked eyebrows, and Isis nodded slightly. No further exchange was necessary and Tricksie slid onto the bed. She moved with all the grace and accuracy of a prima ballerina, but nevertheless Josh was disturbed.

The shift of weight roused him, and he stretched like a long brown cat, rubbed his face drowsily and murmured, 'Isis? Whassamarrer . . .' still half in sleep.

'Nothing, sweetheart,' answered Tricksie immediately, and Isis admired the way she eased her slim form between the lying man's legs and took up a position of near prayer-like kneeling.

Josh's eyes fluttered open, and both women smiled at his instant and total disorientation. His mouth dropped open, and stayed that way for ten whole seconds, then he matched their grins with a wide one all of his own.

'Well, this is an unexpected pleasure, Mizz Turing,' he murmured, his eyes flicking momentarily to Isis's, checking for her smile. When she blew him a kiss, he returned his attention to Tricksie. 'What is this? An initiation ceremony?'

'Team meeting, Josh,' said Isis crisply, pulling her special chair up next to the bed, then dropping her bare body into it. She could reach them both from its cushioned comfort.

'We're going to work very closely together from now on,' she continued, tongue firmly in cheek, yet getting hotter and more serious by the second. This wasn't a computer trip any more . . . It was two real beautiful people she cared for. 'So this is your compatibility check. I hope you don't mind?'

'No, I don't mind at all,' Josh said, trying to sit up and being firmly pushed back down again.

'Just lie back and think of England or whatever,' Tricksie said pertly, 'This won't hurt a bit.'

'I'm sure it won't,' he ground out as Tricksie's soft red lips plunged down on his penis, and his hips bucked up convulsively to meet her. As she began to draw on him, sucking and licking and wholly engulfing him, he turned to Isis and reached for her hand, his expression strangely pleading.

'Yes,' she whispered, taking his fingers in her own, and holding his look until his eyes snapped closed in extremis.

It was an exquisite tableau, and as Isis took it in, her other hand flew to her crotch. Tricksie was bent to her work now, her wine-red hair tumbling forwards across Josh's thighs and hips and belly, but not quite concealing her mouth on his cock. Her lush lips were stretched around him, and as she watched, Isis recalled that same bulk in her own mouth a few hours ago. That same salt taste on her tongue, those same harsh cries echoing in her ears.

She was barely aware of her own small noises as her best friend gave pleasure to her lover. To *their* lover. There was delicious heat in her loins, but she felt confused, at first, by the way she perceived it. The sensation was 'stroking', her reason told her calmly . . . but every nerve-end in her vulva screamed 'suction'.

'This is weird,' she whispered, but doubted if either of her lovers could hear her now.

She laughed softly when she realised what was happening, then gasped as Josh's hips started pumping strongly and Tricksie gulped and moaned around the orgasming obstruction in her mouth.

Isis sighed and writhed herself, her fingers remorseless on her clitoris as she melted in a white-hot, tri-partied climax.

But even as she spasmed, even while she sighed and sobbed, she knew it wasn't really her own hand she'd come by.

Mad as it seemed, Pleasurezone itself had given her *their* pleasure, and probably given hers to them. She smiled and fell back in the chair, pressing her own wet flesh, squeezing Josh's hand, and sending out her swelling heart to Tricksie.

You're a clever girl, Isis, do you know that? she told herself as her soul expanded in a new gold dream . . . then encountered two others, each just as happy.

You don't even have to switch the damn thing on any more!

Postcard from Esme

(225)

Dear Readers

As you can see, I'm taking it easy at the moment. I've been so hard at it in the Nexus offices recently, that the publisher has let me take a little holiday. I'm writing this from my country retreat, and even though the weather isn't as exotic as it could be, I've managed to compensate with various sporting activities that make me glow all over. Even though I'm not at the Nexus offices this month, I'm keeping a watchful eye over the books that are being published, and

I've just time to tell you what's on offer this month and next.

November sees the release of one of my favourite Nexus books of the year, *Return to the Pleasurezone*. Using a sexual time-machine, the characters cross the centuries from Ancient Egypt to Edwardian England to realise their filthiest fantasies in the most imaginative ways.

Also published this month is *Annie*. She is a very pretty young maid, but somewhat wayward and in need of a little discipline. Taken into service in a very disorderly house, her strict guardians ensure that she gets it!

The Black Lace book this month is *Outlandia*, a bodice-ripping yarn set on the South Sea island of Wahwu in the nineteenth century. Shipwrecked Englishwoman, Iona Stanley, is crowned living goddess of the island and treated to the lavish attentions bestowed upon her by a host of virile islanders. That's the kind of holiday I fancy next year.

December sees the publication of a volume of very kinky stories. *The Fantasies of Josephine Scott* must surely rate as one of the most comprehensive collections of corporal punishment tales ever told. Stories like these will be familiar to those naughtier readers of specialist magazines such as *Kane* and *Janus*. A spanking good read, I'd say!

Melinda and the Master is by Susanna Hughes, author of the *Stephanie* series. Staying in the world of jet-setting seduction, the beautiful and submissive Melinda is loaned by her husband to a millionaire businessman for one year to cater to his unusual sexual tastes. After spending one year in slavery, will she even want to return to her former way of life?

Black Orchid is the title of our Black Lace book next month. Now here's a story dear to the heart of every hot-blooded woman. An exclusive and discreet health spa which guarantees to please its female patrons in evey possible way. On offer at the Black Orchid Club are Jacuzzis, saunas, massage rooms and the services of a troupe of exquisitely proportioned male staff, who are there to cater to every whim. One member, Maggie, likes the place so much she ends up doing the hiring and firing.

Well, I must away now to my research work. I'll be back next month with more book information for you all.

Cheerio for now.

Esme ♥

THE BEST IN EROTIC READING – BY POST

The Nexus Library of Erotica – almost one hundred and fifty volumes – is available from many booksellers and newsagents. If you have any difficulty obtaining the books you require, you can order them by post. Photocopy the list below, or tear the list out of the book; then tick the titles you want and fill in the form at the end of the list. Titles marked 1993 are not yet available: please do not try to order them – just look out for them in the shops!

CONTEMPORARY EROTICA

AMAZONS	Erin Caine	£3.99	
COCKTAILS	Stanley Carten	£3.99	
CITY OF ONE-NIGHT STANDS	Stanley Carten	£4.50	
CONTOURS OF DARKNESS	Marco Vassi	£4.99	
THE GENTLE DEGENERATES	Marco Vassi	£4.99	
MIND BLOWER	Marco Vassi	£4.99	
THE SALINE SOLUTION	Marco Vassi	£4.99	
DARK FANTASIES	Nigel Anthony	£4.99	
THE DAYS AND NIGHTS OF MIGUMI	P.M.	£4.50	
THE LATIN LOVER	P.M.	£3.99	
THE DEVIL'S ADVOCATE	Anonymous	£4.50	
DIPLOMATIC SECRETS	Antoine Lelouche	£3.50	
DIPLOMATIC PLEASURES	Antoine Lelouche	£3.50	
DIPLOMATIC DIVERSIONS	Antoine Lelouche	£4.50	
ENGINE OF DESIRE	Alexis Arven	£3.99	
DIRTY WORK	Alexis Arven	£3.99	
DREAMS OF FAIR WOMEN	Celeste Arden	£2.99	
THE FANTASY HUNTERS	Celeste Arden	£3.99	
A GALLERY OF NUDES	Anthony Grey	£3.99	
THE GIRL FROM PAGE 3	Mike Angelo	£3.99	
HELEN – A MODERN ODALISQUE	James Stern	£4.99	1993
HOT HOLLYWOOD NIGHTS	Nigel Anthony	£4.50	
THE INSTITUTE	Maria del Ray	£4.99	

LAURE-ANNE	Laure-Anne	£4.50	
LAURE-ANNE ENCORE	Laure-Anne	£4.99	
LAURE-ANNE TOUJOURS	Laure-Anne	£4.99	
Ms DEEDES ON A MISSION	Carole Andrews	£4.99	1993
Ms DEEDES AT HOME	Carole Andrews	£4.50	
Ms DEEDES ON PARADISE ISLAND	Carole Andrews	£4.99	1993
MY SEX AND SOUL	Amelia Greene	£2.99	
OBSESSION	Maria del Rey	£4.99	1993
ONE WEEK IN THE PRIVATE HOUSE	Esme Ombreux	£4.50	
PALACE OF FANTASIES	Delver Maddingley	£4.99	
PALACE OF SWEETHEARTS	Delver Maddingley	£4.99	
PALACE OF HONEYMOONS	Delver Maddingley	£4.99	1993
PARADISE BAY	Maria del Rey	£4.50	
QUEENIE AND CO	Francesca Jones	£4.99	1993
QUEENIE AND CO IN JAPAN	Francesca Jones	£4.99	1993
QUEENIE AND CO IN ARGENTINA	Francesca Jones	£4.99	1993
THE SECRET WEB	Jane-Anne Roberts	£3.99	
SECRETS LIE ON PILLOWS	James Arbroath	£4.50	
SECRETS TIED IN SILK	James Arbroath	£4.99	1993
STEPHANIE	Susanna Hughes	£4.50	
STEPHANIE'S CASTLE	Susanna Hughes	£4.50	
STEPHANIE'S DOMAIN	Susanna Hughes	£4.99	1993
STEPHANIE'S REVENGE	Susanna Hughes	£4.99	1993
THE DOMINO TATTOO	Cyrian Amberlake	£4.50	
THE DOMINO ENIGMA	Cyrian Amberlake	£3.99	
THE DOMINO QUEEN	Cyrian Amberlake	£4.99	

EROTIC SCIENCE FICTION

ADVENTURES IN THE PLEASURE ZONE	Delaney Silver	£4.99	
EROGINA	Christopher Denham	£4.50	
HARD DRIVE	Stanley Carten	£4.99	
PLEASUREHOUSE 13	Agnetha Anders	£3.99	
LAST DAYS OF THE PLEASUREHOUSE	Agnetha Anders	£4.50	
TO PARADISE AND BACK	D.H.Master	£4.50	
WICKED	Andrea Arven	£3.99	
WILD	Andrea Arven	£4.50	

ANCIENT & FANTASY SETTINGS

CHAMPIONS OF LOVE	Anonymous	£3.99	
CHAMPIONS OF DESIRE	Anonymous	£3.99	

CHAMPIONS OF PLEASURE	Anonymous	£3.50	
THE SLAVE OF LIDIR	Aran Ashe	£4.50	
DUNGEONS OF LIDIR	Aran Ashe	£4.99	
THE FOREST OF BONDAGE	Aran Ashe	£4.50	
KNIGHTS OF PLEASURE	Erin Caine	£4.50	
PLEASURE ISLAND	Aran Ashe	£4.99	
ROMAN ORGY	Marcus van Heller	£4.50	

EDWARDIAN, VICTORIAN & OLDER EROTICA

ADVENTURES OF A SCHOOLBOY	Anonymous	£3.99	
THE AUTOBIOGRAPHY OF A FLEA	Anonymous	£2.99	
BEATRICE	Anonymous	£3.99	
THE BOUDOIR	Anonymous	£3.99	
CASTLE AMOR	Erin Caine	£4.99	1993
CHOOSING LOVERS FOR JUSTINE	Aran Ashe	£4.99	1993
THE DIARY OF A CHAMBERMAID	Mirabeau	£2.99	
THE LIFTED CURTAIN	Mirabeau	£4.99	
EVELINE	Anonymous	£2.99	
MORE EVELINE	Anonymous	£3.99	
FESTIVAL OF VENUS	Anonymous	£4.50	
'FRANK' & I	Anonymous	£2.99	
GARDENS OF DESIRE	Roger Rougiere	£4.50	
OH, WICKED COUNTRY	Anonymous	£2.99	
LASCIVIOUS SCENES	Anonymous	£4.50	
THE LASCIVIOUS MONK	Anonymous	£4.50	
LAURA MIDDLETON	Anonymous	£3.99	
A MAN WITH A MAID 1	Anonymous	£4.99	
A MAN WITH A MAID 2	Anonymous	£4.99	
A MAN WITH A MAID 3	Anonymous	£4.99	
MAUDIE	Anonymous	£2.99	
THE MEMOIRS OF DOLLY MORTON	Anonymous	£4.50	
A NIGHT IN A MOORISH HAREM	Anonymous	£3.99	
PARISIAN FROLICS	Anonymous	£2.99	
PLEASURE BOUND	Anonymous	£3.99	
THE PLEASURES OF LOLOTTE	Andrea de Nerciat	£3.99	
THE PRIMA DONNA	Anonymous	£3.99	
RANDIANA	Anonymous	£4.50	
REGINE	E.K.	£2.99	

THE ROMANCE OF LUST 1	Anonymous	£3.99
THE ROMANCE OF LUST 2	Anonymous	£2.99
ROSA FIELDING	Anonymous	£2.99
SUBURBAN SOULS 1	Anonymous	£2.99
SUBURBAN SOULS 2	Anonymous	£3.99
THREE TIMES A WOMAN	Anonymous	£2.99
THE TWO SISTERS	Anonymous	£3.99
VIOLETTE	Anonymous	£4.99

"THE JAZZ AGE"

ALTAR OF VENUS	Anonymous	£3.99
THE SECRET GARDEN ROOM	Georgette de la Tour	£3.50
BEHIND THE BEADED CURTAIN	Georgette de la Tour	£3.50
BLANCHE	Anonymous	£3.99
BLUE ANGEL NIGHTS	Margaret von Falkensee	£4.99
BLUE ANGEL DAYS	Margaret von Falkensee	£4.99
BLUE ANGEL SECRETS	Margaret von Falkensee	£4.99
CAROUSEL	Anonymous	£4.50
CONFESSIONS OF AN ENGLISH MAID	Anonymous	£3.99
FLOSSIE	Anonymous	£2.50
SABINE	Anonymous	£3.99
PLAISIR D'AMOUR	Anne-Marie Villefranche	£4.50
FOLIES D'AMOUR	Anne-Marie Villefranche	£2.99
JOIE D'AMOUR	Anne-Marie Villefranche	£3.99
MYSTERE D'AMOUR	Anne-Marie Villefranche	£3.99
SECRETS D'AMOUR	Anne-Marie Villefranche	£3.50
SOUVENIR D'AMOUR	Anne-Marie Villefranche	£3.99

WORLD WAR 2

SPIES IN SILK	Piers Falconer	£4.50	
WAR IN HIGH HEELS	Piers Falconer	£4.99	1993

CONTEMPORARY FRENCH EROTICA (translated into English)

EXPLOITS OF A YOUNG DON JUAN	Anonymous	£2.99
INDISCREET MEMOIRS	Alain Dorval	£2.99
INSTRUMENT OF PLEASURE	Celeste Piano	£4.50
JOY	Joy Laurey	£2.99
JOY AND JOAN	Joy Laurey	£2.99

Please send me the books I have ticked above.

Name   ....
Address   ....
              ....
              .... Post code ....

Send to: **Cash Sales, Nexus Books, 332 Ladbroke Grove, London W10 5AH**

Please enclose a cheque or postal order, made payable to **Nexus Books**, to the value of the books you have ordered plus postage and packing costs as follows:

UK and BFPO – £1.00 for the first book, 50p for the second book, and 30p for each subsequent book to a maximum of £3.00;

Overseas (including Republic of Ireland) – £2.00 for the first book, £1.00 for the second book, and 50p for each subsequent book.

If you would prefer to pay by VISA or ACCESS/MASTERCARD, please write your card number here:

— — — —   — — — —   — — — —   — — — —

Signature: _____